Pregnant in Pennsylvania

JASINDA WILDER

Author's Note

Clayton, PA is a fictional location, although if you happen to venture to a little place called New Oxford, Pennsylvania, you may notice a few similarities. These are intentional. Most street names are real; all businesses and persons are fictional, but the overall feel of downtown Clayton is, hopefully, a lot like New Oxford.

1

"HEY, MOM?" AIDEN, MY EIGHT-YEAR-OLD son, is on the floor, playing with LEGO® bricks, building what looks like is going to be a robot.

"Hmmm?" I'm absently scrolling through Facebook gossip about the new principal at Aiden's elementary school, but mostly watching Aiden build his robot.

"Why did Principal Mackey quit?"

I look away from my phone and focus on Aiden. "What? Oh—he didn't quit, honey, he retired."

"What's the difference?"

"Quitting would mean he decided he didn't want to work there anymore, like he got a new job or something. But Principal Mackey is *retiring*, which means he's not working at all anymore."

Aiden uses his teeth to pry apart a couple of pieces, spitting one out and placing the other in a particular spot. "So what's he gonna do all day, then?"

I laugh. "I don't know, sweetie. Golf? Work in his garden? Travel with Mrs. Mackey?"

He uses his teeth to pry apart two more pieces. "Sounds boring."

"He's been a principal for thirty-eight years, so maybe he's ready for some boredom," I say. "Don't use your teeth, Aiden. You have, like, three of those orange piece-remover things."

He rolls his big gray eyes at me. "Yeah, but Bobber chewed one up, I lost one, and the other one is in this huge pile somewhere," he says, gesturing at the big box of Lego pieces. "Anyway, my teeth work just as good."

Bobber is my parents' dog, and a mischievous little thing.

"But your teeth might break," I say.

"Dude, it's fine." His slightly too-long blond hair dangles in front of one eye, and he brushes it away absentmindedly.

I frown at him, nudging him in the ribs with my toe. "Don't call me dude, *dude*."

He wiggles away from my toe—his ribs are his most ticklish spot. "Okay, okay!" He settles back on the floor when I stop tickling him. "I won't call you dude… buddy."

"Don't press your luck, *buddy*," I tease. "I was gonna do pizza for dinner, but I could make grilled chicken and broccoli instead…"

Aiden shoots me a horrified expression. "Have mercy, Mommy dearest! Anything but that!"

I laugh, tickling him again with a toe. "Don't you forget it, mister."

Aiden cackles, squirming away and tossing Lego pieces at me in self-defense.

Our doorbell rings, just then—three times in quick succession, followed by the sound of the door opening: it's my best friend, Cora. "Is there *tickling* happening in this room?" she says by way of hello, jumping into the living room with her hands clawed.

Aiden scrambles to his feet with alacrity. "Nope! There was no tickling happening."

"I think there was!" Cora says, her voice energized with wicked glee. "I know the sound of tickling, and I WILL NOT BE DENIED!"

I laugh as Aiden takes off running, scattering Legos everywhere as he tries to escape Cora; it's hopeless, though—Cora loves nothing as much as to tickle Aiden until he begs for mercy. Indeed, the pursuit is short—Cora corners him by the couch, wraps him in her arms from behind, and tickles his ribs until he's half crying and begging her to stop.

She stops tickling, but doesn't let go right away, peppering his forehead and cheeks with kisses until he's ripping free with a fake disgusted shudder, wiping at his face.

"You always get lipstick on me, Aunt Cora," he complains.

She licks her thumb and extends it toward him. "Here, I'll get it off…"

"NO! That's even worse! It's bad enough when Mom does it!"

Cora pretends to shuffle sadly to the couch, slumping down onto it as if he's ruined her entire life. "Fine, whatever, see if I care. No more tickles, no more kisses."

Aiden sighs, a sound of exhausted long-suffering. "Don't be dramatical, Aunt Cora. You can still kiss me, but you've gotta slow down with the tickling. I almost peed my pants." And, in fact, he's doing the pee-pee dance, poking at himself.

I laugh. "Well *go*, then, you big goofball!"

He rabbits off at a run for the bathroom, the door slamming, the toilet seat clanking loudly.

Cora flops onto her back on the couch. My best friend since forever, Cora is my diametric opposite in just about everything. Where I'm a homebody, she's a party girl; where I'm quiet, she's loud; where I'm reserved and cautious, she's outspoken and bold. She gets us into trouble, and as Miss Sweetness-and-Light-and-Innocence, I get us out of it.

She's been hauling me out to parties for our entire lives and I always try to resist, only to succumb to her wheedling in the end. Which is what's about to happen.

Aiden comes back into the living room, plops back down on the floor, and goes back to playing Legos.

"So." Cora sits up, curly, glossy black hair swaying. Her bright green eyes twinkle mischievously. "School starts up next week."

I play dumb. "Yep. Summer goes by fast."

She scoots across the couch in a comical series of

hops. "And you've barely done anything all summer."

I roll my eyes at her, standing up and heading out onto my little back porch, so we can sit and talk out of earshot of Aiden. "I rode bikes with Aiden, took him to the pool, went to movies, spent a week with my parents in Florida," I tell her as we sit down. "I'd hardly call that nothing."

"Yeah, but that's all Aiden, Aiden, Aiden." She uses a whiny tone of voice when she says his name. "What about Cora? How many times have you been out with Cora, Cora, Cora?"

"He's my son, Cora." I pin her with a serious look. "His behavior is just starting to level off."

She sighs. "I know, I know. But I'm just saying, literally everything you do is with Aiden. You have, like, zero personal life."

"I'm a single mother, babe. I hate to break it to you, but that's sort of par for the course."

"Your parents live ten minutes from here, and they're retired. You know they'd watch him more if you asked."

"Cora, come on."

She doesn't back down. "*You* come on, Elyse. I'm not saying go out every night, or bring a bunch of guys home, but at least meet me for drinks once in a while." She glares at me. "I'm forced to *pretend* to be best friends with Vivian Pratt because my real, *actual* best friend won't ever go out with me."

"You love Vivian," I say, sighing. "She's fun."

"Sure, but I haven't been best friends with her *since birth*. It's not the same."

"Is there a point to all this?" I ask.

"One week before school starts and I demand that you party it up with me *once* this summer. Meaning, tonight. Right now." Cora blinks innocently at me like a cartoon character—I can all but hear her eyelashes going *tink...tink-tink*. "I already talked to Mom, and she's expecting Aiden at seven. She has pizza on speed dial, a whole season of *Ninjago* downloaded on her iPad, and Dad is bringing ice cream home on his way back from golf." Cora has referred to my parents as Mom and Dad since fifth grade, when things in her own home life went...er...somewhat sour, let's say, and my parents basically adopted her.

I sigh. "Of course you fixed things with my parents behind my back."

"They agree with me, I'll have you know," Cora says, her voice arch. "They want to see more of Aiden, and they think you need to start getting out more."

"I don't *want* to start getting out more."

"You need to go out on a date someday, Elyse. It's been three years." Her voice is quiet, now.

I fiddle with my phone, waking it up with my thumbprint and then putting it to sleep again. "I've been on lots of dates—"

"Aiden doesn't count," she interrupts.

I groan. "Why do you want me to go on a date so bad? And who with? Lewis Calhoun?" Lewis is the only remotely eligible bachelor in our tiny town—also known to be the town supplier for a certain smokable substance currently illegal in our state.

"You need to get laid, Elyse," Cora says, watching me warily.

"Cora!"

"Don't act so shocked—it's true, and you know it. It's been three years since your divorce from Daniel, and we both know that what you were getting when you were married to him was…well, subpar is putting it kindly."

"Why are we talking about my former sex life with my ex-husband?" I ask.

"Because your sex life with Daniel sucked. You told me more than once that he would finish and go to sleep before you even started getting close. You complained about it a lot, actually. And then, when things started to go really sour, your sex life dwindled away to nothing. And you've become steadily more introverted ever since."

"It wasn't *that* bad," I argue.

Cora splutters a raspberry. "You timed him once, remember? Three minutes from first grope to final thrust."

I groan. "Can we *please* stop talking about this?"

"Fine. But my point is, you need to move on. You need to at *least* go on a date with someone. Anyone. Even Lewis Calhoun. Who, yes, is a small-town drug dealer, but he is also super hot and really funny."

"And a *drug dealer*." I pop my eyes at her. "I'm a guidance counselor. I can't be seen with the town pot slinger."

Cora snorts. "Pot slinger? I don't think anyone in the history of ever has called it that."

"Whatever. The point is, no."

"No to Lewis? Or no to going out?" She grabs my hand and gives me pleading eyes—and this is where she gets me. "Please? Tonight will be low-key. A few bars, a few drinks. Maybe some dancing at Vinnie's, and karaoke at Field's. Please?"

"I hate karaoke," I point out.

"No, you hate *sober* karaoke. You love it after a few drinks."

"This can't be a repeat of last time," I warn, with a glare.

Last time she dragged me out for "a few drinks," we somehow ended up calling Monty the tow truck driver to take us home, and then spent the rest of the night riding with him on calls, and annoying his dispatcher by monkeying with the CB.

"Nope. It won't be anything like that. Scout's honor."

"You were never a Girl Scout, Cora," I point out, "so that oath means nothing."

"Fine." She pulls her phone from her back pocket and tosses it on the table, placing her palm on it. "I swear by my precious iPhone Eight Plus—my baby, my addiction—that we will be good and there will be no trouble whatsoever."

Considering how seriously Cora takes social media, that's actually a very convincing oath.

"Fine," I sigh. "But we can't be out late, and we can't do anything stupid."

"We'll be perfect angels," Cora promises. "Slightly drunk angels, but angels nonetheless."

2

I STUDY MYSELF IN THE FULL-LENGTH MIRROR ON THE back of my bedroom door. I sigh, because I'd almost forgotten how nice it feels to dress up, to put on some sexy lingerie and a little black dress and some strappy little heels.

"I actually look pretty good!" I say to my reflection.

This is, however, a little piece of positive self-talk to combat all the negative thoughts running through my head:

Your ass is getting big.

Your hips are bigger now than when you were pregnant with Aiden.

Your boobs are getting saggy.

You have those little flaps of fat hanging out under your armpits.

Your thighs shake like Jell-O every time you take a step.

I shut the thoughts down and force myself to say one positive thing in response to each negative thought:

My hair is long and shimmery and beautiful.

My skin is tan and smooth and basically flawless.

I've lost five pounds in the last three weeks—a small victory, but still a victory.

I am beautiful, and the numbers on the scale can't change that.

I'm curvy and sexy, and I'm rocking the heck out of this little black dress.

I give myself one more look, checking for flyaways in my hair, smudged lipstick, VPLs, or bra straps that might be sticking out. I'm five-seven, with reddish auburn hair and hazel eyes that shift from green to brown to gray depending on what I'm wearing and my mood—right now, my eyes look more green than anything. My body is…well…in college and before Aiden, I had a pretty darned amazing body—an hourglass figure, perky breasts, plump but firm hips and butt, and not a lot of extra weight…just enough to make me soft and curvy. Then I had Aiden, and a few—ten or fifteen—pounds never quite left, and then things happened with Daniel and I suffered a long-term bout with depression and packed on a few more pounds—like, twentyish. After the divorce and more depression and more struggles, I finally managed to drag myself out of the emotional pits and went to work on trimming down; I'm almost back down to where I was before I had Aiden. Within ten pounds, which, considering where I started—almost forty pounds overweight—is a heck of win in my book.

A huge part of that win has been learning to shut down and combat the negativity—most of which echoes the things Daniel said to me during the worst of our marriage, when things were dissolving, and I was letting myself go, and he began showing his true colors.

I smooth my hands over my hips, twist to take a look at the rear view: not bad, and getting better. And, I remind myself, I'm my own harshest critic. Cora, my parents, and people around town let me know they see me differently than I see myself, but it's awful hard to shut out that nasty little voice once it starts whispering its lies.

I smile at myself. "You're beautiful, and you're going to have fun tonight."

"I agree," Cora says from behind me, surprising me. "You're sexy as hell, and all the guys in town are going to want to bang you."

I whirl, smacking her playfully on the arm. "Inappropriate!"

She just waggles her eyebrows at me. "It's not inappropriate if it's true."

I snort. "Um, something can be true *and* inappropriate, Cora."

She just makes a mocking face and sticks her tongue out at me. "Whatever. Quit being lame."

"I'm not lame! I'm a mother and a guidance counselor," I insist.

"Neither of which makes you a nun!" Cora fires

back. "You're thirty-two, which means you're in your sexual prime—you're allowed to have fun! You're allowed to have a sex drive!"

I sigh. "Yeah, well, I don't. And I haven't for a long time."

Cora smacks her forehead with her palm. "No kidding! What do you think I'm trying to change? Duh! Now let's go!"

She drags me out of the bedroom, and I have to hop to finish buckling the straps on my heels. Aiden is already waiting by the front door, his Nintendo Switch in his hands, tongue running along his lower lip as he plays Mario Kart. He has his overnight bag on his back—Ninja Turtles, of course—packed with pj's, clothes for tomorrow, toothbrush and toothpaste, and his battery-backup alarm clock...which is, secretly, also his nightlight. He's still young enough to not like a totally dark room, but too big for a real nightlight.

"Ready, kiddo?" I ask, grabbing my purse off the counter and transferring phone, wallet, key ring, and a few other odds and ends into my little black cross-body clutch.

He pauses his game and looks up, and does a double take, his face contorting through several expressions. "Wow, Mom, you look..." he struggles for a word. "Different."

I laugh. "Hot, you mean, right?"

He fake barfs. "No! Eew! You're my mom—I'm not allowed to think you're hot!"

"So I just look *different*, huh?" I press, just to watch him squirm a little.

And squirm he does. "Well, yeah. I mean, you always look nice, but…" He hesitates. "I can just see a lot of your…legs."

I almost never dress up anymore, so I imagine it's kind of weird for him to see me like this. I kiss his forehead. "I'm just messing with you, buddy." I ruffle his hair—which is platinum blond, like his father's. "Ready to go see Grandma and Papa?"

"Yep!" He turns off the Switch and puts it into his backpack. "I'm gonna eat a whole pizza all to myself."

Being single and childless, Cora has by the far the cooler car of the two of us—a yellow convertible Mini Cooper. She has the top back, and Aiden is chattering a million miles a second as he sets his backpack behind the passenger seat, opens the driver's side door and climbs behind it into the back seat. He spends almost as much time in Cora's car as he does mine, so she keeps a booster seat for him in her trunk, which she's gotten out and placed in the back for him.

He buckles up, fishes his gas station aviator sunglasses out of a front pocket of his backpack, and slides them on his face.

"Ready to go, Maverick?" I ask, sliding into the passenger seat.

"Maverick? Who's Maverick?"

"Only the coolest fighter pilot ever!" I say. "Although, you may be a little young for *Top Gun* references."

"I feel the need—!" Cora starts, as she backs out of my driveway.

"The need for speed!" I finish, as she guns the throttle enough to bark the tires.

"What are you guys talking about?" Aiden asks.

"It's a movie, bud," I tell him, as Cora navigates our way out of my subdivision—safely, and within the speed limit, I might add—toward my parents' house which is five miles away. "We'll watch it when you're older."

"Why not now?"

"Because there are bad words in it."

"So? Tommy MacMillan says *dammit* all the time."

"He shouldn't," I say. "And neither should you."

"I won't. I promise!"

Cora eyes me over the top of her sunglasses. "You know, we watched that movie when we were around his age."

"Yeah, and we got in trouble for quoting it at school." I lift an eyebrow pointedly. "Or rather, *you* got in trouble for telling Isaiah Roberts to take you to bed or lose you forever."

"I was nine and I didn't know what it meant," she says. "You sang 'I've Lost That Loving Feeling' all day every day for a week and a half, until Mrs. Thompson threatened you with a week's worth of extra homework you if you didn't stop." Cora laughs. "And babe, you *can't* sing."

"Then why you do make me do karaoke?"

"Because it's hysterical! You're so serious about it! Like, give you three or four glasses of cab sav and you think you're Whitney Houston or something. I love it."

"See if I let you drag me out to karaoke night ever again," I grouse.

She snorts. "You're helpless to resist me. I have the Force."

Uh-oh—a *Star Wars* reference…Aiden is off and running now, babbling breathlessly about Han and Luke and Chewie and lightsabers and that one scene where—

I laugh at Cora, who used that reference on purpose, because her favorite pastime is winding Aiden up on his favorite subjects and watching him go.

We get to my parents' place after a short drive and pull into their long, winding driveway—they live outside town on a few acres of tree-shaded rolling hills: paradise for an energetic eight-year-old. Mom is on their covered front porch cross-stitching when we arrive, a glass of iced tea on the floor beside her rocking chair. She stands up as Cora parks her Mini Cooper, then ambles down the front steps, squatting down to welcome Aiden's full-sprint hug.

"My favorite grandson!" Mom says, peppering him with kisses until Aiden squirms away.

"I'm your *only* grandson, Grandma, so I'd better be your favorite," Aiden says, wiping Grandma-kisses away with the back of his hand.

"Oh. I suppose that's true. Well, how about you're

my favorite…eight-year-old!"

Aiden tilts his head to one side. "Hmmm. How many other eight-year-olds do you know?"

Mom laughs, ruffling his hair. "Oh my, lots and lots."

"Oh yeah?" Aiden challenges. "Who?"

Mom leads him up the steps to the screen door. "I used to teach second and third grade, remember?"

Aiden nods slowly. "Oh yeah. Before you retired." He glances at me, recalling our conversation. "Mr. Mackey retired, and now we're gonna have a new principal."

Mom looks at me. "I didn't know Terry was retiring."

I nod. "It was kind of sudden, I guess. He was planning on another year or two, but after Linda's health scare earlier this summer, I guess they decided he was just not going back. It was only announced a month and a half ago, and they already had a new guy going through the interview process when they announced Terry's retirement."

"You know anything about the new principal?" Mom asks, as we watch Aiden head straight through the house to the backyard, chasing Bobber, Mom and Dad's King Charles Cavalier Spaniel.

I lean against their kitchen island, idly spinning the Lazy Susan. "Not much. I've been too busy preparing for next year to do much sleuthing. I know his name is Mr. Trent, and he's a younger guy from…Connecticut?

Massachusetts? Somewhere around there. I was reading a Facebook thread about him before Cora showed up." I shrug. "I know they put out a newsletter, and I'm sure I got it, but I figure school is starting in a week and I'll just meet him then. Those newsletter write-ups don't really tell you much."

Mom nods, laughing as Bobber cuts a tight turn and Aiden, trying to follow, goes rolling across the grass—only to be lick-attacked by Bobber. "Okay, dear, we're all set here. You don't worry about a thing. Have a good time, okay?"

"He announced that he's going to eat a whole pizza by himself," I say, quirking an eyebrow. "Don't let him do that, okay?"

Mom keeps a straight face. "Why not? He's a growing boy." When I start to protest, she waves me off with a laugh. "Of course not! What kind of a grandmother do you take me for?"

I raise both eyebrows, now. "The kind who sent him home with me after he'd eaten an entire chocolate bar?"

"That was your father, as a matter of fact. I was on the phone with Nancy and when I got off, they'd polished it off. I said they could only have half to split between them."

I laugh. "Which they took to mean, half each."

"Right, and your father being your father, *accidentally* let Aiden have most of his half too."

"You know you can't take your eyes off either one

of them for more than two seconds when they're together," I tell her.

Mom sighs. "I know. Your father is reverting to his
childhood more and more with every year he's retired,"
she says. "I'm tempted to tell him to go back to work
before I go bananas."

Cora groans. "Okay, okay—once you two start gab-
bing, you never quit. I have a fun evening planned and
time's a-wasting."

Mom bumps Cora with her hip. "Don't you be im-
patient with me, Cora Marie. There's plenty of time
for whatever shenanigans you're planning."

"I do not engage in *shenanigans*," Cora says, acting
offended. "I am the picture of a proper lady."

Mom barks a disbelieving laugh. "If you believe
that, then you need to your memory checked, young
lady."

Cora grabs me by the arm and hauls me away. "I
know better than to fall for that game! You're trying to
get me to play 'do-you-remember', and I'm not falling
for it!"

Mom just laughs. "Drat! You saw through my trap!"

"Bye, Aiden!" I call, loudly enough that he can hear
me through the house. "I love you! Be good!"

"Bye, Mom!" Aiden calls back, and I hear his feet
stomping across the hardwood floors, and then the
screen door creaks open and slams closed, and he's
leaping from the top step, sprinting across the gravel
driveway, and skidding to a stop to hug me. "I can't let

you go without a hug!"

I kneel, squeezing him until he groans. "Not too many sweets!" I tell him, after at least ten kisses. "Don't let Grandpa get you guys in trouble."

Aiden makes a big show of crossing his fingers and putting them behind his back. "I won't! Don't you worry about a thing, Mom! Grandpa and I will have extra veggies and NO chocolate."

I laugh, letting him go and head for the car. "Yeah, I don't believe that for a second. Be good, I love you!"

"*You* be good!" he says over his shoulder, running back for the house. "Love you more!"

Cora shoves me into the passenger seat and slams the door. "Okay, okay, okay—you love him, he loves you, and goodbyes have been said. Let's go!"

I buckle up, laughing at Cora. "You are in a godawful hurry, aren't you?"

She does a three-point turn and heads down my parents' long driveway and then heads for downtown. "If I don't drag you away, you'll linger for an hour, talking to your mom and hovering over Aiden." She smirks at me. "Plus, I want to make it José's Cantina for happy hour."

"Ohhh dear," I sigh. "Two-dollar margaritas and three-dollar tacos."

"Exactly—two-dollar margaritas," she says. "But if I slip an extra buck or two in there, Freddy will make 'em top-shelf."

"You mean, if you let him stare at your cleavage

he'll make them top-shelf."

She shrugs. "And? He's old enough to be our dad, but he's a lonely, single old bartender and there's no harm in letting him look, is there?"

I just laugh. "You're ordering them, not me, so you do you, babe."

We make it to happy hour at José's, and I watch from our booth as Cora flirts shamelessly with Freddy—who is a fixture in our little town. She returns with two giant, overflowing, top-shelf margaritas, which I'm sure will also be mostly tequila: part of the reason Freddy is a fixture is that he's notoriously liberal in the way he pours liquor, especially if you're a female and willing to play along with his heavy-handed but harmless flirtation.

Cora, of course, draws the gazes of every male in the joint as she carries our drinks to our table—she's wearing tight black skinny jeans that show off her toned legs and generous booty, paired with three-inch stilettos that work wonders for her already-wondrous backside. She's got on a sequined silver sleeveless top with a plunging neckline, lots of glittery bangles on her wrists and ridiculous huge eighties hoop earrings. Classic Cora style: over the top, but it just somehow works for her.

She relishes the attention, glancing slyly this way and that as she flounces across the bar, scoping out the scene. When she finally sits down across from me, I take a sip of my margarita.

"Wow—I mean...*wow*." I make a face—the drink is pretty much 95 percent tequila with a faint coloring of margarita mix. "You are so shameless, you know that?"

She preens. "Yep. I've got it down to an art." She rolls her eyes at me. "You know as well as I do that Freddy is totally harmless. He just likes to have fun and flirt with pretty women."

"I'm referring to your little prance across the bar, actually," I say. "Could you be any more obvious?"

She just snorts, sipping her drink and sighing in bliss. "A real Freddy Special. Mmmm." She waves me off. "They're all old married coots. Not a single guy in the joint."

"Because Lewis is, very literally, the only single guy in town," I point out.

We live in Clayton, a tiny little hamlet in south central Pennsylvania, the kind of village you have to take rural highways to get to, a place where everyone knows everyone, and everyone's business is the topic of conversation all day long. I was born and raised here, went to the elementary school Aiden goes to—Terry Mackey was my principal, and my mom was my third-grade teacher—and I graduated from the high school where I'm now a guidance counselor. I've been to the weddings of every male between the ages of eighteen and fifty in town, and the whole town was abuzz with gossip when my marriage was dissolving. Everyone knows Lewis Calhoun has had a crush on me since fourth grade, and that I wouldn't touch him with a ten-foot pole, as good-looking and funny as he may be...mostly because I know for a fact what *really* happened with him and Jenny Renfield in tenth grade. His little pot-selling operation is the most well-known secret in town. His uncle is a county sheriff deputy, but he looks the other way.

Cora sighs. "What is it with you and Lewis, for real? His pot business is harmless. He only sells to, like, eight or nine people, and they're all people who should get medical but can't or won't. He doesn't sell to kids, and he's discreet. It's not like he's out behind the gym forcing crack on the freshmen."

"I know." I shrug. "I'm just not interested, and never have been." I eye her. "What is it with *you* and Lewis, for real?" I counter.

She echoes my shrug. "When was the last time you had a conversation with him? He's a really good guy, once you get to know him."

"I'm sure he is," I say, and then frown at her. "Wait...when have you had conversations with Lewis Calhoun?"

Cora shrugs, a picture of studied innocence. "Oh, you know just...here and there."

My frown deepens. "Methinks the lady doth protest too much."

She rolls her eyes at me. "Is it suddenly illegal for me to have perfectly innocent conversations with people?"

"No," I say. "But if you've been talking to Lewis,

you'd think I'd know about it."

She sighs, rolls her eyes, and shakes her head. "I sat next to him at a township meeting a few weeks ago, if you must know."

"Do you remember the thing with Jenny in tenth grade?" I remind her.

Cora raspberries at me. "Oh, let that go, Elyse. That was, what...fifteen years ago? They were kids, and it's not like Jenny was innocent in the whole fiasco either, remember? She was just more vocal about making sure everyone knew *her* side of the story, and Lewis just let everyone believe what they wanted, since he was already the black sheep of not just the school but the whole town."

"Let me guess, that's what you guys talked about at the meeting," I venture.

She shrugs. "Among other things."

Our conversation wanders after that, from high school reminiscences to the latest gossip—Alan Peters is *definitely* sleeping with Amy Andersen, Cora insists, and she's sure Macy Peters knows but Bill Andersen doesn't—to the various and endless other tidbits of rumor and news and gossip.

After about an hour and a half later, and two high-octane Freddy Specials each, Cora decides it's time to move on. We leave her car in the parking lot at José's and walk the two blocks down the street to Field's for karaoke, where she shoves another too-sweet tequila drink in my hands and signs us up to sing "Total Eclipse of the Heart." We're three numbers out, just enough time to finish the first drink and start on the second, which I down a little too fast. I'm tipsy enough to think karaoke will be fun, but not tipsy enough to not get nervous.

Finally, we're up. I clutch my sweating glass in one hand and the mic in the other, and Cora and I belt out our song—I lean into her and close my eyes, pretending it's just her and me in my bedroom, blasting it on my boom box and singing into hairbrushes. When I open my eyes after the song is over and suck down a mouthful of my drink, it's to scattered applause from the crowded bar.

And as I look out at the crowd I see a pair of brown eyes watching me rather intently.

Cora and I step off the little stage and head for our table, and I feel those eyes following me. I take my seat—ripped vinyl cushions at a battered, sticky Formica table, with a metal napkin dispenser, a rocks glass full of tiny pencils, and a stack of request slips. I try to be surreptitious as I shift in my seat so I can scope out the owner of the eyes; he's sitting a few feet away, alone at a table, sipping Labatt Blue from a bottle.

He looks like he's pretty tall, with wavy brown hair swept to one side, wearing a blue polo tucked into a pair of chinos, a brown leather belt, and sensible shoes. Odd outfit to go to a karaoke bar in, but whatever.

I don't know him—that's what's intriguing.

His eyes, too, are part of his charm. They are

warm, exuding good humor and kindness.

I kick Cora under the table. "Who's that?" I ask, cutting a meaningful glance at the newcomer.

Cora gives him a quick, blatant once-over, and shrugs. "I dunno. Tourist, probably, judging by the nerdy getup."

I laugh. "Tourist? Since when do we get tourists in Clayton?"

"There's an accountant conference happening in Lancaster," she suggests. "Maybe he was trying to get there and got lost?"

I roll my eyes. "Lancaster? If he's going there, he's *really* lost."

She glances at him again. "He *is* pretty cute. You should go talk to him."

Pretty cute? Puppies are pretty cute. Babies and kittens and newborn calves are pretty cute. This guy is... handsome. He doesn't fit the "hot" bill, because his features are more classically handsome than Hollywood magazine hot. His hair is neatly but casually styled, his clothing is conservative and plain, but fits him well. Another glance at his shoulders and arms tells me he works out, and the midsection of his polo is flat, meaning no belly.

And he has a five o'clock shadow going on, and those eyes. They're intelligent, curious. Eager. Inviting.

Interested.

"Go talk to him. Get him to buy you a drink."

I shake my head. "I don't need another drink. I

need some water."

Cora elbows me. "Fine, water *and* a drink. You can't poop out now, Elyse."

I frown at her. "I'm not pooping out, I'm just drinking intelligently—drinking water to keep from getting dehydrated."

Cora shakes her head. "You've had, like, five drinks in three hours, and we're getting a cab home."

"A cab? What cab? There are no cabs in Clayton."

Cora snickers. "Well, a ride home, at least."

I eye her warily. "Cora?"

"Elyse?"

"What do you mean by 'a ride'?"

"A designated nondrinker to drive us safely, legally, and responsibly home."

"*Cora.*"

She throws up her hands. "Monty, okay? I have his cell number, and I'm going to text him when we need a ride home, and he'll swing by in his rig and drive us."

"Cora!" I can't help laughing even as I scold her. "I don't want to ride home in Monty's tow truck! It smells like cigarettes and old farts."

"It smells like cigarettes and *new* farts," she corrects. "And would you rather walk home? Because I have no intention of sobering up enough to drive."

I sigh. "Cigarettes, old farts, *and* new farts."

"And *safe.*"

"It's *Monty.*"

Monty Elkhorn: forty-nine years old, lives in stained

mechanic's coveralls too small for his enormous beer belly, sporting a graying hobo-Santa beard, stinking of BO and American Spirit cigarettes...given to rambling in his heavy, grumbling voice about whatever enters his head. Monty lives alone in a single-wide about six or eight miles outside of town, in a little clearing—he calls it a "holler"—with electricity he ran himself. Lock your keys in your car? Call Monty, he'll shim your window. Break down? He'll tow you, or run you to the gas station so you can pick up some gas. His tow truck is a Vietnam-era military surplus two-ton truck he modified into a tow truck himself. Monty is super helpful to have around town, and we've all needed his help at some point, but using him a cab service seems...I don't know. Weird.

She just waves her hand at me. "Exactly. It's Monty."

I sigh. "Fine, whatever."

"Now that *that's* settled, go talk to Mr. Prep Academy over there." She indicates the handsome newcomer with her drink.

"That's judgmental. Just because he's dressed nicely doesn't make him a nerd."

"His chinos look like they've been pressed *and* starched."

"They're just new."

"Go talk to him!"

"No!"

She eyes me with mischief in her eyes. "I'll sign you up to sing again...and I'll make you do ABBA."

"Fine!" I huff, because I know Cora well enough to know she'll do it, and ABBA is sacred—you don't do ABBA karaoke unless you can pull it off, and I definitely can't pull it off...I'm sober enough to know that much.

I run my fingers through my hair, glancing at Cora. "Is my makeup okay?"

She winks at me. "You're sexy. Now go!"

I get up and suck in a deep breath.

I'm about to make my way to his table when I hear a smooth, warm voice. "I hope you're not leaving already," the voice says. "I was just coming by to see if you wanted another drink."

I look up, and it's him. Up close, he's more than handsome—he's breathtaking.

3

"I WAS JUST COMING OVER TO TALK TO YOU, ACTUALLY," I say, and I'm proud of myself for not freezing.

His warm, kind, intelligent brown eyes pierce mine. "I thought you sounded awesome, by the way. Almost as good as Bonnie Tyler herself."

I roll my eyes and laugh. "Okay, whatever you say."

"For real! You and your friend killed it!"

"Well, thanks. Are you doing a song?" I ask.

He gestures to the bar, and I go with him. "You want another drink?"

I nod. "Sure." Sam the bartender comes over, and I catch his attention. "One more of whatever it was Cora had you make us."

"And another Labatt Blue, and the tab to me."

"You don't have to do that," I say.

He just laughs. "Well, that *is* how buying a lady a drink typically works, you know."

"True," I say. "So, you never answered. Are you doing a song?"

He laughs again and shakes his head. "Heck, no! I didn't know this was a karaoke place when I came in." The bartender slides us our drinks, and my new friend hands over a credit card, then turns to me. "My name is Jamie."

"I'm Elyse," I say, and we shake hands—his hand is warm and strong, and he doesn't let go right away, his eyes drilling into mine.

"It's wonderful to meet you, Elyse."

"Same." I consider asking him if he's new in town, but it's pretty obvious he is, so I don't. "If you don't know Field's is a karaoke joint, then you probably haven't been to Vinnie's either."

He shakes his head, taking a swig of beer. "Nope. This is the first place I've been."

"Vinnie's has live music on Fridays and Saturdays," I tell him. "The cover band is a bunch of local guys, but they're pretty decent. Good enough to dance to, at least."

"You want to finish these and head over?" he asks, gracing me with a bright, friendly smile—his eyes, though, are more than friendly, and the look in them gives me butterflies.

"Sounds good to me," I tell him. "Let me just tell my friend the plan."

Jamie indicates the table Cora and I had been sitting at—it's empty. "Looks like she had other plans."

I sigh, turning back to the bar, and to Jamie. "She'll be at Vinnie's."

"Probably not that many other options, huh?"

I laugh. "Nope, not really. We went to José's for dinner, and then here for karaoke, which only leaves Vinnie's for dancing. There are only the three places in town. You want something else, you have to go over to Hanover, and that's almost six miles away, or York, and that's almost twenty."

"Wow, six whole miles, huh?" he says, teasing.

"Around here, that's a long way. If you live in Clayton, you rarely leave Clayton."

His eyes twinkle. "I mean, what else could you possibly want? You've got three whole bars."

"I don't know, I wouldn't mind a Walmart or a Starbucks."

He just waves his hand. "Nahhh. Overrated."

I laugh. "Yeah—convenience and variety...*so* overrated."

"Right? Shop local!" He frowns, rubbing his chin. "Where do you get groceries around here, though?"

"Well, you have two options. Clayton General has pretty all much the essentials—soda, milk, juice, cereal, canned goods, alcohol, frozen stuff, meat, cheese, produce, all that stuff. Benny's Keg Stand, which we all just call Kegger, has a few other basic odds and ends in a little section near the back, and he's open later than the general store."

He shakes his head. "Wow. So, what if you need more than that?"

I shrug. "These days, you order online. If you want

to shop in-person, you have to go to Hanover, because they have an ALDI, a Food Lion, and not one but *two* Walmart Supercenters."

Jamie sighs. "Ahh, so Clayton is small-town living."

"For most of us, it's all we know, and we wouldn't trade it for all the Walmarts and Starbucks in the world." I finish my drink. "You ready to check out the glory and wonder that is Vinnie's?"

He tosses back the last of his beer and sets it on the counter. "Sure am. Lead the way.

I laugh. "Well, it's literally right across the street, so if you get lost on the way, you have issues."

Jamie laughs as we exit Field's and stand on the sidewalk. "Yeah, kinda hard to get lost around here, I guess."

Our main street is US-30, running east to west— if you're coming east into town it's called Lincoln Highway, and if you're exiting town to the west, it's called Lincoln Way West. Bisecting downtown into quarters are Carlisle Street to the north, and Hanover Street to the south; where Carlisle, Hanover, and US-30 all intersect is a large traffic circle, so we don't even have a stop light—otherwise we'd be just another one-stoplight town. We're not even that...we're a blip on the map, a quick bump around the traffic circle through our cute, quaint little town, and then out again onto US-30.

The island at the center of the traffic circle is known, ironically, as the Town Square. It's a small, round park crisscrossed by sidewalks in a pattern that resembles a tic-tac-toe board. At the center, in the very middle of the island, is a fountain, ringed by concrete, with a flagpole in the middle, and war memorials listing the veterans from Clayton who have served in wars ranging from the Revolution through Desert Storm. There are park benches here and there on opposite sides of the Town Square, and you'll often find locals sitting there, chatting, exchanging gossip, feeding the pigeons, and watching the sparse traffic wheel slowly around the circle.

Field's is on the southwest corner, Vinnie's is on the northwest, Clayton General is on the northeast corner, and Kegger is on the southeast. There's a post office next to Vinnie's, a pharmacy next to Kegger, and a few mom-and-pop retail shops fill in the rest. Clayton Methodist is on Carlisle to the north, and Emory Presbyterian on the corner of Hanover and Lincoln Way West, a few doors down from Kegger. There's a dentist, a family medical practice, our town's sole lawyer—John Michael Gregory, Esquire—as well as a few private homes, owned by the wealthiest and most influential citizens. José's is east down Lincoln Highway about half a mile, and there's a VFW lodge about a mile west on Lincoln Way West, but you only go there if you're a military vet, or desperate for one-dollar-pour off-brand light domestic beer served in reused Solo cups

It's a quaint, quiet, sleepy little town that hasn't

changed much at all in the last hundred and some years. Walking through Clayton is kind of a time warp back to the eighteenth and nineteenth centuries—especially when Pa Chantry rides his vintage buckboard into town, pulled by his mules, Ethel and Lucy, or when Jim Parnell, Mack Lackey, and Harrison Graves decide to ride their horses to Vinnie's instead of driving a car. Nobody local blinks an eye at that stuff, although the rare tourist or visitor we sometimes get usually does a heck of a double take. Pa Chantry gets the majority of the confused looks, though, with his chest-length black beard, meerschaum pipe, and faded black Stetson—this being Pennsylvania, most assume he's an Amish transplant or visitor when, in reality, he's just one of the town oddities.

Speaking of whom—Pa's buckboard is parked outside Vinnie's, Ethel and Lucy chomping happily in their feedbags, tails swishing idly.

Jamie does what most nonlocals do at the sight: he tilts his head, frowns, and then glances at me curiously. "Is that part of a reenactment or something?"

I laugh. "Nope. That's just old Pa Chantry. He's a quirky sort of guy. You'll know him when you see him. He lives on a hundred-some acre farm south of town, and he works it the same way as his father, grandfather, and great-grandfather did, without any modern tools or equipment. I've never been to his place myself, but I hear he doesn't even use plumbing or electricity, even though he has it."

Jamie quirks an eyebrow at me. "Takes real dedication to the old ways to use gas lamps and an outhouse when you have electricity and a toilet."

"Dedication…yeah, that's one word for it."

We head across the street, cutting across the empty town square; the fountain splashes merrily, the spraying water and gently flapping American flag, Pennsylvania flag, and M.I.A/P.O.W flag lit by a quartet of yellow floodlights. All the parking spots around the circle are all full, and Vinnie's is thumping and chugging with the strains of "Smoke on the Water" as covered by Johnny and the Walkers, Clayton's only musical act, who have played classic rock covers at Vinnie's every weekend for the past twenty years. The door to Vinnie's is propped open by an empty keg, on which is sitting a bored-looking Al Vincent, a burly ex-Navy veteran and owner of the town "gym"; the quotes are because the gym is literally just an old abandoned warehouse with boarded-up windows, which Al has filled with cast-off, secondhand free weights, benches, stands, and machines, and charges five bucks a pop to go in and work out; he makes decent money at it, too, because it's the only place, except the big box gyms in Hanover, to lift weights.

"Elyse, how are ya?" Al says, extending his closed fist to me.

I tap my knuckles against his. "Okay, Al. You?"

He shrugs a heavy shoulder. "Eh, it's all good. Busy night for these parts."

I snicker. "Meaning Bob and Rick already went at it?"

"Bob said the Nittany Lions suck, and Rick said the Steelers suck even worse, and then they started swinging." Al shakes his head, shaggy black hair shaking. "Had to pop Rick one on the jaw to get him to slow his roll. They're arguing strategy, now, so it won't be long before one of 'em tries swinging again."

"I'll be sure to stay out of the way then," I say.

Al just laughs, a hearty chuckle. "Ehhh, they're both clobbered. You could knock over either one of 'em yourself." He turns a baleful, interested gaze on Jamie. "Don't know you, bub."

Jamie doesn't seem fazed by the less-than-friendly welcome from Al. "That's because I'm not from around here." He extends a hand to Al, which I foresee him regretting in three...two...one: Al squeezes hard, and I watch Jamie go pale, wincing, but he doesn't make a sound and doesn't let go until Al does, and then Jamie only makes a fist once and then shakes his hand a couple of times. "I'm Jamie. Nice to meet you."

Al nods, suitably impressed by Jamie's "manly" endurance of his notoriously brutal handshake. "Yep. You too."

We head in, and the intense vibrations from the perpetually too loud sound system wash over us, bass thudding in our guts, drums rattling and thudding deafeningly. Johnny's guitar shrieks and howls as he works on one of his extended guitar solos. The air is smoky, despite the statewide ban on smoking indoors. Vinnie still allows it, and so do the rest of us. The stage is in the front by the plate glass window, with a few stage lights on the ceiling bathing the band in bright yellow, red, and blue; the bar itself runs the entire length of the building from front to back along the right side, with a little space cleared in front of the stage for dancing. Booths line the left side, and round four-top tables fill the rest of the space. The back door is propped open as well, with Matty Murphy, the other Clayton tough guy, sitting on another empty keg, playing a game on his cell phone.

Vinnie's is crowded with the usual assortment of regulars—the hard-drinking farmers at the bar, their wives gossiping in the booths behind them, a few of the younger residents dancing and milling by the bar. Vinnie's is a small place and the modest crowd—a hundred-some souls—makes it seem very crowded. When you factor in the crowds at Field's and José's, pretty much everyone who lives within thirty minutes of downtown Clayton is represented here, with a few exceptions, like my parents and a handful of other non-drinkers. Clayton being what it is, there's not much to do around here at night aside from sitting at home and watching TV, or hitting one of the bars and drinking, and it's not hard to figure out which one most people choose.

Jamie nudges me. "Bar, booth, or dance floor?" he says, leaning close and speaking into my ear to be heard over the band.

I smirk at him. "Was that your idea of asking me to dance?" I respond, putting my lips to his ear.

He grins back. "It was my way of asking if you wanted to dance, or just sit and talk."

"Drinks first, then dance!" I hesitate, and then smile even more widely. "And then sit and talk."

The bar is crowded enough that he grabs my hand and holds on as we weave through to the bar, sliding between Abe Cowell and Grady Masterson, two of the oldest, orneriest, and hardest drinkers in Clayton, who are perched on their usual stools dead center of the bar. They give me terse nods, and stern, wary stares at Jamie, who lifts a hand to catch the attention of Sam, Vinnie's bartender—yes, both bartenders at Field's and Vinnie's are named Sam, one of Clayton's many odd coincidences. Jamie orders me a tequila sunrise, gets another beer for himself, and then we get a table where we leave our drinks before heading to the dance floor.

Johnny and the Walkers are into a rollicking rock-abilly version of "Hard Day's Night" and we're in the thick of the crowded dance floor, bumping into people as we move to the music. I'm not the best dancer, but after a few drinks I don't really care—I'm oddly relieved to find that Jamie is about the same: he won't win any dance contests, but he's confident and carefree, and he dances close to me.

His eyes stay on mine, and our bodies sway closer and closer, like two planets being pulled toward each other by the inexorable force of gravity. Time slips and distorts, and I finish my drink—Jamie takes it and vanishes, returning with two more drinks for us, and some water. A nice gesture but, at this point, the water is insufficient to make a dent in my buzz. We drink, and we dance. Johnny and the Walkers play through their repertoire of classic rock covers, from Led Zeppelin to Poison, Van Halen to The Allman Brothers, with a few pop hits turned classic rock thrown in for fun—their most popular pop covers include "Oops, I Did It Again," "Genie in a Bottle," and "Bye Bye Bye." Which are their ideas of "modern pop." If it's newer than the year 2000, they won't play it.

I've lost track of time and the number of drinks I've had, and the universe is spinning a little when I lean into Jamie. "I need to sit down, and I need, like, forty waters."

He nods. "Same here."

His hand in mine, Jamie leads me off the dance floor and to a back-corner booth far away from the dance floor and close to the pool tables and dart boards, where it's nominally quieter. I slide into the booth facing the bar, and watch as Jamie weaves, only a little unsteadily, back to the bar. He comes back moments later with two empty pint glasses and a clear plastic pitcher of water. He slides into the booth facing me, pours us each a glass of water, and we both drink greedily.

He jerks his head backward, indicating the band. "They're actually pretty good!"

I laugh. "Good thing, because they're the only act in town!"

A brief silence, punctuated by each of us refilling our water. And then Jamie leans across the table. "So. Tell me something about yourself, Elyse."

I decide to lead off with the potential deal breaker. "I'm a single mother to an eight-year-old."

Jamie just nods, totally unfazed by this information. "Eight is a fun age. Girl? Boy?"

I need a second to recover from his unexpected response. "Boy. His name is Aiden."

"Aiden, huh? Where is he tonight?"

"With my parents." I lift my chin at him. "And what about you?"

"Divorced, no kids, just transferred to the area for a new job." He lets the silence between us stand—a relative silence, since the bar is noisy with the band and the crowd—but only for a moment. "Since I'm curious about you, I'll tell you about me first: I'm thirty-five, and I was born and raised on the East Coast—Nashua, New Hampshire, to be specific."

"I'm thirty-two, and I was born and raised right here in good ol' Clayton." I smile as I offer my next fact. "I've actually never been west of Cleveland, South of Pittsburgh, or north of Philly."

"So you're a lifelong P-A girl, huh?"

I nod. "Yep. Well, I went to college in Baltimore, but that's still close enough that I came home on the weekends to eat and do laundry, and then moved right back here after college." And that's all I'm saying on *that* particular subject.

"Until my recent transfer, I'd never left the Nashua area, except for a weekend in San Francisco a few years ago, and a road trip to the Pacific Northwest with some friends during college. So I get it. As small as it is, Nashua is a bit bigger than Clayton."

I laugh. "A postage stamp is bigger than Clayton. We're a blip on the map, and our town is more than an hour from the nearest major city. If we *had* a stoplight, we'd turn it off at night, and if we could roll up sidewalks, we'd do it." I shrug, sighing. "But...it's home, and I love it."

"Never thought of leaving?" Jamie asks.

I make a face. "Of course I have! My entire teenage years were spent daydreaming of moving to New York City. And then I went to the University of Maryland, and Baltimore was so huge to me it was overwhelming. I was honestly relieved to be back home."

Jamie pours us each a third glass of water. "Oh, man. You've never been to New York?"

I widen my eyes and shake my head. "God, no! I'd probably have an anxiety attack in the first ten minutes!"

"If Baltimore was overwhelming, I'd say if you ever do visit the Big Apple, go with someone who's been there before. It's its own world, let me tell you."

"Did you live there?" I ask.

He fiddles with the saltshaker, pouring a bit of salt on the table and balancing the shaker on one end.

"Heck no! I visited a couple times, but the thought of trying to live there full-time?" He shudders. "I break out in hives just thinking about it."

"Well, Clayton is as far from the Big Apple as you can get, I'd say, actual distance notwithstanding." I knock over the saltshaker, and then try to balance it in the salt like he had; I fail repeatedly, and we both laugh.

The pitcher of water is empty, and Jamie nudges it toward me. "You want more?"

I shake my head. "Nah. I've had so much water at this point that my belly is all sloshy, as Aiden would put it."

"It's all water too, I'm sure," he teases.

"Yeah, well…" I shrug, and then meet his intriguing brown eyes. "I've had fun," I say.

"Me too."

Silence.

"I'm gonna go potty," I say, and then groan at myself. "To the bathroom, I mean. Because I am actually an adult."

Jamie just laughs. "Spend enough time around kids, and you tend to pick up some of their mannerisms."

When I come out of the bathroom—shaking my hands dry because all Vinnie has in there to dry your hands is an aging air dryer that feels like having a geriatric poodle breathe on your hands—the booth is empty. Odd.

I'm wondering if he left, or if he went to the bathroom when I feel two warm hands clap me on the arms and spin me around.

"Elyse! I'm so proud of you!" Cora is in rare Cora form—meaning, she's had as much to drink as I have, but less water. "You're macking on the hottie in the starched chinos!"

"His name is Jamie, and I'm not sure where he went, actually." I arch an eyebrow at her. "And literally zero people say macking anymore, by the way."

She wiggles her eyebrow. "He's in the bathroom. He had to adjust himself."

I frown. "How do you know that?"

"Because I've been spying on you from the bar!" She gyrates her hips. "You guys were dancin, and drinkin', and talkin'! And the eyes you were making at him? Oooh, baby. Gettin' spicy up in here!"

"I think you've had enough to drink, Cora."

She rolls her eyes at me. "It's my last hurrah of the summer, *Elyse*. Don't shit on my parade."

"Rain on your parade, you mean?"

"Whatever. My point is—" she wraps an arm around me. "My point *is*...he's in the bathroom, and when he went in, he was adjusting a nice little semi, because he's, like, the *most* into you."

"Cora!"

"What?"

"Have some water."

She shakes her head. "Nope, nope, nopety, nope, nope. Monty is on call! Monty the Mountie, to my rescue."

"You didn't make him any promises, did you?"

She frowns at me. "Aside from cold hard cash in exchange for his professional services? No. What do you take me for?"

"A crazy person who does crazy things when she's drunk, and you're drunk."

"If it was Lewis Calhoun, I'd be telling a different story. But, alas, Lewis Calhoun is a *lone wolf*, and he's too cool for bars." She sighs sadly. "And I'm not drunk enough yet to just show up at his place."

"Good idea," I say, drily. "You never know, he might be in the middle of a drug deal."

She rolls her eyes at me. "Oh, let that go, already. He's from *Clayton*—he's not John Gotti."

I frown at her. "Was John Gotti a drug dealer? I don't think he was."

"Oh shut up with your facts. You know what I mean." She pokes me in the chest. "Let's get back to the important stuff—namely Jamie, he of the starched and pressed chinos, and how you're into him, and he's coming out of the bathroom right now."

"Cora—"

She backs away, points at me. "Go with it!"

"I'm going *home*!"

"Yeah, you are…in the *morning*!" she says, turning and vanishing into the crowd on the dance floor.

"Cora! I'm not—" and then I cut myself off because Jamie is headed this way, shaking his hands.

"Those hand dryers are the single least effective

thing on the planet, I think," he says by way of greeting.

"I know, right? I think Vinnie has a Go-Fund Me to have them replaced with those fancy Dyson air blade things."

"I'd fund that," he says. And then, after a long, significant look, he nods at the exit. "Want to get out of here? I could use a walk and some fresh air."

"Sounds good," I hear myself say.

Because it does sound good to get out of the close, humid air of the bar, away from the noise and the crowd. It would be nice to spend time with Jamie, and enjoy some quiet conversation.

He heads for the front door, but I catch his hand. "Back door," I tell him, leading him that way. "No point fighting through the crowd."

I wave at Matty as we pass him. "See ya later, Matty," I sing-song.

He just juts his chin at me with half a glance. "See ya, Elyse. You're walking home, right?"

"Well, I'm not driving anywhere, that's for sure," I promise him. "I don't even have my car here."

"Good." Matty is fifteen years younger than Al but just as big; he's not much friendlier than Al if you don't know him, but to us locals, he's a teddy bear with a heart of gold. Matty and I went to school together all our lives, but he never left like I did. He's always making sure nobody drives home after too many drinks, and has been known to deliver people's cars to them after they walked home.

"Keep an eye on Cora for me, will you?" I ask.

He snorts. "Yeah, okay. Let me just go right ahead and stop her from doing crazy shit."

I laugh. "Just don't let her hurt herself, or do anything too stupid."

"I got you." His eyes go to Jamie, and then back to me. "You're good?" His voice is quiet, and he seems somehow more threatening when he uses his quiet voice; I'd fear for Jamie, if I said no.

I smile at him. "I'm great. Thanks, Matty."

He just nods, and goes back to the video game on his phone. "See ya 'round."

The alley behind Vinnie's is bordered by a chain-link fence, beyond which are the backyards of the houses of Oak Junction. The road here is paved in some sections, original cobblestone in others. A single whitish-yellow streetlamp hangs from a power line overhead, casting a broad shadow over the alley beyond the pool of light. The music and chatter from Vinnie's are loud, even out here, and my ears ring in the relative quiet.

A dog barks in the distance, and another answers.

As if on some unspoken cue, Jamie and I begin walking, turning left onto Carlisle and heading north. We are quiet for a minute, and then he asks me about my favorite music, and that leads to a story from Jamie about seeing Dave Matthews Band's concert at The Gorge in 2002, days after his twenty-first birthday, which was part of a road trip a few friends had surprised him with. We talk about all sorts of things as we amble slowly up Main Street, leaving downtown behind. His hand is in mine—our fingers are twined together, and it seems like the most right and perfect thing ever.

My head is fuzzy, and I'm a little tipsy still, but I'm lucid enough to absorb every moment of this—Jamie's low, quiet, smooth, pleasant voice relating a funny story, his hand in mine, the sense of anticipation just from being with him. I watch him as he talks—he uses his left hand to gesture, not letting go of mine with his right. He's animated, and an amazing storyteller. His features are even, symmetrical, and handsome. His jaw-line is strong, his hair no longer quite as neatly combed as it was when I first saw him, and he's all the sexier for it. The shadow of stubble on his jaw makes me weak in the knees, and when his eyes cut to mine, I feel all melty.

"Is there somewhere around here we can get a cup of coffee?" Jamie asks.

I laugh. "At this time of day? Yeah…no."

He pauses, looks at me. "Um, so then…do you want to…come over? For coffee?"

My heart thuds, pounds, and I swallow hard. It's just coffee. We're just going to hang out and talk and have a cup of coffee. That's all.

"Sure," I say. "Sounds good."

We're in the Oak Junction neighborhood now, on North 3rd, the third street north of the county highway. Clayton's planners, being the creative types that they obviously were, numbered the roads in the same way on the other side of the highway, only there, it's South 1st and so on. Brilliant, I know. The houses here are old but well-kept, with deep front porches and steep concrete steps, tiny lawns in front, and shared backyard spaces fenced off in some places, but not in others.

North 3rd ends at Washington, which takes you back to the county highway, and we make a left on Washington. We only go a quarter of a mile when Jamie comes to a stop outside a house painted a pale blue with a sea-foam green door, white shutters, and small, neat box shrubs on either side of the front door.

My hands tingle. My chest aches, and my heart is hammering. A little voice deep inside tells me I should rethink this, but that voice is too small and too quiet— there are other, louder voices that drown it out. Voices that remind me how handsome Jamie is, and how much fun I've had with him this evening, and how easy he is to be around, and how it's been such a long, long time since I've been so attracted to anyone.

How long it's been since…well…everything.

I let out a breath and shuffle a little closer to Jamie, so my chest brushes his and I'm staring up into his warm, intense, eager brown eyes; there's no mistaking the shift in the atmosphere between us, or what he's suggesting, and what I'm agreeing to when I say:

"Let's go in." I find his other hand with mine.

4

I FOLLOW JAMIE INTO HIS HOME. IT'S DARK INSIDE, WITH only a faint silvering of moonlight on the hardwood floors; there are shadows and silhouettes—a sectional couch, an end table, a lamp, a recliner, an ottoman, a low rectangular coffee table, stacks of boxes, a vacuum. A doorway shows the kitchen in shadow—more boxes occupying most of the floor space, the sink and a window over it look onto the backyard. To the left of the living room as you walk in the front door is a staircase leading up to the second floor; at the top of the stairs is another window letting in a shaft of silver moonlight

We stand in the darkness and the silence for a moment, side by side, hand in hand. My heart pounds. Anticipation sings in my blood.

For the first time since I met him, the silence between us is awkward.

"I just moved in," he says, by way of explaining the obvious. "Haven't had time to do much unpacking."

My breath comes short, and my hands tremble.

I turn to face him, intending to say something, anything, just to break the ice. Something pithy and stupid about moving, perhaps. I see him in shadow: his hair is a mess, ruffled, wavy, a strand draping over his forehead. I can't help myself—I brush the tendril aside with a fingertip. His eyes fix on mine again. The silence is no longer awkward but rippling with tension, anticipation.

"Elyse," Jamie murmurs.

"Jamie?"

"I'm going to kiss you."

"Thanks for the warning?" I say, smiling up at him.

His palms cup my cheeks, and he slides a few inches closer and now my breasts brush his chest, and I wonder if he can feel my heart slamming against my ribcage. I keep my eyes open, as his are, until the moment his lips touch mine. I swallow my heartbeat desperately, and my fingers lift, trembling like sparrows unsure of a branch, to rest on his shoulders. It's just a touch of his lips at first, a questing. Testing my reaction, perhaps.

Jamie brushes my cheekbones with his thumbs, and I suck in a deep breath as his lips press harder against mine and I feel the first pulse-shattering tease of his tongue against my teeth. The kiss deepens, and I feel his hair clutched in my hands, his scalp on my fingertips as I pull him closer, angling upward, lifting on my toes to meet his kiss, to delve deeper yet.

I'm breathless and the world is spinning.

His hand drifts through my hair, hesitates on my back just between my shoulder blades, and then dances and trips down. One hand is on my cheek, the other is at the small of my back, hesitating, waiting. I press against him, and I feel his heart hammering as hard and wild as my own. I feel all of him, and I can feel how much he wants this.

The kiss breaks, just for a moment—his eyes open, and our eyes meet, and I know he's waiting for the refusal, watching for the demurral.

Instead, I lift up on my tiptoes and kiss him. I taste him, then. His tongue finds mine, and his hand continues its descent. My breath leaves me in a rush as he cups my backside and pulls me tighter against his body.

I deepen the kiss, clutch at his shoulder and rake my hand down his spine.

The only light is moonlight, and the only sound is my pulse in my ears and the sound of our kissing.

Jamie breaks the kiss, just enough that his lips can move, and his whisper resonates in my gut: "Upstairs?"

"Please," I breathe.

He turns, and his hand finds mine and I follow him up the darkened stairs, and we turn the corner at the top and my hand runs along the cool wood of the banister. My pounding pulse ratchets faster yet as we reach the bedroom at the end of the hall. A window lets in silver moonlight—the moon itself is full and framed in the window. There is a bed, a four-poster with a nightstand to one side, a bureau with a round mirror, a closed closet, and more boxes, some opened, and a few large black garbage bags full of clothing. The bed is neatly made, with a throw blanket folded over the foot.

Jamie lets go of my hand as we enter his bedroom, and turns to face me. "Elyse, I…" he trails off, doesn't finish.

"You what?" I ask.

He shakes his head, his eyes leaving mine and roaming down my body, traveling slowly back up. "God, you're beautiful."

My knees don't want to stay locked. My hands shake. My mouth is dry and my throat is seized, and my stomach is fluttering. His words land like bombs, and their detonation shakes me free of my nervous paralyzation.

I step closer to him, run my hands over his chest, and then untuck his shirt from his pants. "Thank you," I whisper.

I feel the alcohol in my system—I know I'm still tipsy, and I know I'm allowing it to circumvent my inhibitions. Sober, I don't know if I would do this. But I also know I'm sober enough that I'm making this decision with full awareness. And I know he's in a similar place—an unsteady step here or there, the scent on his breath, the expression in his eyes; but his hands are steady, and his words are clear.

A tense, thick silence.

And then his lips slant across mine and I'm dizzied by the sudden passion of his kiss. This isn't a tender questing, or a hesitating exploration—this is raw need unleashed. I match it with my own, groaning as his tongue tangles with mine and his hands caress my back, and then cup my bottom and I arch my back and press into his touch in a silent but loud *yes, please, more*. I seek his skin under his shirt and he's gathering the hem of my dress in his fingers, and my eyes are closed; I feel the spin of the world around me, but his body steadies me even as his kiss dizzies me further. I don't know if it's the alcohol or the wild passion making me unsteady on my feet.

I pull his shirt off of him, and fumble at his belt while he tugs the stretchy fabric of my dress up over my hips and then his hands clutch and caress at my bare thighs and buttocks, and then his belt is undone and his pants are sagging. The wild kiss becomes desperate, lips missing lips and stuttering here and there—I tilt my head back to offer my throat to him, and he kisses it; he's fumbling at the zipper of my dress and I'm blindly seeking his skin, trying to remove his pants and underwear without opening my eyes, without losing the press of his lips on my flesh or the scouring thrill of his lips on mine.

I feel a blast of air as he finally lowers the zipper and my dress hits the floor.

The moments then all tangle and braid and slip and twist—it's all a blur of heart-pounding kisses and his hands on my naked flesh. I feel his desire in my fist and our bodies are pressing and writhing; his breath is hot on my skin and his low male murmur and my high breathless delicate groan mingle in passion. I feel the bed under me and Jamie above me; we move in word-less synchronization, in perfect unison.

I'm naked, utterly bare to him, and I feel his hands everywhere, inciting moans in me and eliciting groans from him as he palms my breast and cups my sex and I caress his arousal and we kiss through groans and kiss through whimpers and I can't stop—there is nothing but this, nothing but Jamie in this moment and the wild dizzying fury of how badly I need this. His back is bare and strong, the muscles rippling and undulating under my hands, which skate downward and I feel his buttocks with a slight dusting of hair flexing and pulsing as his need becomes too much. I'm whimpering because my own desire is a mad explosion of heat in my belly and a flood of damp in my core, and there's nothing, nothing, nothing in this universe except Jamie. I hear tinfoil tear and feel his hand move clumsily and desperately between us, and then his mouth covers mine once more and I wrap my legs around his waist and welcome him into me and we're moving together. I clutch at him and cling to him, writhing beneath him. He is everywhere, above me, around me, inside me. This is not mere pleasure, god no—this is so much more.

This is pure, unadulterated ecstasy.

He groans, and I cry out.

He moves desperately, wildly, an unrestrained animal passion driving him to grunt my name in a guttural chorus, and I'm wrapped around him, every limb clinging to his sweat-slick body, writhing in synch with him as we explode together.

Our lips stutter together, and I taste his moans and he sucks in my whimpers and we explode and explode and explode and our voices are raised together, and I've never ever known anything like this, never known such heights of wild, furious passion.

After a too-short eternity, it fades and I'm left sobbing with the quaking aftershocks.

He's gasping for breath.

I'm so dizzy.

I can't breathe.

Wave after wave continues to shake through me, leaving me trembling and helpless as Jamie rolls to his side and gathers me in his arms—I don't question his embrace; I'm too dizzy, too breathless, too helpless.

Moonlight bathes me in quiet silver as I drift in unfamiliar arms that nonetheless feel like home.

The sky through the window is dark gray tinged with pink as I wake.

Arms are wrapped around me.

Male desire is hard and thick behind me, and his breath is ragged, and his hands clutch at my breasts, and desire wakes in me fully alive and ravaging, ravenous. I twist in those strong arms and bury my mouth on his and we are lost together in bold touches and desperate caresses and possessive clutches.

I bite down hard on his shoulder as he fills me and I weep as I'm stretched to bursting, moving raggedly as he shows me without words how beautiful I am, and yet I hear his voice in raw breathless whispers—"So beautiful, Elyse. You're so beautiful…"

And I know I'm doing something wrong, something terrible, something deeply forbidden but I'm too caught up in the delirious mad joy of the ecstasy Jamie infuses in me with his every touch, every movement, every kiss to even think of what could be so wrong about such incredible perfection.

I cry, sobbing, whimpering as I come apart.

His groans as he joins me are as ragged and helpless and breathless as mine.

I fall asleep again, with our arms wrapped around each other.

5

I**T'S FULL DAYLIGHT WHEN I WAKE AGAIN. THERE'S A SOFT** snore beside me, and awareness ripples through me.

Jamie.

I remember it all—every moment. It's all burned with crystal clarity into my mind. Meeting him. Drinking with him at Field's, dancing with him at Vinnie's, talking for who knows how long over drinks and endless glasses of water. Walking and talking with easy familiarity.

His home.

His room.

His bed.

His hands, his kiss.

Earth-shaking sex.

World-altering sex.

I'm breathless even now at the memory of it.

I glance over at him—he's sleeping, and he looks boyish in the vulnerable innocence of sleep.

I glance at the bedside table: there's a box of

condoms hastily ripped open, a strip of foil pack-ets hanging out of the opening of the box, and two opened, empty packets.

I vaguely remember him putting one on the first time, but the second time was a mad, wild rush of pas-sion, and I was half asleep and thought perhaps I was dreaming and all I really remember is him and the fury of immediate bliss at his touch, the erotic thrill of our union.

There are two empty packets, so he must've worn one the second time, put it on before I was fully aware.

I feel a rush of worry, a blast of panic—but we used one both times. It's fine. I'm fine.

I leave the bed in slow, careful movements; I hon-estly can't believe I did that with Jamie—that I let it go so far, so fast, knowing so little about him. I don't know his last name, or what he does. I do know a lot about him, though—that he grew up in New Hampshire, that he's a got an older sister who's a marketing exec in Manhattan, and a younger brother studying law at Columbia.

I know we're both fairly recently divorced.

He knows I have an eight-year-old son named Aiden, and I know he has no children, but that he does want them someday.

We both love Dave Matthews Band even though it's kind of passé at this point.

We both love *Sixteen Candles*, *Tremors*, and *St. Elmo's Fire*.

And Hootie and the Blowfish.

We can both quote *Robin Hood: Prince of Thieves* pretty much word for word.

And I know that sex with Jamie was, without question, the most amazing thing that's ever happened to me.

I also know this was a one-night stand, and that I have to get out of here, get home, showered, and changed and go pick up Aiden—we have back-to-school shopping to finish, and I can't pick him up from my parents' still smelling like sex and wearing last night's clothing.

I find my underwear and step into them—my bra is under the bed, and I have to lay on the cold hardwood floor to get it. My dress is out in the hallway, inside out, and his bright red boxer-briefs are inside out on top of my dress. I shrug and wiggle into my dress, zip it up, and spin in circles, looking for the rest of my things.

My purse—where is my purse?

I find it downstairs on the floor by the front door, along with my shoes. I step into them, settle my purse over my shoulder, and sneak as silently as I can out the front door—the hinges protest and the knob rattles, and the screen door screams as I open it and thunks loudly closed despite my best efforts to be quiet.

My heels thwack on the concrete steps.

I dig my cell phone out of my purse and glance at it as I head toward the county highway, which is less than half a mile from here; I have sixteen missed calls from

Cora, ranging from one in the morning to less than twenty minutes ago, as well as…it looks like forty-two text messages.

I hear a sprinkler going, and look up to see Mrs. Himmler, self-appointed head of the Clayton Busybody Society, watering her roses and watching me very, very intently.

Hooo, boy. Looks like all of Clayton will soon know about my little walk of shame. Yay.

I ignore the voicemails and texts from Cora, opting to call her instead once I'm safely out of earshot of Mrs. Himmler and Jamie's house. It only rings half a ring before she picks up.

"ELYSE GABRIELLE THOMAS! WHERE THE *HELL* HAVE YOU BEEN?" she shrieks, so loudly that I have to pull the handset away from my ear.

"I'm doing the walk of shame, Cora," I say, keeping my voice low.

"What? You're—you…you *what*?" She stutters to a stop, quieter now.

"*I slept with him*," I hiss.

"The guy from the bar?" She's incredulous. "You went home with the guy from the bar? The one with starched chinos and the blue polo?"

"Yes, Cora."

"Holy crap holy crap holy *crap*!" She's breathless with excitement. "Tell me everything!"

"I'm on Washington Street and I need a ride home. I'll tell you everything after I've had a shower and coffee." I hesitate, thinking back to how wasted she'd been last night. "How are you awake right now? You were even more drunk than I was!"

"Yeah, but I do it more often, so I recover better. Plus, I've been so worried about you not returning my calls or texts that I couldn't sleep, even being super drunky-fish."

"I'm sorry," I say, genuinely contrite. "I didn't mean to worry you."

"Must've been good," she speculates, still angling for immediate info.

I laugh. "You have *no* idea. Now come get me."

She sighs. "I'm already on the way. I'll be there in less than five minutes."

"Make it two, because Mrs. Himmler saw me leave."

"Ohhh boy. The Busybody Society is going to have a field day with this one, Elyse."

We've called Mrs. Himmler and her circle of elderly retiree friends the Clayton Busybody Society since we were in junior high when they would watch our every move and report back to our parents and grandparents.

"No kidding."

"I'm turning onto Washington now. Get ready for a quick getaway."

I hear her engine and a soft squeal of tires, and then she's braking to a hard a stop beside me, the black top up and her windows open, "Where the Streets Have No Name" is blaring from the speakers. I slide in, buckle up, and kick off my heels, toss my purse in the foot-well, and thud my head back against the headrest.

"Holy cow, Cora."

She snorts. "Who even says holy cow anymore, Elyse? For real?"

"Shut up. I'm in no mood for your crap."

"Says the woman who called me at six-oh-four in the morning for an emergency walk of awesome pickup."

"Walk of awesome?"

She nods. "I don't believe in the concept of a walk of shame. You have nothing to be ashamed of. You're an adult and you had an enjoyable evening. That's nobody's business but your own."

"Yeah, well, all of Clayton is going to make it their business."

"Ignore them! This stupid town can and will gossip about literally anything and everything, and you know it. So just ignore it."

"Easy for you to say," I grumble.

Cora eyes me. "Really? Easy for me to say? And why would that be, Elyse?"

She halts at the stop sign at the highway and then turns left to head east toward the town square. My house is in East Clayton, the neighborhood occupying the southeast quadrant of Clayton—mirrored on the opposite—southwest—side by...you guessed it, West Clayton. They're both distinct neighborhoods, even though they both border on Pleasantonville. Basically, if you have money, you live in Pleasantonville; if you're not well off but not poor either, you live in East or West Clayton, if you're somewhere between poor and East/West Clayton, you live in Oak Junction, and if you're flat-out poor, you live in Grand Manor. In a place like Clayton, there's a certain subtle, unspoken, but very real socioeconomic status that's directly tied to where you live, and those who feel it the most acutely are the kids in middle and high school.

We're approaching my street, Walnut Drive, and I hold my answer until we pull into my driveway, the third house on the left. She shuts her car off and eyes me. "Seriously—what did that mean?"

I sigh, shrugging. "Just that you don't care what people think, and never have. I do, and it's harder for me to shrug the gossip off like you can."

"Oh." She seems to deflate. "That's not what I thought you meant."

I give her a baleful glare. "Really, Cora?"

She rolls a shoulder. "Whatever. Go take a shower while I make coffee. I need the deets."

"Deets?"

"People still say that," she protests.

"No, they don't. Or if they do, it's either ironically or they're hopelessly out of touch and trying to sound like they're not."

She laughs. "How do you use *ironically*, anyway?"

We head into my house—there are still Legos all over the floor, and the TV is on, the *Lego Movie* DVD home screen illuminates the living room.

"You're an English teacher," I say. "Aren't you supposed to know the definition of irony?"

"Yeah, I know the definition of irony, but that's a different thing than using a colloquialism or slang term ironically."

"So basically, nobody really understands what irony really means, and we're all just pretending we do?" I ask.

"Exactly!" She whacks me on the butt. "Shower! I need details, and I need them now!"

"I'm going, I'm going."

I take my time showering, and it's hard to not relive last night. I want to remember it forever, but I'm also a little scared to look too closely, because I'm worried if I do, I'll start a downward spiral of one-night stand guilt. Once I'm finally clean, my hair washed and conditioned, my legs shaved, and I've blow-dried my hair and dressed in comfy clothes—yoga pants and a long-sleeve T-shirt—I follow the scent of brewed coffee to my kitchen. Cora is at my kitchen table, sipping coffee, munching on a Pop-Tart, and scrolling on her phone.

"I can't believe you still have this junk in your house," she says, lifting the pastry. "I thought you gave up this kind of stuff a long time ago."

I laugh. "I did! I thought I threw out all that stuff—where'd you even find it?"

"Back of your pantry."

"And you're *eating* it? That's got to be leftover

from when we moved in!" Which was three years ago; I bought this after selling the house Daniel and I had owned together.

Cora just shrugs. "It *is* a little stale. Whatever. I was munchy."

"I have real food, you know."

"That requires cooking. I barely slept last night and I'm not in the mood for culinary exertion." She gestures at the mug of coffee on the table near hers. "Sit and spill the juicy stuff, sister."

Cora knows me better than pretty much anyone—she's poured my coffee and put ice cubes in it, because I like my coffee at a temperature most people would call cold, which I call not burning my tongue to cinders.

I sit, sip at the coffee, and spend a few minutes just breathing. Cora knows better than to rush me, so she just idly browses through the news app on her phone until I'm ready to talk.

"Best sex I've ever had," I say, by way of introduction.

She almost spits out her coffee, coughing and wiping at her lips. "What?"

I nod. "For real. It was…magical."

"Magical," she repeats.

"I've never felt anything like it in my life."

"Ever?"

"Ever."

She stares at me. "Dude. Then why did you sneak out? Did you leave your number?"

I shake my head. "Nope."

She frowns. "Why?"

I shrug. "I don't know. I just…the thought of going through all that awkwardness was just…no. We didn't even exchange last names, or what we do."

"So?"

"So…it was a one-night stand."

"Why does it have to be just that?" she asks. "Why couldn't it be, like, a four-month stand or something?"

I laugh. "That's stupid. I'd get attached, or he would, and I'd be tempted to bring him around Aiden, and it would just be good sex and not a real relationship and it would eventually end and Aiden would get hurt. I mean, you can't base a relationship off of sex, even amazing, truly magical sex. It has to be based on friendship and trust and…and reality."

Cora rolls her eyes at me. "Yeah, because that worked out *so* well for you last time."

"Your relationship with Hank," I say, referring to her longest relationship, which ended…unhappily, shall we say. "What was that based on?"

"Incredible sex."

"Exactly." I lift an eyebrow at her. "And did it last?"

"For five years, yes."

I sigh. "And do I have to remind you what happened?"

"NOPE!" she says, too loudly. "What about you, though? You and Daniel were high school sweethearts. You never even dated anyone else—like, ever, did you?"

"No…"

"So, how do you know what happened with the hottie from last night was a fluke? Or the reverse, that sex with Daniel was just that bad? You don't know."

I sigh. "We did break up sophomore year of college, remember?"

"For, like, two months. And then you got back together."

"Yeah, and I wasn't a nun for those two months, was I?"

She snorts. "No, but there was just the one guy, what, three times? Hardly counts as a broad field of study."

I frown. "Why are we dissecting my sexual history?"

"Because you said it was the best sex of your life, and yet you're willing to just…poof? Let it go without looking back?"

I shrug. "It's safest."

"Was he just passing through?"

"No. He'd just moved in, but we didn't stop to do a tour, if you know what I mean."

"There are not that many options. You know you're *going* to run into him again, right?"

"Jim and Janine Morrow moved last fall, and I know their house finally sold a few weeks ago, but I haven't heard anything about to whom. There's the new principal, and I heard he's already hired a new gym teacher because Amy Erhart transferred to the middle school. Plus, Brad Caldwell was talking the other day about how he hired a couple new guys at the automotive shop. So there are actually quite a few options as to who Jamie could be." I sigh. "And if I do run into him, we'll be adults about it. It happened, and it was good, and we're both moving on."

"Are you sure it wasn't just amazing because you were drunk?"

I sigh. "I mean, sure, there's probably an element of that. But I remember everything perfectly—and I mean...*everything*. And it was amazing."

"Amazing how?"

I hesitate. "I don't know. He just made me feel... beautiful. Wanted. Desired. It was...passionate."

She eyes me curiously. "Passionate?"

I shrug. "I don't know how else to put it."

"Was he...big?"

I snicker. "Yes."

"Good with his hands?"

"*God* yes."

"And his mouth?"

I blush, stupidly; my fingers have, somehow, drifted up to brush my lips as if to relive where his had been, and I immediately snatch them away and tangle them on my lap. "Well, he's an amazing kisser, I'll tell you that much."

"Did he kiss *both* sets of lips?"

"Cora!" I say, whacking her across the arm. "Nasty!"

"It's not nasty, it's hot, and you know you like it. You told me Daniel did it once and you really enjoyed it but you never got him to do it again, and you were always pissed about that."

"Yeah, and if he had, I'd have been more likely to… you know…to him. But he didn't, so I didn't."

"Because he was a selfish asshole."

"That too."

"What about this guy—what was his name? Jamie?"

"Yeah, Jamie. And no, he wasn't selfish, not at all. And no, we didn't do…*that*. Either direction. We just… it was…it happened so fast, you know? Not that *it* happened fast…I mean, once we got to his house and started kissing, that was it. There was no stopping it."

"Wow."

"We woke up in the middle of the night…or maybe closer to dawn, I don't know what time it was. And we did it again."

"Sober?" Cora asks, eyebrows lifted.

"Yeah. Or, mostly. We were both kind of half asleep, but it was…in a way, it was almost hotter than the first time."

"That's a little weird, to be honest."

"What is? That it was better the second time?"

"No, that there was a second time way after the fact. Most of the one-night stands I've ever had, and there have been…a few…it was like, you have sex half drunk and you keep at it until the buzz wears off, and then one of you leaves, or you pass out and one of you sneaks out. You don't wake up halfway through the night, sober, and have, like, *intimate* sex. That's weird."

She shrugs. "But more power to you, if it worked for you."

"It was amazing." I frown. "But now that you call it into question, it *was* kind of…intimate."

"Which is why I'm saying you should've stuck around. Maybe it could've become something. God knows you need someone to help you get over Daniel's stupid ass."

I sigh. "I'm as over him as I can get. We haven't heard from him in over a year, and the last time we did hear from him it was a generic birthday card for Aiden with a twenty-dollar bill inside, and he'd signed it 'Dan.'" I shake my head. "He *never* went by Dan, it was always Daniel. And who signs a birthday card for their own child with their first name?" Cora's eyes narrow, and I realize I'm getting worked up. "*I'm* over him. As in, I'm over our relationship. I'm not in love with him, I don't miss him, and I hope I never see him again, but that is just for myself. I'm mad for Aiden, and that's different. Aiden deserves a father. Our personal problems shouldn't mean Aiden doesn't have his dad. I've never said a bad thing to Aiden about Daniel and I never will, and if Daniel comes back and indicates he wants to be a part of Aiden's life, I'd let him. I'd have an anxiety stomachache the entire time, but I'd do it for Aiden."

Cora's smile is gentle. "I know, babe. I know you would." She sighs, and then smiles more brightly. "I'm glad you had last night, at least, though."

I laugh. "Me too."

"So. What are we doing today?"

"Back-to-school shopping," I tell her, glad and sort of sad at the same time to be moving on from the topic of Jamie and our one, magical night together. "Aiden still needs a new pair of gym shoes, a few more folders, and like, eight million glue sticks."

"So…we're making the drive out to Walmart, then?"

I sigh. "As much as I don't want to, yeah."

She shrugs. "Fine by me. I want to browse their book section anyway. My little library is a bit sparse."

"Didn't you spend something like a hundred dollars on books for your classroom library last year?"

She rolls her eyes. "Don't get me started. Kids borrow them and don't return them."

"So make a sign-out system. Like, hold their grade hostage until they give the book back."

Cora just sighs and waves a hand. "I could, and I threaten to do just that every year, but the kids who don't return the books are the ones that probably don't have any books of their own at home, and I just sort of conveniently forget. Every kid deserves to have books at home."

"You're too good for your own good."

She widens her eyes and whispers conspiratorially. "DON'T LET MY SECRET OUT!"

I just roll my eyes, laughing. "It's not a secret to anyone who knows you, Cora."

"I *do* have a certain reputation around town, Elyse."

"That's just a holdover from high school."

"I *did* sleep with Ellen Baldwin's husband senior year."

I snicker. "That was the talk of the town for *years*. I still can't believe you went through with it."

"He was a DILF! Or, not a dad, just a hot older guy." She shrugs. "Ellen and Cooper were basically divorced by then anyway. It's not like they were happily married. They weren't even living together—and hadn't been for almost a year. So I like to think I slept with Ellen Baldwin's *ex*-husband, except for a minor technicality."

I just laugh. "Yeah, minor technicalities like actual signed divorce papers. No big deal."

"She was just mad because Cooper told everyone I gave better head than she did."

"CORA KATHERINE PEARSON!"

She grins salaciously. "Which is true. I do give amazing head."

"CORA!"

She rolls her eyes at me. "Oh stop being such a prude, Elyse. Sex is normal. Everyone has sex." She frowns. "Except for Pa Chantry, I think."

I laugh. "Actually, I heard from Margie Nelson that Pa Chantry and Dot Wannamaker get it on. In his barn. A *lot*."

Cora shakes her hands, making gagging sounds. "Oh my god, oh my god, *eeew*. Why would you tell me that?"

I laugh harder. "Because sex is normal, and

everyone has sex."

She glares at me. "Exactly! So why are you such a prude about me discussing my exceptional fellatio skills?"

I just sigh and shake my head. "Because I'm just more conservative about it than you, I guess."

"Which is because you've basically only ever had boring married people sex with boring Daniel Thomas. You never really got a chance to be wild and do crazy stuff. I know that much for a fact, because you told me that you and Daniel almost never had sex in any position except missionary."

I sigh again. "Can we *not* go back into my erstwhile sex life with my ex-husband? Please?"

"Fine. Which positions did you and Jamie do it in?"

I bite my lip, grinning. "Missionary, the first time. The second time, on our sides facing each other."

She frowns at me. "Super weird, Elyse. You and Jamie had sex, sober, half-asleep, on your sides facing each other?"

I frown back. "Yeah, why? It was incredible."

"That's the most intimate and personal way you could possibly have sex, Elyse, you do realize that, right?"

I shrug. "I mean, I guess. It just happened. I woke up, he was, *ahem*, right there, if you know what I mean. And I just...I needed him, and it just happened."

She's still frowning, shaking her head. "I'm telling you, Elyse—that's not normal. You should have left him your number. Or better yet, had breakfast with him."

I just shake my head back at her. "No. I told you—I can't afford to get involved with anyone right now. Aiden and I have things worked out. We're good. I'm good."

Cora sighs. "Whatever. You're a big girl; you can make your own decisions. But just let it be known for the record that I think there could have been something better than a one-night stand in it for you."

"Duly noted. The committee will take your comments under advisement." I glance at my phone. "Time to get Aiden from my parents' and go to Walmart."

"Are we getting more Legos?" Cora asks.

I laugh. "You know he'll beg, and you know I'll give in."

"Yay! We need a new set."

"You guys built the last one in, like, an hour!"

Cora loves building Lego sets with Aiden—it's part of their thing. She just grins at me. "It was too easy. We need a challenge."

"Yeah, I know. He's been wheedling me for a Technic set for months."

"OOH! YES! I've wanted to do one of those for years!"

I shake my head at her. "Then you can pay for it. Those sets are crazy expensive."

"Deal."

We tidy up the house, and then get in my

secondhand, eight-year-old Ford Focus to pick up Aiden. We spend a few minutes with my parents, chatting, and then start the drive to Walmart. It's easy to get wrapped up in the comfortable, familiar patter between Cora and Aiden. It's easier yet to get caught up in back-to-school shopping, getting my office at the high school ready, going over files from last year, and making notes to check in with this student or that one, helping the other counselors finalize schedules, and work out scheduling conflicts, and attending staff meetings.

Jamie slips slowly from my mind over the week that precedes the start of the school year. I let myself think about that night sometimes when I'm alone, and if I need a little…stress relief, but that's a dangerously slippery slope, and I start to avoid even that. Best to just let the past be in the past—focus on Aiden, on the new school year, and on my students.

By the time the first day of school rolls around, I've all but put Jamie out of my mind.

And that's for the best.

6

"AIDEN!" I SHOUT, FOR THE SEVENTH TIME IN five minutes. "LET'S GO!"

Of course, my son chooses today, the first day of school, to be the slowest, pokiest, slowpoke on the planet. Usually, he's up and at 'em by six thirty or seven regardless of what time he went to bed, but today? Oh no. Today, he slept in. And I, not wanting to wake him until necessary, let him sleep. Figuring we'd make up the time by hustling a little bit. Only, he's foiling those plans by doing everything as slowly as possible. He ate his eggs at a sloth's pace. Hung around over his toast for ten minutes. Took another five minutes to drink his juice; all the while, I'm running around like a chicken with my head cut off, trying to get myself ready, get all his stuff ready, and eat my own breakfast while scurrying this way and that, forgetting things.

And then—AND THEN...as we're heading out the door, already running five minutes behind schedule, he says he has to go to the bathroom.

And stays in there for FIVE MINUTES.

"Aiden Daniel Thomas, what in the world are you *doing* in there?"

"I'm poopin', Mama. I'm almost done."

I facepalm myself. "Now? You had to go *now*?"

"When you gotta go, you gotta go. That's what Papa always says."

"Yeah, and buddy, we have GOT to go! You are going to be late for school!"

"So? It's the first day. It's not like we're gonna actually do anything important."

"That's not the point. You can't be late the first day of third grade."

"Okay, okay, keep your pants on. I'm coming."

I hear him wash his hands, flush the toilet, and then he comes out, still wrestling with the zipper, which is stuck at the bottom.

I glare at him when he stops messing with the zipper and glances up at me. "Do *not* tell your mother to keep her pants on, Aiden. It's disrespectful." I sigh. "Let me guess, Papa says that to Grandma?"

He shrugs, not willing to rat out his Papa. "I plead the second."

I laugh. "You mean, you plead the fifth. The second amendment is gun rights, buddy."

"Oh. Whatever," he says, still trying to get the zipper to work. "The fifth, then."

"And that just means you're not willing to say anything which might incriminate you. It's basically admitting guilt."

He sighs and gestures in frustration at his zipper. "Can you help, please? It's stuck."

I fix his zipper and then hand him his backpack, which is stuffed to overflowing with the mind-boggling amount of folders, glue sticks, crayons, Kleenex, more glue sticks, colored pencils, markers, more glue sticks, a pencil box, a binder, packets of colored construction paper, and did I mention glue sticks?

"Are you finally ready, now?" I ask him.

"Yep."

"Are you sure? You're not missing something? Like, say, oh…I don't know, your shoes?"

He glances down and wiggles his toes, which are clad in socks, but not shoes. "Oh. Oops."

I hand him his shoes. "Put them on in the car, champ. We have to go. You're going to miss the first bell at this rate."

"Okay, Mama."

I ruffle his hair as we leave the house. "Good thing you're cute, Aiden."

He just gives me a saucy grin as he climbs into his booster and buckles up. "Grandma always says I'm gonna end up catching me a world of trouble with this grin of mine."

I sigh. "And they encourage it."

"Yep, they do."

"Okay," I say, preparing to back out. "You have your shoes?"

"Yep."

"And you're putting them on and tying them tightly?"

"Yep."

"You have your backpack?"

"The thing weighs at least a billion pounds, so I don't think I could forget it."

"Yeah, well, once you give Mrs. Crenshaw your supplies, it'll be empty again except for a folder or two."

I glance at him in the rearview mirror as we head for the school complex—a large plot a few miles north of downtown Clayton; the complex houses the adjoined middle and high school, the elementary school, the New Oxford Public Library, and the county police station, along with the various athletic fields.

"And do you have your positive attitude and eagerness to learn?"

He rolls his eyes at me. "Yes, Mama."

"Don't you roll your eyes at me, young man—I'll pick 'em up and roll them right back at you."

He just snorts. "That's dumb."

"Mom jokes, kiddo. Get used to them."

We pull up to the elementary school as the last of the drop-off line of cars pulls through. I pull to a stop at the front of the line, put the car in park, and get out. Aiden is already out and jogging for the door, backpack bouncing heavily.

"Um, excuse me, mister!" I call out. "Hugs and kisses and first-day photos!"

He stops, hangs his head, turns around with an

elaborate show of drama, and drags his feet back to me. "I'm gonna be late, Mama!"

"And whose fault is that?"

"Yours?" he says, grinning, eyes twinkling mischievously.

I laugh, kneeling down and hauling him in for a tight hug, giving him a truly embarrassing number of kisses, until he squirms and writhes away.

"Okay, pose for the first day of third-grade photo!"

"*Mom!*" he huffs. "There's no time for photos! The bell's gonna ring!"

"There's always time for photos."

He poses, giving me a cheesy grin and two thumbs-up, and I snap several photos.

"Okay, now flash me a three on both hands like gang signs," I tell him.

He rolls his eyes. "I don't know what gang signs are, but they sound stupid."

I laugh. "You're probably right, but it'll be funny. Just hold up three on both hands and look tough."

He does the pose as requested, and then comes over. "Can I see?"

I show him the photos, and he picks the ones he likes best—which is our deal whenever I want to post photos of him on social media: he gets input on which photo, and veto power if he really hates it.

I smack him on the butt. "Now go! I love you! Have a great first day, okay?"

"You too! Love you, Mama!" He jumps up, gives

me a kiss on the cheek, and then runs inside.

I clap my hands over my heart as he slips inside, struggling with the door, stopping halfway through to wave at me before vanishing. "Stop growing up so fast, Aiden," I whisper to myself.

I brush away a lone tear—first day of kindergarten, I sobbed like a baby; first day of first grade, I cried enough that I had to reapply my makeup in the car before I went in to work; first day of second grade, I cried, but not enough that I had to redo makeup. Third grade? Only one lonely little tear. It still feels like I'm sending a piece of my heart into that building, though.

I summon my breath and my courage, and head back to my car. There are a few other stragglers dropping their kids off late, and the busses are trundling away from the bus drop-off line, diesel engines grunting and rumbling. I hear the bell ring as I slide in behind the wheel, buckle up, and put the car in park...

I get about two feet when I happen to glance in the rearview mirror, and see Aiden's Star-Lord lunchbox on the back seat.

"Crap." I let out another few unladylike words my mother would scold me for using, and then brake to a stop and throw the car in park again. I'm going to be late myself, now—I have an 8:15 appointment with Jen Hurley, and it's currently eight thirteen, and I still have to get over to the high school, park, get to my office... yeah, I'm going to be late.

"Darn it, Aiden." I lean to the back seat, snag the

lunch box, and throw my door open.

I leave my car running and the door open as I jog toward the front door of the school—at the same time, I'm whipping off a text message to Liz, the main office secretary, letting her know I'll be a few minutes late for my appointment with Jen. I glance up briefly as I reach the doors, then back down at my phone, finishing the message as I yank the door open. I hit "send" and launch myself through the door, intent on jogging to the office as fast as I can in my navy-blue knee-length skirt and red wedge heels.

I slam into a hard male body and bounce backward, dropping my phone and Aiden's lunchbox with a loud clatter. I feel myself reeling backward, off-balance, with nothing to catch myself on. It happens in slow motion, as such accidents always seem to do. But then a pair of hands catch me, and I smell something male and familiar and comforting and arousing all at the same time. Warm, kind, intelligent brown eyes lock onto mine.

"Elyse—are you okay?" His voice is low, a smooth, intimate murmur.

I blink. "Um." I find my feet, and my voice, as yank myself out of his arms, smoothing my hands over my skirt and tugging my slate gray V-neck blouse back into place. "Yeah—yes. I'm fine, thank you."

My phone is at my feet, and Aiden's lunchbox is a few feet away, open, the contents spread across the floor. I kneel and grab my phone first—I have a thick rubber case on it, because I'm prone to dropping it and can't really afford a new one, so thankfully, the device escaped the fall unscathed, except for a new scratch on the screen protector.

Jamie kneels and scoops Aiden's lunch back into the box, snaps the cover closed, and now we're standing facing each other, a little too close for my comfort, and his eyes are piercing, penetrating, curious.

I blink at him, struggling to process what's happening. "You—you're..."

"The new Clayton Elementary Principal," he finishes.

"I—um." My brain is blank.

This is Jamie. The man I slept with eight days ago. The man who utterly rocked my world with unbelievable, mind-blowing, earth-shaking sex. The man I ran out on without so much as a note.

My son's principal.

A coworker, seeing as we work in the same district.

"You're Jamie Trent," I manage.

He smirks. "That's me."

"All I ever saw in the district email newsletter blast about you was that your name was J. Trent and that you're from the East Coast, and a grainy thumbnail photograph." I lick my lips, and his eyes follow the movement of my tongue. "You—god, it's you."

"It's me." He glances behind himself, into the building; he has a walkie-talkie on his belt, crackling with a staticky voice requesting his presence in the fourth-grade classroom. "I have to go."

"Me too," I say. "I'm late for work."

"Where do you work?"

"The high school. I'm a guidance counselor."

He nods, and I can see he has a million questions, a million things to say, but the walkie-talkie is blurping again, requesting Mr. Trent go to Mrs. Fredrick's room. "I really have to go, but could we talk at some point?"

I swallow hard. "I—um. I don't know. I don't think that's a good idea." I back away. "I have to go. I was supposed to meet a student five minutes ago."

"Elyse—"

I whirl, speed walking back to my car, pulse pounding in my ears.

"Elyse!" I hear him behind me, and then he catches up with me. "Aiden's lunch."

Somehow it ended up back in my hands, and I thrust it at him. "Oh, um, yeah. He—he forgot it."

Jamie takes it from me, fiddling with the metal clasps, his eyes on mine. "I'll get it to him."

"Thank you."

I get into my car and drive away, a little too quickly for safety. I glance in the rearview mirror and see Jamie in his starched and pressed gray chinos, well-worn dark leather dress shoes, and a pale blue button-down dress shirt with an explosively colorful tie. His hair is neatly combed, his face carefully shaven. He's watching me even as he lifts the walkie-talkie to his mouth to reply. When I turn out of the parking lot, he goes back inside.

Somehow, I can still feel his eyes on me.

The surprise, the intrigue.

The attraction.

I'd half hoped I'd imagined everything that had happened that night—or that my buzz had played it up to be more than it was.

But no...

I felt it, he felt it. There was a definite charge in the air between us.

I park in the teacher lot at the high school and hustle inside, working hard to put Jamie out of my mind. I whirl into the office, out of breath and flustered. My appointment, Jen, is sitting in one of the uncomfortable gray chairs lined up outside the guidance counselors' bank of offices.

She smiles at me brightly, waving. "Hi, Mrs. Thomas!"

I smile back. "Hi, Jen. I'm so sorry to keep you waiting. It's been one of those mornings, you know?"

She shrugs. "Oh, it's not a problem—trust me. I'm missing AP Calculus, so feel free to take your time."

I laugh. "We'd better get you back to class as soon as possible, then, shouldn't we? Wouldn't want you to get behind in an AP course."

Jen rolls her eyes. "Please, I was doing calc for fun in tenth grade. Math is kinda my thing, you know? If it was history or Lit, it'd be different."

I unlock my office and usher her in, flipping on the lights and setting my purse under my desk as I settle in. I look Jen over—she's grown up a bit since junior year, matured some since the last time we saw each other. Somewhat plus-sized, Jen's struggle with body image and body positivity is a constant factor in our ongoing discussions. She's a beautiful girl, with long black hair and beautiful, expressive green eyes and clear, pale skin, but she's struggled for years to accept herself because of her weight. She comes from a troubled home, as well, and I suspect—though she's never outright said so—that someone in her home is constantly berating her and beating her down emotionally, especially in regard to her body. She's a brilliant girl, one of the top students in our school, and a school favorite in our peer tutor program.

Jen gathers her long, thick, loose black hair in her hands and settles it over a shoulder, shifting uneasily in the chair while I close my door and wake up my computer. Logging into my system, I find my notes from the last conversation I had with Jen, at the end of last year. I bring up her schedule. "Wow," I tell her. "You've really piled it on for yourself this year, Jen—AP Calc, AP Physics, Ancient Civ, Modern Lit, fourth-year Spanish, peer tutor hour, and independent study with Mr. Lakoda."

Jen nods shyly, ducking her head. "Yeah, it's a little ambitious, I guess."

"The independent study with Mr. Lakoda, that's advanced math, right?"

She nods again. "Yeah. He's going to take me into math beyond what's taught in even the AP curriculum.

I've already taken most of the tests for calc this year—I did them over the summer. I basically don't have to go to first hour at all if I don't want to, because the real work is coming from the independent study hour, but I had to take the course to have enough credits for graduation."

"I imagine your peer tutor schedule is already filling up. You had a waitlist last year, didn't you?"

She smiles, hesitant and unsure. "Yeah, I guess. I helped Rob Krasansky pass math last year, and he was about to fail out completely and be put on academic probation from the football team."

I laugh. "And that sealed your fate as the best tutor ever, because without Rob, the football team wouldn't have had a season at all."

"I don't do sports," she says, "but that's what they tell me."

"I went to a few games with Aiden," I say, "and his name was called every other play."

She rolled her eyes. "He told me he set a record for rushing yards and most sacks in a season, but don't ask me what any of that means, because I have no clue."

I frown. "My dad watches football with Aiden, so I know a tiny bit. I think rushing is how many yards he ran with the ball, and a sack is when someone tackles the quarterback before he can throw the ball."

She snorts. "Sounds like Rob—running around and hitting people."

I laugh. "Pretty much. Although, you know, he also

set another record last year? Most number of volunteer hours in a school year."

Jen's eyebrows rise. "Really? What'd he volunteer for?"

"He helped Clayton Methodist bring meals to retirees and other low-income families in the area. He basically ran the program, and railroaded most of his teammates into doing it with him. It was pretty cool, actually."

Jen sighs. "Rob is misunderstood, I think. He's a really nice guy, if you can get past the jock armor he puts up."

"Kind of like how you're actually a really cool girl, if you can get past the shy and insecure armor you put up?"

Jen doesn't answer right away. "It's not armor, Mrs. Thomas."

"Get you talking about math or physics, and you're the most confident girl I know. Take you out of that context, though…"

Jen lifts a shoulder. "Out of that context, I get lost, that's all."

"Did you have a good summer?" I ask.

She shrugs noncommittally, her face a little too blank. "It was okay."

"What'd you do?"

"Read a lot. Mostly books on advanced math and biographies on famous or influential mathematicians."

"Did you meet anyone new?"

Her face falls. "No, I didn't."

"Did you try?"

She stares at her shoes. "Not really."

"Come on, Jen. We talked about this. You can't hide behind academics your whole life. You'll only ever meet someone if you put yourself out there and try."

Jen nods, shrugs. "I know, I know. But I just don't...I don't know how. And if I did put myself out there, I'd just get rejected."

"How do you know?"

Her eyes flare, anger rising. "Because look at me, Mrs. Thomas! You know what else I did this summer? Not one, not two, not three, but *four* different diets, none of which worked for more than two weeks."

I sigh. "Jen, it takes more than a couple weeks. And just because you mess up once or twice doesn't mean you failed the whole thing. And plus, there's more to meeting someone and being with someone than what you look like or how much you weigh."

"I guess, but..." she trails off.

"But what?" I prompt.

"But that's all I see, and it's all anyone else will ever see." Her expression was so despondent it was heartbreaking. "Everyone knows I'm smart, that's why they all want me to tutor them. Rob was single when I tutored him, and he acted like...like I was a talking robot, or his sister, or something. He couldn't have been less interested in me if he had tried. I wasn't a girl to him, I was just...a tutor. Someone to help him at math so he could keep playing football."

"Jen—"

"He wasn't mean about it, don't get me wrong. He was nice, a lot nicer than I expected him to be. He just…he didn't see me like…like that."

"Do you like him?" I ask.

She shrugs. "I mean, sure. Who doesn't? He's really good-looking. But did I *like* him? I knew he didn't and wouldn't ever see me like that, so I didn't bother letting myself feel that for him. There wasn't any point."

I want to make excuses for him, or offer some kind of explanation. But I don't. She'd see through them, and I've experienced similar things myself, so I know where she's coming from.

"You have to be confident in yourself, Jen. You have a lot to offer, sweetheart. You're an amazing person. You're not just smart, you're beautiful, and you're fun to talk to and to be around. So be confident!"

She smiles at me, but I can tell it takes some effort. "I'll try."

I tap a few notes into her file, and then turn back to face her. "So. You said your schedule this year is a little ambitious. Do you feel comfortable with it? I think there's some wiggle room to move things around if you want."

She shakes her head. "It'll be a lot of work, but it'll keep me busy, and that's a good thing. I can do it."

I take her hands and squeeze. "Great. I'm glad to hear you sound so confident in yourself!"

"I'm a work in progress?" She says this as if trying to sound hopeful.

I squeeze her hands again. "We all are, Jen—we all are."

We arrange to meet again in a couple of weeks to check in, make sure her schedule is still working—and so I can evaluate her mental and emotional well-being. She leaves, and my next appointment comes in hard on Jen's heels: Michael Prescott, a close friend of Rob Krasansky's, another star football player—Michael is a young man in whom still waters run deep, and I always look forward to chatting with him.

My day is filled with meetings and appointments, one after another in such quick, nonstop succession that I barely have time to catch my breath let alone ruminate about my run-in with Jamie this morning.

And the next week is the same—I'm pretty much the only guidance counselor at the school: there are, technically, two others, but one, John Ward, is retiring at the end of this year after forty-five years at the school, and has pretty much checked out, and the other, Allison Howell, is the kind of guidance counselor who's just in the wrong line of work…she doesn't like kids and is angling for a job in the district office so she can get away from the day-to-day grind of having to talk to teenagers all day every day. Which leaves me to take the lion's share of actual counseling work—resolving scheduling conflicts, listening to upset students, reading college entrance essays, advising athletes on academic probation toward being eligible to play again, and a million other odds and ends that fall between the cracks of the administrative staff.

Which means, for most of that week, I'm too busy to think about Jamie. I run Aiden to school, go to work, pick Aiden up, take him to football—he's playing in a tackle youth league this year, and my poor mama's heart has a hard time watching him spend all that time getting roughed up, but he loves it and is thriving—and then we swing by Grandma and Papa's for dinner and then we go home and start it all again. Sometimes, in the small hours of the morning right before my alarm goes off, Jamie's face flits through my mind. Sometimes, as I'm drifting off to sleep, I drown in a half-formed memory of his hands and mouth and body. Sometimes, in the middle of the night, I wake up aching and needy with his name on my lips.

And I tell myself it's just loneliness and lust.

It will pass.

It has to pass, doesn't it?

7

IT'S THREE FORTY-FOUR, AND I'M PACKING UP TO LEAVE. It's been another nonstop, jam-packed day of last-minute schedule changes, withdrawals, and IEP meetings. Aiden's dismissal bell rings at 3:45, and he has to be at the football field by four, and there's always a five- or ten-minute wait in the pickup line...

I'm rushing.

I log out of my system, put the computer to sleep, arrange the stacks of papers I need to go through tomorrow into priority piles, unplug my phone and toss it into my purse, check my desk one last time, and then exit my office, shutting off the light and preparing to lock the door behind me.

And there, in front of me, is a student with mascara-laced tear tracks running down her face. Tina Brokaw, four-point-oh student, president of the mock UN, debate team captain, head cheerleader, shoo-in for prom queen...Clayton High School's premier It Girl. She's always put together and perfect—blond hair, brown eyes, fashion sense far beyond the understanding of the residents of this little town.

"Tina," I say, shocked to see her here, and to see her crying like this. "What's the matter?"

She sniffles, trying to stifle the flood of tears, but she can't get words out. "I—I…"

I suppress a sigh as I flip my light back on and set my purse back down. "Come in, honey. Sit." I hand her a box of Kleenex and close my door. "Take a minute, and then tell me what's going on."

"Everything!" she wails. "Everything's wrong!"

"Well, can you break that down a little for me?"

She dabs at her eyes, sniffling again. "I don't know where to start." She sucks in a breath, holds it, and lets it out shakily.

I slide my phone from my purse. "Okay, well, why don't you think about where to start while I let the elementary school know I'll be late picking up Aiden, that way we'll have plenty of time to talk."

I call the elementary office and let Peggy know Aiden will have to stay with the latchkey kids until I'm done here. When I hang up the phone and set it aside once more, Tina has herself more composed.

"First, Jake dumped me."

I wince. "Wow, that's unexpected. You guys have been dating for a while, right?"

"Since the summer before ninth grade! He's going to college in Arizona and doesn't want to do a long-distance relationship. But why *now*? Why not just break up after the school year? It's three weeks to homecoming, and what about prom? We were going to be prom king and queen! Who am I supposed to go to prom with? Rob? Like, no!" She takes a steadying breath. "I don't get it. I just don't understand."

"I'm sorry, Tina. That's rough. Sometimes guys just do weird, inexplicable things."

"No kidding. I didn't realistically expect us to keep dating past high school, since he's going to Arizona State and I'm going to Brown, but…I just thought we'd finish high school as a couple, you know?"

I offer a sympathetic smile. "I'm sorry, Tina. I wish I knew what to say besides that." I sigh. "You'll meet someone in college, though, right? High school sweethearts are great, but maybe this is for the best, you know?"

"Nice try, Mrs. Thomas. The problem is that his timing just sucks," she says, half laughing, half crying.

"So. That can't be the only reason you're in here crying, can it? You'd go to your girlfriends to cry about a breakup, not some old lady."

Tina rolls her eyes at me. "You're not old, Mrs. Thomas. I have an older sister who's almost the same age as you."

I roll my eyes back at her. "Leslie, yes, I know. We went to school here together, you realize."

"I got a C on a test in Mr. Lakoda's independent study." She says this with utter shock, and no small amount of despair.

I wait for the rest. "And?"

"A C! I don't *get* Cs, Mrs. Thomas! I'm not *allowed* to get Cs. I might as well have just gotten a zero!"

"Tina, honey, it's one C. It won't affect your overall GPA. And I'm sure if you talk to him, Mr. Lakoda will let you get some extra credit to make up some of the difference. He taught Leslie too, so he's well aware of the expectations your parents have."

"That doesn't matter. I've already talked to him and I'm staying to help him grade freshmen algebra tests all next week for extra credit. That's just not the point. Mom and Dad don't accept Cs, not on homework, not on quizzes, not on tests. And he won't let me retake it!"

I sigh. "It's a pretest, Tina. Mr. Lakoda doesn't weighthose very much at all. It will be okay."

"YOU DON'T UNDERSTAND!" she wails. "If it's not an A-plus in *everything*, it's a failure. I've been accepted at Brown already, but me being able to go at all rides on maintaining perfect grades through graduation. Anything less than perfect, and they'll just send me to Penn State or something. I *have* to get out of here, Mrs. Thomas. I know you understand."

Perfect grades, no exceptions. I remember very well Leslie making similar complaints.

"Get the extra credit. Mr. Lakoda doesn't do retakes and never has, so you're out of luck there. But he's generous with extra credit, so you'll still be able to finish the year with a perfect grade in his class. So…just take a breath and do what you can, okay?"

She lets out another shaky breath. "Okay."

I surreptitiously check the time: 3:54. I have to get Aiden soon—the youth league coach is obsessive about punctuality, and if a player is late, he doesn't get as much playing time in the next game.

"Is there anything else, Tina?"

She nods, but hesitates. "I…I think Jake and I had… an accident."

I blink. "You…you *think*?"

She nods. "I'm…late."

"Oh. Oh my." I bite my lip. "Have you taken any tests?"

She shakes her head. "No. Not…not yet. I'm too scared. And I don't know how to get one anyway—at least, not without everyone knowing." Her eyes widen. "I can't do it, Mrs. Thomas. I just can't. I can't be stuck here! A single mom stuck in Clayton? My life would be over. Mom and Dad wouldn't lift a finger to help. They'd call it getting what I deserve. You *know* that's true so don't try to bullshit me."

I wince, biting my lip. "Yeah, I know."

"What do I do? They won't help. They won't approve of me…" She shrugs, trails off meaningfully. "… fixing it, either."

"No, probably not."

"So…what do I do?"

"What about your sister?"

Tina frowns. "What about her?"

I hesitate, and then out a long sigh. "Look, Tina— as a counselor and an adult, I feel obligated to present all the options to you. But...I'm also a single mom in Clayton, okay? Your life won't be over. You may have to put some things on hold, and come up with a new plan, but your life wouldn't be *over*. And, speaking as a mom, it's the most incredible and rewarding thing you'll ever do. It's hard, yes, and it feels impossible sometimes, yes...especially if you're doing it without a husband or boyfriend, but—"

"Your parents help you, Mrs. Thomas. They *care*. Mine would see this as me being a failure and they'd want nothing to do with me or the baby—*ever*."

"Tina, listen—I know. Okay? I know. I know very well what your parents are like. I do. But there are other avenues for help. If Jake wouldn't step up, there are other good guys in this town." I sigh. "I just...I have to make you aware of that option. Keeping it, I mean assuming you're actually pregnant."

She winces at the word, and tears streak down her cheeks all over again. "Pregnant," she breathes.

I nod. "But, as someone who's been a teenager stuck in Clayton, I get it. But I also get...the other side. And I know how your parents are, and I get how hard it would be to raise a kid alone in this town."

"Hard? Try impossible."

"So, having presented the option of keeping it, there *are* other options."

"I just don't see how. I have no money, Jake won't be any help so there's no point even involving him—"

I fix her a stern look. "Tina. You *have* to tell him. He

has a right to know. Even if he reacts as you expect, you owe it to him to tell him. That's nonnegotiable."

She winces, but nods. "I know. I will."

"Promise me you'll talk to him?"

"I promise."

"Okay. Well, I know there's not exactly a lot of love lost between Leslie and your parents…"

Tina snorts derisively. "You can say that again. She comes back once a year for Christmas and New Year, and it's tense and awkward and she takes off again as soon as she can, and I don't see her coming back at all once I'm out of their house." She frowns. "You think she'd help me?"

I nod. "She's enough older than you that if you go into Baltimore or Washington or even Harrisburg, a clinic wouldn't ask too many questions as long as you had an adult with you signing off like she's your mom."

"What about the money?" Tina asks. "She's not exactly rolling in it."

"She'd help. And Jake has been working at Caldwell Automotive for a couple years now, and he has a responsibility to you, and to this situation." I sigh. "I hate this for you, Tina. I really do. I'm a mom, and the thought of not having Aiden?" I shudder, shake my head. "But I understand your situation, and that you feel you may not have another viable option. And I want to see you handle this situation safely and responsibly."

"Responsibly would have been not letting this happen in the first place," she mutters. "I feel so stupid."

"Well…" I sigh, because there's no arguing with that logic. "Just…learn from it?"

"Yeah, I guess." She tries a smile. "Thanks, Mrs. Thomas."

"It's what I'm here for." She hesitates. "Is there anything else?"

Tina shrugs. "Would…would you—I'm scared to call Leslie. Could you just…sit here with me?"

I nod, smiling. "Of course, honey."

So, I sit while Tina calls Leslie, and I listen and offer encouraging smiles as Tina haltingly explains the situation to her older sister, who works in communications in Boston. Leslie is stunned, and then upset, and then agrees to help Tina resolve the situation in any way she can.

By this time it's four fifteen, and Aiden is super late for practice. He may even end up missing it entirely.

Tina ends the call, and sits fiddling with her phone. "Um, what about Jake?"

"What do you mean?"

"How…how do I tell him?"

"Just sit somewhere private with him and tell him the facts."

"He'll blame me."

"And if he does, he's an asshole," I say. "Because it takes two, if you know what I mean."

She smiles. "Yeah, that's true."

"Just tell him, Tina. Don't drag it out, don't wait. Go find him right now, tell him you have to talk to him."

"He's at football practice."

"So wait till it's over. But do it today." I glance at her. "Although, you should probably take a test to be absolutely certain. It is possible to just miss periods. Stress especially can do that."

"I don't think it's stress." She smiles faintly. "But it's a nice thought."

"Take the test while Jake is at practice."

"If I get a test at the pharmacy, Mr. Van Hess will tell everyone."

I wince. "True. Mr. Van Hess is a card-carrying member of the Clayton Busybody Society."

Tina chuckles at that. "He's the worst of them, I think. I love that name for them. Lisa and Taylor and I call them the Gossip Gang."

I snicker. "That's a good one. I think everyone has their own name for them." I consider, and then an idea springs on me as Cora walks by my office with a stack of papers. "Cora!"

She glances at me, and I wave her in.

"What's up, buttercups?" Cora says in a singsong. She glances at Tina. "Why the long face, Brokaw? I have your pretest here, and you'll be pleased to know you scored a hundred and six percent."

I glance at Tina. "I have an idea. Cora has been my best friend my whole life, and I trust her implicitly. The question is, do you trust me?"

Cora's eyes narrow. "Are we wiling?"

I frown at her. "Are we what?"

"Wiling. Using our womanly wiles." She wiggles her eyebrows. "I heard you and Jake broke up and I thought maybe we were conspiring to get him back by homecoming."

I shake my head. "Nothing so fun as that, unfortunately." I glance at Tina again. "Yes or no?"

Tina nods. "Yes." She looks up at Cora, and then the door; Cora nudges the door closed and sits on the edge of my desk.

"Ohh," Cora breathes. "This is something serious."

Tina nods, and Cora's eyes fly wide.

"You're pregnant?" Cora guesses.

Tina nods again. "I—I think so."

"You *think*?"

"That's where you come in, Cora. She needs a test, but if she goes into the pharmacy…"

"Mr. Van Hess will have the whole town talking about it in under five minutes," Cora finishes.

"Exactly. He'd also start talking if I got one."

Cora nods, following my logic. "But he wouldn't bat an eye if I did. He'd assume I let one of the town drunks knock me up."

"Mrs. Pearson!" Tina says, laughing with shock.

"Everyone always assumes the worst about me, Tina," Cora says, waving a hand. "I'm used to it." She smiles at the distraught girl. "I'd be glad to use my black sheep status to get you a pregnancy test."

"Thank you," Tina whispers.

Cora wraps her up in a hug. "It'll be okay. Come

on, let's do this. You can use my bathroom."

"Come in and talk to me tomorrow, after you talk to Jake, okay?" I say to Tina.

She nods. "I will." She sniffles. "Thanks, Mrs. Thomas. You're the best."

"I'm here if you need me, Tina. Always. Even when you're not a student anymore, okay?"

Another nod, and then Cora and Tina are headed out of the main office, which is empty except for Alice Frank, a para-pro, who's making copies in the copy room.

It's four thirty, and now that Tina's crisis has been handled, I fly into motion, shutting down and locking up my office and power-walking to my car. I rush over to the elementary, where there are only two kids left on the playground with Mrs. Emory, the latchkey program supervisor, watching over them.

Aiden is not at the playground, and I'm low-key panicking.

Mrs. Emory sees me and hurries over. "Ah, Elyse! I was getting worried about you! You're never this late."

"I had a last-minute student crisis," I explain, peering past her at the playground, scanning for Aiden. "Where's Aiden?"

"Oh, he was getting really upset about being late for football practice, so Mr. Trent walked him over to the field. I think he tried calling you, but you didn't answer."

I haul my phone out of my purse and see I have

three missed calls from the school, and a voicemail—I listen to it:

"Hi, Elyse, this is Jamie Trent, principal at the elementary school." His smooth voice is all business. "Aiden is here with the latchkey kids, but he's getting pretty antsy to get over to football practice. The field is just over behind the administrative building—but you know that, obviously. Anyway, I'm going to walk him over there. He said he'd have to sit out an entire quarter of his next game if he's late, and I wouldn't want that for him, and I know you wouldn't either. I know how last-minute meetings can be. So…hopefully you get this message and call me back. I'll be at the field until you get there."

Instead of calling him back, I thank Mrs. Emory and then drive from the elementary over to the practice field parking lot, which is on the far side of the school complex acreage. I see the kids in their huge pads and oversized helmets lining up and practicing plays, with Coach Barnhart yelling direction and encouragement and criticism from one side. There's a little quarter-stand of bleachers on this side of the fence, and the bleachers are filled with parents watching their kids practice. I spy Jamie by himself, arms resting on the fence, watching the practice.

Shoot, shoot, shoot.

Now I have to talk to him.

I leave my car, hike my purse onto my shoulder, and cross over to stand beside Jamie.

"Thank you for bringing him over," I say.

Jamie grins at me. "Oh, no problem. I didn't want to be presumptuous or whatever, but Aiden was getting really upset at the prospect of being late."

I laugh, nodding. "He's the team captain, and their star catcher and runner. He takes his responsibility as team captain very seriously."

Jamie chuckles. "Receiver and running back," he corrects.

"Same thing." I eye him. "Did you play?"

He nods. "Yep. Third grade all the way through college."

"Really? What position?"

"Quarterback."

"Were you good?"

He shrugs. "I did okay. I had plans for my life that didn't include football, so once college was over, that was it." A glance at me. "Your son is very good."

I smile. "He is, isn't he? He loves it. I'm just scared of him getting hurt."

"Eh, he'll be fine. The training and equipment is getting better every year." He eyes me again. "Elyse, I—"

I cut in over him. "Jamie, please. What happened, happened. It was..." I blink, hunt for something to say. "I really had a great time with you. But you're... you're my son's principal, and we work in the same school district, and...I'm a single mom. I can't—I can't afford..."

"Distractions." Jamie's voice is carefully neutral.

"Right."

"You didn't have to sneak out."

"I woke up, and…" I shrug. "I didn't want to make things awkward."

He laughs. "A little late for that."

I laugh, too. "Yeah, I guess so. You could've knocked me over with a feather when I realized you were the new principal."

Jamie nods. "Yeah, it was…unexpected." He laughs. "Shouldn't have been *too* much of a shock, though, considering how small this town is."

"True, I just wasn't expecting to literally bump into you."

Awkward silence. Part of me wants to say more. Wants to talk about that night. Another part of me wants to run, to cut this conversation short and avoid him forever.

He's seen me naked.

He's touched me, intimately.

He's been *inside* me.

He's slept beside me.

And yet, in some ways, he's a total stranger.

And a coworker.

And my son's principal.

I'll have to see him every day.

"Thank you again for bringing him here. I had a student come in with a crisis right as I was leaving."

"Did you get the crisis resolved?"

I shrug. "Mostly. As much as I could manage in the moment."

Another long, awkward silence as we watch Aiden and his team practice a play where the quarterback throws the ball to Aiden, who's supposed to run it downfield.

"Elyse, about...us." He glances at me as he says that last word.

"Jamie..." I hesitate. "I think maybe it'd be best if we just let it be."

He sighs. "If that's what you want, then okay."

"It's more about what's best. For Aiden, especially."

He nods. "Yeah, okay. I get that." He pats the fence, smiles tightly at me. "I'll see you tomorrow morning at drop-off?"

"Yep. Assuming I can get Aiden out the door on time."

Jamie chuckles. "Kids can be tricky like that. Getting them all to come in from recess is always interesting."

"I bet."

Jamie waves at me, and the moment is...supremely awkward. "Bye, Elyse."

"Bye, Jamie."

He's gone, then, sauntering across the field toward the elementary school, arms swinging loosely, sun outlining his broad shoulders and strong frame.

He's handsome. And kind. Loves children. He's thoughtful. Goes out of his way to take care of people.

He was a considerate, generous, amazing lover, and

I can't stop thinking about it.

But…

Daniel seemed to be all that at the beginning too. Mostly.

Some of it anyway.

And then he just…left. It was inevitable, after a certain point, but whose fault was that? Mine? His? Both of ours? I don't know. I just know the idea of trusting someone else is…almost impossible to even consider.

I just can't.

Aiden already sees Jamie every day in the role of principal—how could I even begin trying to introduce him as my boyfriend?

God, just the thought of having a "boyfriend" is beyond bizarre. I haven't had a boyfriend in…fifteen years? How do you even do that? When is the right time to introduce your boyfriend to your impressionable eight-year-old son? Especially when said boyfriend is said eight-year-old's principal—how does *that* work?

It doesn't.

It can't.

I push Jamie out of my mind and focus on Aiden, who's making catch after catch, run after run. Practice ends, and Aiden runs up to me with his helmet in his hand, his pads still on, his practice jersey grass stained, and his hair sweaty.

"Mom! Did you see me? Coach says I totally crushed it today!"

"I watched, buddy! You were doing great! You

made pretty much every catch!"

"I practice catching during recess. Coach says I have the makings of a star receiver. He says I might even break some records, if I practice hard."

"I have absolutely no doubt that you will, baby." I smile at him. "Go get your pads off and meet me at the car. Grandma made lasagna for dinner tonight."

We eat dinner with my parents at least three or four nights every week, just because it's more fun to eat with them than just the two of us alone, and now that my mom is retired, it gives her something to do during the day, while taking dinner prep off my job to-do list. I honestly don't think I could have succeeded as a single mom half so well without my parents.

"Yay! Lasagna! I'm gonna eat pretty much the whole thing by myself. I'm starving!"

I laugh. "Well, you know Grandma. She probably made you a whole dish to yourself."

He takes off his pads on his way to the locker room; a millage rate on taxes from a few years ago paid for a brand-new equipment and locker building for all the various sports that happen at this complex of fields. The building services sports which range from baseball to soccer, football, and softball, with youth, middle school, high school, and adult leagues in each. The building is amazing, actually, with room enough for lockers for each team and each sport, laundry facilities for washing jerseys, and equipment storage. It is great, because I don't have to haul around stinky pads and jerseys, and Aiden doesn't have to worry about forgetting his pads at home, or in my car.

Once he's changed, he climbs into his booster and buckles up, chattering a mile a minute—I have a feeling he'd be running a commentary regardless of whether there was even anyone around to hear.

"—And then I was playing DB against Jimmy, and I intercepted him like six times! He was getting mad, but it's not my fault I'm so much better than he is! And know what? During school today, Mr. Trent came around to all the classrooms and read his favorite book. His favorite book is *Fox in Socks*, and it's super funny the way he reads it. He goes really, really fast, almost like he's rapping, and we were all laughing so hard. And then, because my class was so good today, he read us an extra story. And know what he read, Mama? He read a *Star Wars* chapter book! He's the coolest. I thought Mr. Townsend the janitor was the coolest, but now Mr. Trent is the coolest and Mr. Townsend is second coolest. It's kind of a tie, though, because I've known Mr. Townsend for pretty much ever and Mr. Trent is new." He barely pauses for breath, and then he's off again. "And know what, Mama? Mr. Trent played football in college! He was on TV! Mr. Henry who teaches art— but you know that, duh, because he taught you art too, only that was like, forever ago—and anyway, Mr. Henry was like, Mr. Trent was a quarterback in college. Mr. Henry said something about Big Ten, whatever that is, and he showed us some parts from an old game from when Mr. Trent was in college, and he could throw the ball *so far*! Like, all the way across the field. But I guess he doesn't really talk about that too much, or something. But how cool is it that our new principal was like sort of famous?"

"So...you like Mr. Trent just because he played football?"

"No! I mean, yeah, but that's not the only reason I like him. He's just cool. He talks to us different than other adults do. You know how some adults talk to kids like we're all still in kindergarten? I hate that. Mr. Trent talks to us like we're...I don't know how to say it. Not like we're adults, but just...normal, I guess. I don't know. Plus, he comes out to the playground during recess and he throws the football and shoots baskets and pushes kids on swings and all sorts of stuff. He doesn't just watch. Plus, he's super great at reading to us. He did voices when he read the *Star Wars* book. His C-3PO voice was almost like from the movie!"

I only just barely stifle a sigh as Aiden keeps singing Mr. Trent's praises all the way to Mom and Dad's house.

It'd almost be easier to shut this whole thing down if Jamie wasn't so darned amazing.

But, alas, he is, and putting him out of my mind is going to prove difficult, very difficult.

8

A FEW DAYS LATER, I'M RUNNING A FEW ERRANDS IN town—grabbing some groceries, dropping bills off at the post office, things like that. Aiden's at practice, and once I'm done with my errands, I head back to the field. After parking, I head for the fence to watch the last few minutes of practice. And, lo and behold, who's there on the field, helping coach? None other than Jamie Trent. He's in athletic shorts, running shoes, a sleeveless tee shirt, and a ball cap. He's working the runners and catchers—receivers and running backs, he called them, while Coach Barnhart works with the boys who line up in front, whatever they're called. Jamie has his group of boys clustered around him, each boy on one knee, hanging on his every word. They're nodding, and shouting "Yes, Coach!" every few seconds, and then they all clap once, in unison, and jump to their feet. They form a single file line to one side of Jamie, who has a pile of footballs at his feet. He bends, grabs a football, spins it in his hands, and then calls out in a loud, commanding voice,

"READY—GO!" and the boy in front sprints forward, and then cuts a hard right turn. Right as the player makes the turn, Jamie dances backward a step, and then rockets the ball at the player, who catches it and jogs to the back of the line, tossing the ball at Jamie's feet. Jamie calls out encouragement to the next player in line—my Aiden. At Jamie's signal, Aiden sprints forward and cuts right, catching Jamie's throw easily. I watch as Jamie goes through the entire line of boys, and then they start again, running a different pattern. Jamie throws easily, naturally, each movement lithe and smooth.

This Jamie is at odds, in my mind, with the Jamie I've known so far, a button-down and pressed khakis and loafers kind of guy—a principal, an educator. It makes my heart skip a beat, watching him coach the boys. He's encouraging to everyone, even when he makes corrections or gives tips for making a better catch. When a boy misses a catch, he tells them it's fine, offers advice, and claps him roughly on the pads or slaps him on the helmet.

Dammit, he's making this hard.

After a few minutes of this, Coach Barnhart calls the end of practice and the boys all gather around him on one knee, helmets off now, sweaty heads bobbing as they listen to him. Jamie hangs back; lets Coach Barnhart make his statements. With his background in football, Jamie could probably take over coaching if he wanted to, but he doesn't seem interested in cutting in over Bob Barnhart's authority, just helping out. Bob has been coaching the youth league since I was a little girl, and he hasn't changed much in the intervening twenty, thirty years—a few extra wrinkles on his weathered face, a little more white to his hair than steel-silver, but he's as he's ever been: red track pants with white strips on the sides, white T-shirt, battered gray New Balance running shoes, a red Nebraska Cornhuskers ball cap, clipboard in one hand and a whistle around his neck.

Coach Barnhart dismisses the boys, and the two men spend a few minutes chatting, discussing football with lots of hand motions and pointing at diagrams on the clipboard. One by one, and two by two, the boys trickle out of the locker room and head for their parents. Aiden sees me at the fence, waves, and half jogs, half walks over; Jamie joins him, a football in his hands, tossing the ball in the air and catching it one-handed.

"You did really great today, Aiden!" Jamie says as they both converge at the fence near me. "Made some really great catches."

"Thanks, Coach!" Aiden is vibrating with excitement, beaming up at Jamie. "I have a question, though."

"Hit me with it, buddy," Jamie says, tossing the ball to Aiden, who catches it with absentminded skill.

"You're my principal, but now you're also my coach, so do I call you Mr. Trent, or Coach, or what?"

Jamie grins, shrugs. "Either one is fine, kiddo."

Aiden tosses the ball back. "I'll call you Coach, then. It's more fun." He takes off running. "How far can you throw it, Coach?"

Jamie laughs. "Farther than that, pal! Keep going! Go deep!" He takes a couple dancing steps forward, the ball cocked back, cupping it. "Here it comes, Aiden!"

When Aiden is at the far end of the field, Jamie takes a hopping lunge-step forward and sends the ball arcing in a perfect spiral through the air—his form is perfect, and I can see the ex-quarterback in his movements. Aiden is watching it while running, checking his forward progress every few steps and then glancing back up at the ball. And as far as he's run already, the ball is clearly going to sail past him.

"Get it, Aiden!" Jamie encourages, more to himself than to anyone else, dancing on his toes as he watches Aiden sprint for the ball. "Come on, kid, make the catch!"

Aiden glances forward one last time, and then leaps into the air, the ball landing in his outstretched hands. He impacts on the ground, the ball tucked against his belly, and rolls with it across the grass a few feet.

"YES!" Jamie says, leaping into the air excitedly. "He got it!" He turns to me, beaming. "Did you see that? That's a ninety-yard bomb he just caught!"

Aiden, however, isn't moving. He landed so hard, I'm worried he got the wind knocked out of him, or hurt himself.

"Is he okay?" I ask, worried.

As soon as the words leave my mouth, however, Aiden thrusts the ball into the air triumphantly, still laying on his back. "I got it!" he shouts.

He leaps to his feet and jogs slowly back across the field to us; when he reaches us, he's still gasping for air.

"Holy cow, Aiden! I honestly didn't think you'd make that catch! Way to go, buddy!" Jamie catches him in his arms and ruffles his hair. "That was *awesome!*"

Aiden is absolutely thrilled. "I know! It was like, the whole field! I thought for sure it was gonna go past me and so I jumped for it and it just landed right in my hands! It was like something from an NFL game!"

"OBJ couldn't have done it better himself," Jamie says. "You've got a heck of a future ahead of you, Aiden. For real. I played football for a long time, and I haven't seen anyone with as much raw talent as you have, like, ever."

"For real?" If Aiden vibrates any harder, he'll jitter away across the field. His grin is ear-to-ear, so wide and bright it's contagious.

"Think I'd lie to you, kid?"

"I dunno. Adults say things they don't mean all the time, especially to kids."

Jamie laughs. "You have a point, unfortunately. But no, I'm telling you the god's honest truth."

Aiden circles around the end of the fence and slams up against my legs, wrapping sweaty arms around my waist. "Did you see that, Mom?"

I kneel down and wrap him in a hug. "Heck yeah, I saw it! You're a rock star, Aiden!"

"Is there any food, Mama?" he asks, his voice hopeful.

I laugh. "How many times have I ever picked you up from football without a snack for you?"

"Never."

I ruffle his hair as I stand up. "There's a protein bar and some chips in the car, on the seat next to mine."

"YAY!" he shouts, and takes off running to the car.

I laugh, shaking my head. "He just spent a solid hour and a half running, and he's still got more energy than I'll ever have," I say.

Jamie smiles, balancing the football on its end on his index finger. "Right? Boundless energy."

"What you said about him being talented at football..." I prompt.

Jamie's eyes lock on mine. "That was no exaggeration, Elyse. I played with guys in college who couldn't make that catch."

"I knew he was pretty good, but some of these kids..." I shrug, chuckling. "They're awful pumped to be playing, and I don't know anything about football, but even I can tell they're not..."

Jamie flips the ball in the air. "They love the game, but probably won't be playing past high school, if that."

"Right."

"When it comes to kids this age, it can be hard to tell. Some kids, they get close to puberty, and they just...bam, they discover athletic ability they didn't know they had. Other kids, like Aiden, are just obviously born with it."

I want to stare into his warm brown eyes for as long as possible. Instead, I twist to glance back at Aiden, who is sitting on the bumper of the car, eating his protein bar and watching a pair of grackles chase a crow away from their nest.

"You know," I hear myself saying, "honestly, when I first met you, I wouldn't have pegged you for the football type."

Jamie laughs, not at all offended. "I was never the quintessential jock. In high school, I was in chamber choir and the drama club and all that. I went to practices and lifted with the team, but the crowd I hung out with wasn't the jocks, it was the drama nerds and choir dorks."

"I bet that went over well with the team," I say.

He snorts. "Yeah, about as well as you'd expect. But they couldn't ostracize me too much and risk making me quit, because I was pretty much our entire offense simply because I could put the ball right in the hands of even the worst catchers, and I was also fairly quick and not afraid of getting hit, so I could run a keep for a few yards. They knew if they alienated me too much, I'd quit and play for the rec league instead, and they'd be screwed."

"Honestly that makes me feel a little better," I say, laughing. "I always thought I was a pretty decent judge of character, so if I had you pegged for one thing and you turned out to be something else, I'd start questioning my judgment."

"Nope, I think you had me just right," he says, and I feel myself blushing at the unintended innuendo; Jamie catches on and rubs the back of his neck. "Oh, god. Um—I mean…" he trails off. "I didn't mean it like that."

"I should go." I make myself say, before I say anything I'll regret.

"Yeah, me too. There's a board meeting and I probably shouldn't show up wearing this."

My eyes flick over him—tanned, muscular calves, strong arms, a five o'clock shadow. "Oh, I wouldn't mind, if I was on the board." I *so* didn't mean to say that.

"*Are* you on the board?"

I laugh derisively. "God, no! I don't even go to PTO meetings."

"Too bad. I'd enjoy seeing more of you."

My heart thumps, twists; I feel the same way. But Aiden's already getting attached to Jamie as coach and principal. I can't add another layer of complexity to that, not for something with no substance or basis beyond a night of hot sex and a little chemistry.

"Jamie…" I sigh, unsure what to say.

He holds up his hands, leaning back against the fence that stands between us. "I'm sorry, Elyse. I know you've said more than once now that it's best we're just friends or whatever, but I just…" He shrugs. "I don't know. We had an amazing night, and I like you a lot."

"I like you too, Jamie, but I can't complicate things with Aiden. His father leaving us was very hard on him, and he's just now starting to really find his equilibrium, you know?"

Jamie nods, not looking at me. "I get it."

"If it was just me…"

He shakes his head, pushing away from the fence. "You don't need to qualify it, Elyse. I really do understand."

"MOM!" Aiden calls. "Grandma probably has dinner waiting. Come on!"

I laugh. "Bottomless pit, that boy."

"All boys are bottomless pits. Just wait till he's a teenager lifting weights and practicing for two hours a day."

I fake a whole-body shudder. "God help me. He already eats me out of house and home."

"Start saving now, Elyse. It'll be like feeding an army. And if he brings over his football buddies, you really *will* be feeding an army."

"Are you trying to scare me? I just want him to stay this age forever."

He laughs. "I think I've heard parents say that at every age."

"Because we never want our kids to grow up, and it just keeps happening faster and faster."

"That's definitely how it seems to go." He's quiet

as he says this, and there's a distance in his eyes, in his voice.

I want to ask about it. He obviously loves kids, but yet he's divorced with no kids of his own. There's a story there, but I dare not ask. I dare not get that close.

"I'm gonna go. Aiden will start eating the car if I don't get him dinner soon."

"Okay. I'll see you around."

He turns away first, striding easily across the field toward the administrative building. I watch him longer than I should.

We're in the car heading for my parents' when Aiden pipes up. "Hey, Mama?"

"Yeah, buddy."

"Can we invite Coach Trent over to Grandma and Papa's for dinner sometime?"

I swallow hard. "Um...I don't know about that, kiddo."

"But he's so cool, and you guys are friends, right? And *everybody* likes Grandma and Papa."

I have a vision: Jamie at the table at my parents' house, laughing as he passes a dish, talking football with Dad, him and Aiden tag-teaming the dishes.

I shake my head to clear the vision. That's not happening. "We'll see, Aiden."

Aiden sighs disgustedly. "I know what *that* means."

I laugh. "Grandma made chicken pot pie," I tell him, in a blatant attempt to distract him. "Are you looking forward to that?"

"Heck yeah! I love Grandma's chicken pot pie." He meets my eyes in the rearview mirror. "You know who else would love it? Coach Trent."

"Aiden, let it go, okay? Please?"

His eyes search mine, and I'm afraid he'll see through me, that he'll see how much I'd like that too. "Okay, Mama."

"Thanks, buddy."

I'm distracted at dinner, that fleeting vision of Jamie is stuck in my head—him, here, in my parents' house, eating with us.

When Daniel and I were together, we didn't come over here very often—he didn't really ever get along with my dad, and the tension made it awkward to bring him over. Then, when he left and we divorced, Mom and Dad became my support system, along with Cora, and I'm here more than I was even during high school. Making up for lost time, I guess.

I can't get rid of that vision, though.

It can't happen, of course, but it's a pleasant fantasy.

Fate is such a bitch.

I can't get away from Jamie Trent. I see him every day at Aiden's football practice, every morning at drop-off, and every afternoon at pickup...until Jamie volunteers to walk over with the three or four other boys who play on the team with Aiden, so they don't have to be picked up and driven around the complex. Every time we see each other, we end up chatting for a few minutes, and each time, it's far too easy. His smile seems to sear into my soul, and his eyes seem to see my every secret.

Surely he can see how attracted to him I am...

Friday, a few weeks into the new school year, Mom and Dad offer to have Aiden stay the night so Cora and I can decompress a little. So, after football practice, I take Aiden to my parents' house, give him hugs and kisses, and tell him to be good, and I meet Cora at José's. Our night out goes swimmingly, at first.

Over tacos and margaritas, we spend an hour discussing the latest Clayton gossip, and our students, and what we'll be covering at the next in-service meeting. Eventually we head over to Vinnie's, skipping the karaoke tonight in favor of a low-key evening. We sit at the booth near the back and sip wine, leaving the dance floor to the others.

Cora is on a rant about her favorite subject: Lewis Calhoun.

"...There's talk his uncle is retiring from the sheriff's department, and if Tony Calhoun retires, word is they'll bring in someone from the outside to take over and shake things up. And then what would Lewis do? Tony has been looking the other way about Lewis's little business for years. It's an open secret, and I've even heard Tony talking about it to his buddies at the bar. Like, it's harmless, you know? It's just a little pot. If

Lewis was trying to sell anything harder, or in bigger weights, he'd have to step in, but as long as Lewis keeps it small and keeps it quiet and doesn't sell to minors, no big deal. And anyway, Tony knows the narc officers in Columbia, which is where he speculates Lewis is getting his supply, and he could easily make a few calls and get Lewis's supply line cut."

I shake my head, snorting. "Cora. Why do you care about Lewis Calhoun's marijuana supply line?"

"Oh, I don't, not really. I'm just interested to see what he does if and when Tony retires."

"He'll have to stop selling, that's what."

Cora nods. "Right, but that's how Lewis makes ends meet. His whole small engine repair business barely lets him scrape by. If Tony retires and Lewis has to stop selling, I'm not sure how he'll manage."

I laugh. "Um…by getting another job, and an honest one?"

"I told him he should start selling his junk art, but he's like, nah, that's just a hobby."

I eye her—that's a new one. "Junk art?"

She claps her hands over her mouth. "I wasn't supposed to talk about that."

"Cora."

She sighs. "You can't let it go beyond us, okay? He's weird about it."

I roll my eyes. "Cora, who would I tell? You're my only real friend in town."

"He salvages things from the scrapyard over in

York, brings them back to his shop, and turns them into abstract art. He's got that whole warehouse, you know? He bought the whole plot including the warehouse and the abandoned manufacturing floor and everything else for an absolute pittance from Gordy Garrison a few years ago just so he could have access to the mechanic's shop. But over the years, he's actually done a lot of work on the place, and he's got quite a backlog of junk art pieces in that warehouse. Pretty cool stuff, actually."

"You've been in Lewis's warehouse?" I ask. He's notoriously reclusive, and very few people have ever been in there.

She shrugs, focusing on her drink instead of meeting my eyes. "Yeah, once or twice. We hang out sometimes."

"Cora?"

She looks up at me finally. "What?"

"What aren't you telling me?"

"Nothing. We hang out sometimes. Literally, that's it. Nothing beyond literally just hanging out and talking."

"That's weird."

She frowns at me. "Why is it weird? He's an interesting guy. We're just friends."

I shrug, shake my head. "You were pushing him on me not that long ago, that's all."

"You'd never date him. I'm starting to think you'll never date anyone." She holds my gaze very intently.

"Even Jamie Trent."

I sigh. I've managed to go this long without an interrogation from Cora, but I knew it was coming. "Can we keep talking about Lewis?"

She laughs. "Nope. Nothing to talk about anyway. He's weird, cool, interesting, funny, artistic, reclusive, kind of mysterious, very attractive, and yes, I may have a little bit of a crush on him and so what—we're not talking about him, we're talking about Jamie Trent, he of the starched and pressed chinos. Who, apparently, is also a big deal football player or something."

I roll my eyes. "That rumor is a bit overstated. He played in college, that's all."

"So he's got a hot body under those chinos and polos?"

"He actually wears button-downs and weird ties more than polos."

Cora rests her chin on her fist and blinks at me. "Oh? Do tell."

"Tell what? There's nothing to tell." I drop my voice, even though the bar is loud and there's no one even within ten feet of us. "Yes, we slept together. Yes, it was absolutely incredible. Yes, I'm attracted to him. No, I'm not going to date him. Yes, he has a pretty great body—he stays in shape, but he doesn't have the body he probably did in college. He has very nice arms and a flat stomach, but not quite a six-pack. A little definition, but not shredded." I laugh and pat my stomach. "Like I have any room to be making judgments on that score, though."

Cora hurls a mayo packet at me. "Oh shut up with that mess, Elyse Thomas. You lost forty pounds through hard work and determination! You're sexy and you have nothing to be self-conscious about."

"I lost forty and put ten back on and can't seem to get it off again. And I did it by not eating garbage and walking a lot."

"Speaking of which, aren't we due to start back with our morning walks?"

I nod. "Yes, we are. I kinda slipped a bit this summer on the walking, but I was pretty active with Aiden. I do want to get back into our before-school walks."

"I've been talking to Trish and Avery and Yvonne, and they want to walk with us."

I sigh—selfishly, I kind of like our walks just being the two of us especially because along with Cora, Trish, Avery, and Yvonne are the heirs apparent to the Clayton Busybody Society. Cora would never admit to being a gossip or a busybody, but she loves keeping abreast of the town news, and she keeps tabs on everyone and always has a line on the juiciest tidbits.

Cora spins her now-empty wineglass by the stem. "Why won't you date Jamie?"

"Do you really have to ask?"

She eyes me. "I know the excuses you'd make."

"They're not *excuses*, they're *reasons*," I insist. "And valid ones, at that."

"Not wanting to confuse Aiden or let him get too

attached when it may not work—that I get. But that's not a reason to not date Jamie at all, just...be careful about it. Go slow. Don't let Aiden know until you're sure it's something that can last."

"Jamie is already all kinds of mixed up in Aiden's life—he's his principal as well as his football coach, now, and Aiden thinks Jamie hung the moon. He'd get one whiff of Jamie and I and be all over it like ants at a picnic."

"What's the real reason, Elyse?"

I groan, tipping my head backward and closing my eyes. "Cora, come on."

"You come on, Elyse. It's not a complicated question."

"Isn't it?"

She sighs. "Not really, no."

I grab her wineglass and mine and slide out of the booth. "I'm going to get us more wine."

She catches my wrist and hauls me back to the booth. "Oh no, you don't."

I slump to the bench. "Why are you digging into this so hard, Cora?"

"Because you're my best friend and I smell bullshit. You *like* him. He likes you, I can tell. There could *be* something, babe. Why not explore it a little?"

"Because he'll hurt me!" I snap, louder and more aggressively than I intend. "He's divorced—and why? What's the story? I'll be the first to admit there's no innocent party in a divorce, Cora. When I had the miscarriage, I shut down. I stopped wanting Daniel—I wanted nothing to do with him, and it wasn't his fault. It wasn't my fault either, and I know that. But I took it out on him."

"That's not quite how it happened, Elyse."

"Close enough. My point is, I'm not innocent."

"And sure, maybe there's a story there, and yeah, Jamie probably holds his portion of the blame for whatever happened between him and his ex-wife, but that's just life. That doesn't mean he's not a good and decent guy at the core. And you know what? Yeah, maybe he will hurt you. You date someone, you get involved with someone, you get hurt. It's inevitable. Hell, we've been best friends our whole lives, literally from birth, and how many times have we pissed each other off and hurt each other's feelings over the years? How many times have your parents had blow-out fights? I remember most of them. I remember when your mom moved back to Montana for two months because she and your dad were fighting so bad."

I sigh. "They worked that out, and haven't had a fight like that since."

"Right! That's exactly my point! And do you think that didn't hurt them both? Of course it did! Your mom *hates* Montana. She got hurt, and your dad got hurt, and it was a huge, giant, messy mess. But their relationship was worth it for both of them, so they figured it out, and they forgave each other. *We* forgive each other. And if Jamie were to hurt you, you'd be faced with two basic choices: either it's worth it and you forgive him, or it's not and you don't. You can't know which one it'll be *when* he does something to hurt you—because he will—until you give him a chance."

"I thought what I had with Daniel was worth it," I say. "I thought we could work it out. I *wanted* to work it out. I didn't want to get divorced. I thought maybe he'd need a month or two away and he'd miss me and miss Aiden, and he'd come back and we'd—we'd—" I blink hard, choking. I stuff it down; force myself to be okay, to keep going. "I thought we'd be a family again. Mommy, Daddy, and Aiden."

"Apparently Daniel had other plans," Cora says, her voice soft. "I know. I wanted that for you, too."

"You did *not*," I snap.

She rears back, hurt. "Yes, I did! And damn you for doubting me, Elyse."

"I'm sorry," I say. "I just meant you never liked him."

"No, I didn't, and I won't apologize for that. I always saw that cowardly center of him. I never thought he'd have the inner strength to weather a life with you. He was a coward his whole life. He let Brad Vostich beat him up every single day for two years and never fought back, never told anyone, never dealt with it. Just gave him his lunch money, literally, and took the beatings. Hell, Brad tried to bully me and I socked him in the jaw, and he left me alone. Your wimp of an ex-husband just took it, because he was too scared to fight back. And it's not like Brad was even that big! Daniel was nice, yes. He was good-looking, yes. But he was also the stereotypical gym teacher, and you know it. He ended up teaching gym because he had no idea what else to do with himself. He had no special skills or talents or dreams. He was just...there. At least now we have Kelly Pruitt teaching gym, and she's fanatic about fitness and health. She teaches gym because she loves kids and loves teaching them to be healthy. It's a calling for her. Daniel just did it as a cop-out."

I sigh. "Can we stop trash-talking my ex, please?"

"Fine. My point is that, yes, I never liked Daniel Thomas, not for one second, not at any point in our lives. I never liked him for you, and I never knew what you saw in him. But—*but...*" She reaches out and takes my hands. "I wanted your marriage to work, for *you*. Because *you* wanted it to. You loved him—god knows why, but you did. He's Aiden's father. You wanted that family, and you had it, and it got taken away from you, and yes, sure, you can shoulder some of the blame because no one is ever totally innocent." She leans forward, squeezing my hands again. "And what I want for you more than anything is for you to realize that you *can* move on from Daniel, that you haven't yet, and that you deserve happiness—you just have to let yourself have it."

"And you think my happiness will come from Jamie Trent."

Her eyes flick over my shoulder, widen a bit, and

then she glances at me, a mysterious smirk on her face. "It's not that I think your happiness *will* come from Jamie, just that I think you *could* be happy with him." She grabs her purse. "And here he comes now—okay, bye!"

And then she's out of the booth and vanishing into the crowd near the bar. I barely have time to register that she's gone before another body is filling the booth.

Jamie.

With two glasses of red wine.

His smile is gentle and hopeful, and he's still dressed for work in tan slacks, a white button-down, and a Teenage Mutant Ninja Turtles necktie loose around his neck, the top button undone, sleeves rolled up, that five o'clock shadow dusting his jawline.

"Hi, Elyse."

I swallow hard. "Hi, Jamie."

9

"**C**ORA SEEMS TO ENJOY LEAVING YOU SWINGING around me," he says, grinning.

I sigh, rolling my eyes. "Yeah, she does."

"Another girls' night out?"

I shrug. "Just Cora and me having some downtime."

He nods. "You and Cora are pretty close, then?"

"You could say that. We were in preschool together and have spent just about every single intervening day together since." I laugh. "Actually, it goes back further than that. We were born the same day, in rooms next door to each other at the hospital. My mom says we were in bassinets in the maternity ward next to each other, and that we were just fated to be best friends for life."

"That's really awesome. I'm kind of jealous of that."

"You don't have any friends like that?"

He shakes his head. "Not really. I mean, there are a couple childhood friends I'm still in contact with, but they're all back in Nashua and I'm here."

"This is kind of an odd place to end up," I say.

He shrugs. "I…I needed a drastic change."

"Well, moving from the capital of New Hampshire to our quaint little Pennsylvania village is as drastic a change as you can get short of leaving the country."

"Yeah, pretty much."

"Mind if I ask why you moved?" I shouldn't ask that. Asking him personal questions will lead to him asking me personal questions…and that's us getting to know each other, and that's entering dangerous territory.

Yet, I just can't seem to stop myself.

He lifts a shoulder. "The divorce." He tilts his head to one side. "Well, that's not entirely true. It's more complicated than that, actually. I was sort of stuck at the school I was teaching at in New Hampshire. They'd just hired a new assistant principal, and the principal was relatively young, like forty-five or so, and was clearly going to be a lifer. I wanted to be in administration. I loved teaching, but I wanted to be a principal—that was my goal from day one. I sent resumés to school districts across the country—I didn't really *want* to move, but I was willing to. And I guess I…well, I sort of overlooked how resolute my wife—my *ex*-wife was about not moving. We were having issues anyway, and I guess I justified it by thinking that a change of scenery might help our marriage, you know? Like, we'd both been born and raised in the Nashua area, and we knew everyone and everyone knew us. And I thought, if it was just us in a new place, and we had to rely on each other, maybe that would fix things."

I wince. "Not so much?"

"No. Like I said, we'd been struggling with... well, issues, I guess, and we'll leave it at that for now. I didn't think it was over, and neither of us had said the D word at any point. I was sending my resumé out all over the place, taking interviews at schools everywhere from Oregon to Texas to Florida, hoping for a principal job, and nothing was opening up. It was just a constant flood of 'not the right fit' or 'not quite what we're looking for.' Meaning, nobody wanted to hire a thirty-something teacher with zero administrative experience as a head principal."

"I mean, don't you usually start as an assistant principal somewhere?"

He laughs. "Well yeah, usually, and I was applying for anything that had the word 'principal' attached to it. Time was slipping away, you know? I'd been teaching for ten years at that point already, and I was eager to start the next phase of my career as an educator." He waves a hand. "And then one day I got a call back from this elementary school in the middle of nowhere in Pennsylvania. Their principal was retiring and they were thinking about hiring someone young and fresh to take over and shake things up."

"And here you are?"

"Eh, not quite." He stares beyond me, seeing the past, I think. "I did the interview, felt confident about it…but also felt a good bit of apprehension about such a drastic move. And the issues Iris and I were having… weren't getting better. They were getting worse, if anything. And when I told her I wanted to take this job, she…well, she didn't respond well. And that's when the D word got dropped—by her, first—not that it matters in the end. She told me she wasn't going to move, and if I wanted to take this job, go ahead, but she'd be serving me divorce papers if I did."

"Ouch."

He nods. "Yeah. And I think once that idea gets floated, you can't take it back."

"No, you can't," I agree, thinking of Daniel.

"So, I told them I needed time to think, and they gave me two weeks to tell them yes or no, but that if I said yes, I'd have as much time as I needed within reason to make the transition happen." He sighs. "But really, I knew I was going to say yes. I just wanted time to see if I could salvage things with Iris."

"Which clearly didn't work."

"No, clearly not." He takes a sip of his wine. "So, by the way, all this was taking place more than two years ago. The school here wanted to have someone lined up and ready to go, wanted to give Mr. Mackey plenty of time to tie up loose ends, you know? He'd told them he was ready to start the process, and so they started looking for a replacement, and it took them a while to find me, and then even after I'd told them yes, Mr. Mackey wanted to finish that year, and then my divorce was taking a long time to settle…"

"Not amicable, then?"

"How many divorces are ever actually, truly amicable?" he asks. "No, it wasn't amicable at all. It was slow, and painful. We separated, sold our house, split most of our belongings fairly evenly, but it just…she was just…" He sighs, shakes his head. "It was insanely hard, and I'll leave it at that."

"So…if you don't mind me asking, how long have you been actually divorced?"

"A year and a half."

"What were you doing in the time between the divorce finalizing and moving out here?"

He shrugs. "Teaching, and trying to prepare myself for being a principal as best I could. Living with my best friend out there, Marc. He's one of those childhood friends I was telling you about. We text a lot, and exchange these long, rambling emails. He's been threatening to come visit me for a while now, but his workload hasn't allowed it yet." He waves. "So, that's the gist of my story."

"Well, I'm sorry you went through that."

"Yeah, thanks. I mean, it brought me here, though, and I'm really coming to love this little town." His eyes fix on mine, and I hear what he's not saying—that it's not the town, it's the people. Me. Aiden.

He swirls his wine—we're barely even drinking our wine. Sipping for appearances now and then, but not really drinking. "So. I showed you mine."

I blush, and then realize he means his divorce story. "Oh. Um." I inhale, hold it, and let it out slowly. "Well…Daniel and I were high school sweethearts. We grew up here together, flirted a lot in middle school, started hanging out freshman year, started dating sophomore year…went to the same college in Baltimore, moved back here afterward, got married, had Aiden." I hesitate again. "Um. Things were…well, pretty good. Not great, but not bad. Just…average. I was—and still am—a guidance counselor at the high school, and he was the gym teacher. We had the house with the fenced-in yard, decent jobs, a baby…I wasn't unhappy. I always wanted to be a wife and a mother. Cora and I used to play house as little girls, and I was always the mom, and she was either the dad or the kid, depending on what we were pretending. Daniel…god, I really don't want to go too deep into it. Um. The salient points of the story are that I got pregnant again. I was happy. I loved being a mom, and even though I knew another baby would definitely make things even harder as we weren't exactly raking in the money, as I'm sure you know…I was happy about being pregnant again."

"He wasn't?" Jamie guesses.

"He was worried about money, about me needing time off, about how we were going to take care of two when it was all we could do to keep up with Aiden as twenty-somethings just starting out in life and marriage and careers." I'm struggling. I don't want to talk about this. Not with him, especially.

He listens sympathetically, his eyes radiating warmth and compassion and interest. "He couldn't hack it?"

I shake my head. "I wish it was that simple, honestly." I swallow hard, several times. "I…I lost it—I lost the baby. Fourteen weeks. A late miscarriage. It was… well, it was a nightmare. There's no other way to put it."

"God, Elyse. I'm so sorry."

I shrug. "Yeah. Um. So, really, that was it. I didn't…I didn't handle it well. I went into a really bad depression, and Daniel didn't know how to help, how to handle me like that. We stopped…um…connecting, I guess you could say, if you know what I mean. I just couldn't cope, and he was clueless. In retrospect, I really needed to get help. And, I mean, I talked to my parents and I talked to my doctor, and I even tried some various medications. So it's not like I pretended I was fine or refused to get help, but…the medication really only made me worse, what with the various side effects and all. So, I think *we* needed help. He needed someone to…" I shake my head. "I'm not going to make this about him or try to put it all on him. It was a big tangled nasty mess, and neither of us coped well, and he ended up leaving."

"He just…left?" Jamie seems puzzled.

"Yep."

"You had a miscarriage and suffered a depression, you two have a son together, and he just…*left*?"

"Yep. He came back a few times to see Aiden, and then it was just phone calls and cards and gifts for Aiden, and then that trickled off, and then I got papers giving me pretty much everything—legal and physical custody, the house and the car, and in return leaving him free of alimony or child support. I signed and that was that." I shrug. "That was three years ago, and we haven't heard from him beyond a random birthday card for Aiden last year."

"I don't understand that *at all*."

I laugh bitterly. "That makes two of us."

"He just left you, his wife, and Aiden, his…what? Five-year-old son? Where did he go? What is he doing? Do you even know?"

I shake my head. "Not really. Cora did some online stalking a few months ago, and he's living in Branson, Missouri, dating somebody named Anne, and is, somewhat enigmatically, self-employed." I shrug. "But that's about all I know, and I don't really care to know anymore."

"I wonder if he's pretending he doesn't have an ex-wife and eight-year-old son," Jamie muses.

"Probably. I guess he's going by 'Dan' these days. All growing up, our whole lives, he was always Daniel. He was adamant about it." I rotate my wineglass, staring at the ruby liquid I'm not drinking. "If he's going by Dan and is self-employed, my best guess is he's 're-invented' himself." I use air quotes around the word. "Whatever. Not my business anymore."

Jamie shakes his head. "I guess I just can't comprehend walking out on Aiden. He's such a great kid. He's funny, he's athletic, he's smart. His teacher, Mrs. Crenshaw, told me just yesterday that he's the sweetest and most helpful student she's ever had." Jamie shakes his head again, frowning. "How do you just walk away from your own kid?"

I fight tears. "I wish I knew, Jamie."

He winces. "I'm sorry. I'm bringing up a lot of painful stuff, aren't I?"

I laugh, a bitter, mournful huff. "It is what it is, right? We all have our stuff."

His eyes bore into mine. "I can see more clearly why you don't want to get involved in anything."

I close my eyes. "Jamie…"

He holds up his hands. "I'm only saying that I get it. You have a good reason for it."

"Aiden didn't take Daniel leaving well at all. He was just confused at first, thought Daddy would be coming back, like he was on a trip. And I had no idea if Daniel was coming back myself, so I wasn't sure what to tell him. And then when it became clear he wasn't coming back, I had to tell Aiden, and…" I blink hard. "He acted out for a long time. He was angry and confused, you know? He had every right to be, and all I could do was…just be everything I could for him."

"Elyse, I—"

"And he's just now starting to be really okay, and not just okay, but happy again. He loves football, he loves third grade, he loves spending time with his grandparents—"

"What about his father's parents?"

I wave a hand. "They moved down to Florida years ago, before Aiden was even born. They send him birthday and Christmas gifts, but he doesn't really know them." I shrug. "Daniel never got along with my parents, and I never really got along with his, so there's not really been much love lost along the way in that regard."

"Gotcha. That's rough, too."

"Not really. He doesn't know them and never did, so he doesn't miss them, because they never factored in his life. My parents love him to pieces. I think they're trying to love him enough to make up for him not knowing Daniel's parents." I smile, then. "And they succeed, I'm pretty sure."

"Well, they raised you, so I can imagine how amazing they must be." His smile is so warm it threatens to melt me into a puddle.

I blush so hard my cheeks are hot. "Jamie, come on."

He lifts an eyebrow. "What? I'm not going to stop thinking you're an amazing person just because..." he trails off.

I frown. "What?" I ask. "Just because what?"

He shakes his head. "I like you, Elyse. I admire you as a mother, I'm attracted to you as a woman, and I just flat out like who you are as a person. I would like to spend more time with you. It can be casual, and it can be whatever you want it to be or not be. I truly get where you're coming from, why you're resistant to starting anything. I'm not going to lie—I'd really love an opportunity to explore us being something more than friends, but if all we can be is friends, I'll take that too."

My heart flips. "Dammit, Jamie." I'm blinking hard. "It's not that simple."

"Why not?" He leans forward, into my personal space. "I'm not asking for anything but a chance to just...talk, sometimes. Spend a little time together now and then, even as just friends. What's complicated about that?"

"Because I like you too, Jamie. But...you know Aiden pretty well by now—you know as well as I do that if you and I started seeing more of each other, he'd sniff it out in a heartbeat."

"And you wouldn't want him to know?"

"Just because there's never been anyone but Daniel, and I don't know how he'd take it." I hesitate. "And he's already attached enough to you as it is."

He smiles. "Heck, I'm attached to him, too. As a principal and coach I'm not supposed to have favorites, but I admit I'm a little partial to Aiden, and not just because he's your son."

My heart is pounding. I want...I don't know. So many conflicting things.

But I keep seeing Aiden's face when I told him his

father wasn't coming back. I keep hearing him crying at night because he thought he'd done something wrong. I keep…I keep seeing my hand, holding a blue ballpoint pen, scribbling my name on a document that made it legally clear Daniel didn't want anything to do with me or Aiden ever again. I keep seeing Aiden holding an envelope with his name on it—no return address—and pulling out the cliché robot birthday card with the twenty-dollar bill in it, and a single scrawled sentence:

Happy birthday Aiden.
    —Dan

Aiden had stared at the card, flipped the cover over to look at the front again. "I've never been into robots. And what am I supposed to do with this?" He had handed me the money, threw the card in the trash, and went outside to play basketball with the neighbors. When I asked him about it, he said he didn't really care, and asked if we could get ice cream. That flat, expressionless look he'd given me when he handed me the money had been heartbreaking.

How could I bring anyone else into his life?

If he got attached to Jamie, started to develop a deeper relationship with him—love him, in something like a father-son sort of way, and then Jamie and I ended up not working out…

His stability was still…fragile. Aiden would never recover from that.

And neither would I.

I already suffered enough Mom guilt for everything Aiden has been through—neither of us can handle putting Aiden through any more heartache.

And honestly, I'm not sure I can take any more myself.

"Elyse?" Jamie's voice snaps me out of my meandering thoughts and back to the present: a back booth at Vinnie's, with Jamie across from me, his deep, piercing brown eyes on mine.

"Hi," I breathe.

"I lost you there for a second," he says.

I swallow hard, holding Jamie's gaze. "I'm sorry." I slide out of the booth. "I just...I can't."

He breathes out a gentle sigh of frustration. "Okay...okay. I get it." His eyes betray hurt, however.

I turn away from that hurt, walk away from him. Out the back door. Out into the alley behind Vinnie's, ignoring Matty's voice calling after me. I don't know where I'm going, only that I'm walking fast, eyes blurring.

"ELYSE!" Cora's voice does break through and halt me.

I stop, clinging to the chain-link fence, which rattles noisily. I turn to rest my back against the fence, and the diamonds press into my flesh.

"Where are you going?" Cora asks, catching up to me.

"I don't know."

"What's wrong?"

I shake my head. "I just...I'm so confused."

She rakes a hand through her long black hair. "Tell me."

"Jamie. He's persistent."

"That's a good thing, yes?"

I shake my head. "I can't go there with him, Cora. I just can't. If it didn't work, Aiden wouldn't ever recover. I can't do it to him."

"But?"

"I like him," I whisper. "A lot."

"Aiden is stronger than you're giving him credit for, Elyse." Cora twists her hair in her hands; coiling it into a knot at the back of her head and then letting it go to bounce around her shoulders.

"He's not," I say. "He's fragile. Daniel abandoned him, and Aiden spent years wondering what he did wrong to make Daniel leave him. He still wonders about that, I think. He probably always will. How can I bring Jamie into his life when there's no guarantee it would ever be anything but..." I shrug, lifting my palms up and then dropping them to slap against my thighs. "But what it was: good sex for one night."

Cora groans. "You don't know that's all it was."

"No, I don't!" I say, a little loudly. "That's the problem! I don't know! If there was some way I could have a guarantee it would work out, that it would last...? I'd jump in and not look back. But there are no guarantees in life, and I can't risk Aiden's well-being for my own benefit."

"So you're just going to be alone the rest of your life because you're afraid Aiden can't handle a breakup you don't even know would happen?"

"I mean, maybe when he's older? I don't know." I push away from the fence. "I want to go home. You can stay—I'll walk."

Cora snorts. "Don't be dumb. Stay here, let me grab my purse and we'll go."

"You're having a good time, Cora. You don't have to leave just because I'm lame." I offer her a tiny smile.

She whacks me on the arm. "Duh, yes I do. That's what best friends for life do."

I roll my eyes. "You're supposed to say I'm not lame."

"Well, you kind of are." She grins at me. "Love you!"

I shake my head. "You suck."

"And quite well, I'm told."

I groan. "You're so nasty."

"No, I just have the libido of a teenage boy and I'm a woman in her sexual prime." She pokes me in my chest. "And I know you, Elyse Thomas. Your libido is just as strong as mine—you're denying yourself. It's not healthy."

"Yeah, you may be right, but I have other consider-ations. I can't just do whatever I want. I wish I could, but I have a responsibility to Aiden, and that has to come first."

She sighs. "You have a point, which I grant you. But I think you're also hiding behind Aiden because you're scared of being hurt again. I think what happened between you and Daniel hurt you a lot deeper than you even realize yourself."

I huff. "Can we just go home?"

She grins mischievously, pulling me by the arm back toward Vinnie's. "One more drink first."

I pull back. "I'm not going back in there."

"He left, Elyse. I watched him go out the front door and walk toward Oak Junction." She hesitates. "He didn't look happy, either."

"Well, no. I keep rejecting him."

Cora breathes out slowly, pressing her palms together. "I've said my piece, and I shall say no more. You know how I feel, I know how you feel, and we don't need to keep having the same conversation."

I let her drag me back inside, and I let her buy me a drink even though I never even finished the glass of wine Jamie bought me—it's still sitting on the table at the booth, actually, next to Jamie's equally untouched drink. I sit at the bar with Cora and listen to her exchange entertainingly witty banter with Abe and Grady—she's the only one who can ever get them to crack a grin, and she does it through a salty, ear-curling variety of vulgar insults and bawdy jokes.

My heart's not here, though. Not in this bar, and not in the conversation.

It's on Jamie. On that hurt look in his eyes, the

resignation in his voice.

I wish I could soothe it. I wish I could take away the hurt, take away the resignation. I wish I could take back my rejections. I wish I could go back and be in bed with him again. Wake up with him, wrapped around him. Wrapped up in him.

But I can't.

I just can't.

10

I MANAGE A WEEK WITHOUT SIGNIFICANT CONTACT WITH Jamie. Which is a good thing.

Only…it sucks.

And I hate it.

I see him in the pickup and drop-off lines, and when I pick Aiden up from football, and that's it. We're well into the school year now, and Cora and I are buried in work, so we barely have time to see each other, let alone spend any time outside of work.

Jamie is everywhere, however, and that makes it hard. He's really thrown himself into the community, working hard to make his presence known and felt, to establish roots. He's helping coach the youth football league, and he's joined the poker group at Vinnie's on Tuesday nights, and he attends community forum meetings—this being the boring small town it is, there's a community forum about something pretty much every week—and he's informally joined the school board. He even goes to Al's gym with Matty and a few of the other younger guys in town.

I just can't get away from him. Which makes my life feel impossible, like some karmic, cosmic joke. Like, hey—here's this great guy, we had a great time, we're attracted to each other, my son adores him, he's everywhere all the time, but I just can't get past my hang-up. I watch Aiden get closer and closer to Jamie, especially on the football field, and it only reinforces my resolution to not get involved with him: Aiden loves him enough as it is. If he got the slightest hint that Jamie and I were dating...well...I honestly don't know how he'd react. Would he be upset? Confused? Excited? A little of everything, probably.

And if/when Jamie and I broke up, I just know for certain that Aiden wouldn't be okay.

So the status quo remains: I try to keep my distance, try to remain neutral, and Jamie gives me looks and smiles that threaten my resolve, and he showers Aiden with attention and praise and it melts my heart, and Aiden talks about Jamie nonstop and my heart cracks and throbs...and I remember what would happen to Aiden if it were to be anything but what it is now, and—

And the cycle starts all over again.

Fifth week of school, a Thursday, two in the afternoon, near the end of the school day. Lots of students, today—lots of questions, lots of athletic eligibility issues, lots of seniors trying to decide on college...a busy day.

There's a timid knock on my doorframe. I look up.

"Mrs. Thomas?" It's Jen.

"Hey, Jen, come on in." I minimize the window I'm working in, put the screen to sleep, and turn to face Jen as she perches on the edge of the seat opposite my desk. "What's up, honey? Is everything all right?"

Jen shrugs, but her lower lip is quivering, and her eyes fill with tears. "I…"

I hand her a Kleenex, and she dabs at her eyes. "Take your time."

She lets out a shaky breath, glances at the ceiling and blinks hard. "Okay, okay." She shakes her hands, as if that will somehow stop her from crying. "Um. So…I kind of asked Rob if he would want to ever go somewhere with me."

I raise my eyebrows. "Wow, Jen! That's awesome!"

She shakes her head. "No, it's not, because he said—"

I hold up my hands. "Let me stop you real quick, Jen. I'll let you finish, but you need to listen to me first. I'm proud of you for taking a step for yourself. For having the courage and confidence to do that. I know how hard and scary that must have been, and I think it's seriously inspiring that you did it at all. It doesn't matter what he said, because the very fact that you had the courage to ask him out is the coolest thing I've heard all year. So be proud of yourself, regardless of the outcome."

She nods, trying to smile and not quite succeeding. "Thanks. I didn't think of it that way."

"That's my job—to give you a different perspective."

"It was the scariest thing I've ever done. Rob is, like, the king of Clayton High School."

I nod. "I know, believe me."

"And so does he," Jen says.

I offer her a sympathetic smile. "So. What did Rob say to you?"

She sniffles, tilts her head backward again, and then takes a deep breath. "He told me he was flattered, but that he wouldn't want to lead me on, because I'm just not his type."

"Oh gosh, the not-my-type excuse," I say, rolling my eyes.

"Yeah. Not his type." She ducks her head.

"And what did you say to that?"

Jen sighs. "Um. I may have gotten a little…testy."

"Uh-oh."

"Yeah. I was like, I'm not your type? Why? Is it because I'm fat, or because I'm smart?"

I frown at her. "Jen—you are *not*—"

She holds up her hands. "I know, I know—you don't have to say it, Mrs. Thomas. I know I'm not fat. I've actually lost fifteen pounds since school started. I've been walking to and from school instead of driving and I stopped drinking soda."

"That's *awesome*, Jen! I'm so proud of you I just can't even!"

She rolls her eyes at me. "Don't try to sound cool, Mrs. T. It doesn't work for you."

I chuckle. "No? Just accept that I'm lame?"

"No! I just meant…you don't need to try to talk like a teenager or whatever to sound cool. You're cool enough without using outdated slang."

"Outdated?"

"The whole 'can't even' thing is pretty much over."

"Oh." I sigh. "See? Lame."

"You're *not* lame. You're your own kind of cool."

I narrow my eyes at her. "That sounds an awful lot like patronization."

"It's not! I swear! You're not just everyone's favorite guidance counselor, you're pretty much everyone's favorite staff member in the whole school." She shrugs. "It's a toss-up between you and Ms. Pearson, and you guys are BFF's."

"I didn't think anyone still said BFF," I say.

Jen laughs. "Hey, I'm not much cooler than you are."

"So I'm *not* cool! You admit it!"

"You're cool precisely because you're not and you don't try to be…it's hard to explain."

I nod. "I'll accept that." I roll my hand in a keep-going gesture. "So. What was Rob's response to your outburst?"

"He got mad. He was like, 'it has nothing to do with your weight, Jen,'" She mimics Rob's deep voice. "So I was like, why, and he was like—"

I interrupt her. "Jen, you're far too smart to be saying 'like' so much."

She groans. "I know, I know. But I'm upset, so… whatever." She waves a hand. "He told me he just didn't think of me like that. He said he likes me as a friend, but that's it. Then he said I hope you understand, and we can totally be friends…it was a douchey cop-out. It was straight from a made-for-TV teenage romance movie where the popular jock lets the smart but awkward heroine down gently, leading her to go through a supposedly drastic makeover that usually just involves straightening her hair, putting in contacts, and not dressing like a dork."

I laugh. "That's…surprisingly specific."

"That's how it felt."

"I'm sorry, Jen. That had to have hurt."

She shrugs. "Yeah, but, I mean…I expected it. I just didn't want to regret not saying anything to him, not even trying. You know? Like, I fully expected him to reject me, and he did, but at least now I have the satisfaction of knowing I tried."

Somehow, her words sting. I shove that away and focus on Jen.

"I'm proud of you, Jen. It took guts to do that, especially if you anticipated rejection from the very start." I smile at her. "I'm impressed…and inspired."

She smiles, a little tearfully. "I guess I just…I wanted to tell you."

"I'm glad you did." I squeeze her hand. "Are you going to be okay?"

She nods. "Oh yeah, I'll be fine. I'm used to

rejection. I'll just keep walking everywhere, and maybe even try to stop eating so much junk food." She grins. "Hey, maybe I'll even have my own makeover montage. Lose a few more pounds, figure out how to dress better…"

"You're perfect and beautiful exactly as you are, Jen," I tell her. "Change to make yourself better, to improve as a human, not because you don't think you're good enough."

"That sounds tricky."

I nod, sighing. "It sure is, and I'm speaking from experience."

Jen rises. "Okay, I have to go. I just needed to talk to someone about Rob."

"Thank you for telling me."

"Thank you for being awesome." She grins at me. "Even if you are a little lame."

I toss a paperclip at her. "Now you're just trolling me."

"Bye!" Jen calls, and is gone in a whirl of teenaged angst.

I sigh. I really do like that girl—she's smart, sweet, and beautiful, but I think sometimes she has trouble believing it about herself. The last one especially.

I plow through another thirty minutes of paperwork, and I'm anticipating the end of the day—there are always a few last-minute stragglers, someone with a question, a crisis that needs to be handled.

Sure enough, as I'm getting ready to lock up and

leave, Tina enters the main office and heads toward my office door. So, I sit back down, toss my purse on the floor near my feet so I can feel it vibrate if my phone happens to go off while we're talking.

"Hi, Tina," I say as she comes in and closes the door behind herself.

"Hi, Mrs. Thomas," Tina says, hesitantly taking a seat.

"So, how did things work out for you?"

She sighs. "I...um." She blinks hard, tears in her eyes already. "Sorry. Um."

I pass her the Kleenex box. "It's okay, honey. Take your time. Say what you need to say."

She nods, takes a moment to find some semblance of composure. "I took the test that Ms. Pearson helped me get, and I...it was positive. I was pregnant." She sighs. "Um. I *am* pregnant."

I blink hard. "Wow, okay. So...your sister couldn't or wouldn't help you get to a clinic?"

She shook her head. "No, it's not that. She took me. I was in the clinic, and the nurse was telling me all the facts and stuff, and I just...I couldn't."

I cover her hand with one of mine. "You couldn't go through with it?"

She shook her head. "No, I just...I couldn't. I had this image of a little baby, and I...I couldn't."

"So you're keeping it?"

She blinks hard again, but tears slide down anyway. "No, I'm going to carry the baby to term and place it for adoption."

"Oh my god, Tina…" I'm actually stunned speechless for a moment. "Why—how did you come to that decision?"

She shrugs. "I just couldn't go through with an abortion, but I also know there's literally no possibility I'd be able to take care of a baby on my own. I… um. I told my parents, and I told Jake. I told them I'm pregnant."

"Wow, so…how did they take it?"

"About as expected across the board. Jake offered money for an abortion, but said he's leaving for college no matter what. So, I can put him on the birth certificate if I keep it, but he wants nothing to do with me or the baby. I told him I was having it adopted, and he was like, whatever." She sniffled. "I guess I never realized what an asshole Jake is."

"A crisis will often show a person's true colors."

"Well his colors are poop brown, because he's an asshole."

I laugh. "Seems so. And I'm sorry he's being like that." I eye her. "And your parents?"

She laughs bitterly. "How do you think they took it?"

"Not well?"

"I'm currently living with Ms. Pearson. You can't tell anyone, though, because I guess she'd get in trouble or something."

I smile at her. "Ms. Pearson is my best friend, so I

already knew."

"Oh, right," she says. "Well, yeah, that's where I am."

"They disowned you?"

Tina nods. "Yep. Mom helped me pack a couple bags of clothes and stuff, and Dad gave me a check for five thousand dollars."

I shake my head. "My god. I don't understand that reaction at all, Tina. I'm so sorry." I breathe out slowly. "So…even after telling them you're having the baby adopted, they still won't help?"

She shrugs. "They said I'm a disgrace to the family, and that I'm on my own."

"So…what are you going to do? Do you know? What kind of help do you need?"

"Well, I called the admissions department at Brown—I had a partial academic scholarship, and I was planning on taking a bunch of loans—Mom and Dad were going to help a little, but it's not like they were going to pay the whole thing. So, Brown said they could hold my scholarship for one year. I'll have to take more student loans out because I won't have Mom and Dad helping." She sighs. "I mean, realistically, I should switch to a non-Ivy League school, because I'll end up with a bajillion dollars of debt, but if I'm going to be going at this alone, I may as well swing big, right?"

"And, with another year, we can even look into getting you some more grants or scholarships, try to defray the costs a little."

She nods. "Yeah, that's true."

"Schedule an appointment with me during school hours, and we'll spend some time working on that, okay?" I pat her hand. "So, adoption, huh?"

She nods. "Yeah. It just...it seems like the best option. I don't know if I'm going to do closed or open, because I've only done a little bit of research. I just...I have a feeling it's going to be the hardest thing I'll ever do. But there's just no way I could manage here in Clayton alone as a single mother. There's just no work, no way to support myself. And I'd...just selfishly, I know that would be the end of my dreams. It'd be a shitty life for me, and for the child. This way, the baby will go to a good, loving family who wants a baby and can take care of one, and I can still work for my own future."

"It will be hard, Tina."

She nods. "I know."

"Well, I think you're incredibly brave, Tina. And please know that I will help you with whatever I'm able to help with, you have only to ask. I'm here for you, no matter what. You're NOT doing this alone, okay?"

She nods, sniffling. "I'm just trying to prep myself to be the talk of Clayton."

"Oh, you're giving the Busybody Society fodder for gossip and speculation and rumor for years to come."

She rolls her eyes. "The last teen mom Clayton had was Emily Johnson—that was ten years ago and they're *still* talking about her."

I lean forward. "Actually, Gina Rhodes was the last teen mom in Clayton."

Tina's eyes go wide. "No way! I always wondered where she went."

"She and Cam Bowers eloped when they discovered she was pregnant. I helped them get their GEDs so they could drop out and elope to Philly. I think Cam is a diesel mechanic, and Gina is doing some sort of sales thing where she works from home. Nail stuff and lip stuff, maybe? I don't know. Their son is three, now."

She smiles. "Good for them. I always liked Gina. She was nice." Tina laughs. "She sort of took me under her wing during gym class my freshman year. I was terrified and had my period unexpectedly and didn't have any pads or tampons, and nobody was my friend. She gave me a pad and took a zero for the day so she could sit on the bleachers and talk to me."

"Sounds like Gina." My phone rings then—I can feel it buzzing. "I'm sorry, Tina, my phone's ringing and I need to make sure it's not Aiden."

"I have to go anyway," Tina says. "Ms. Pearson is taking me into Hanover to pick up a few things."

"Bye, honey."

"Bye!" she calls, and she's out the door.

I snatch my phone out of my purse—it's a number I don't recognize, but some urge or instinct has me answering. "Hello?"

"Elyse? This is Jamie."

"Jamie, hi." I close my eyes and breathe.

"Um, so…Aiden got hurt playing football today."

I bolt up out of my chair, immediately heading for the door. "What? Where is he? What happened?"

"I'm on the way to the county hospital with him right now. He's okay, he just…he twisted his ankle pretty badly."

"Is it broken?"

"No, I don't think so. Sprained, most likely."

"Can I talk to him?" I ask, jogging to my car.

"Yeah, of course. Here he is."

"Mama?" His voice is strained, as if he's trying desperately to be tough—but he's still an eight-year-old boy who wants his mom.

"Baby! Mr. Trent says you sprained your ankle?"

"I was catching a ball like that time I did when you saw it, and I landed wrong. It's all swoled up and bruised."

I'm already out of the parking lot—driving a little too fast, but my baby is hurt. "Does it hurt a lot?"

He sniffles. "Yeah, it hurts pretty bad. I cried a little when it first happened, but I'm trying to keep it together."

I can't help a laugh. "Oh, buddy. I'm gonna meet you at the hospital, okay?"

"Okay." He's quiet a moment. "Mom? Will I ever be able to play football again?"

I sniffle a laugh. "I'm sure you will, but probably not this season." I sigh. "And, you know, there *are* safer sports you can play."

"But I *love* football. And I'm really, really good at it."

"Aiden, honey—we'll see, okay? For right now, let's just focus on getting your ankle all better."

"It hurts, Mom."

I make a sympathetic sound. "I know, honey. Mr. Trent will get you to the hospital and they'll help make it better, okay?"

"Okay." He whimpers. "I'm gonna give the phone back to Coach Trent now."

"Okay. I'll see you soon."

The line rustles and I hear Jamie's voice. "We're pulling into the hospital now. I'm not his parent or guardian, so…"

"I'm almost there."

"Okay, see you in a minute."

I toss my phone into my purse, which is sitting on the passenger seat. The last couple miles to the hospital seem to stretch out into infinity, taking far longer to drive than I imagined. I'm so tempted to nail the pedal to the floor that I force myself to put the car on cruise control at just above the speed limit.

When I finally get there, I find the emergency room nearly full—mostly kids dealing with sports injuries, a farmer with a bloody towel wrapped around a hand, and several pregnant women in labor. Aiden is sitting sideways in a chair, his foot propped up on Jamie's knee, a Ziploc bag full of ice resting on a towel on his ankle; he has Jamie's phone in both hands, turned to landscape, and I hear the telltale sounds of *Ninjago*. Jamie is half watching the show with Aiden, and half keeping an eye out for me.

I hustle over to Aiden and drop to a knee beside him, wrapping him up in a hug. "Hi, Aiden, honey. How are you?"

He shrugs away from my hug. "Mom! It's the new season! It's not on Netflix yet. Coach Trent bought it on Amazon Prime so I could watch it."

I laugh. "Well, things can't be *that* bad if *Ninjago* is more important than hugs from your mother."

"Coach Trent calls it distraction therapy. If I'm watching my favorite show, I'm not thinking about how bad it hurts."

Jamie smiles down at me. "You've got quite a trooper here, Elyse. He's amazing."

I hate that I have butterflies at the way he smiles at me. "Thank you for getting him here." I glance at Aiden, enthralled in the show, wincing now and then as he shifts. "And for buying that episode for him."

He shrugs. "I bought the whole season, actually. I wasn't sure how long we'd be here, considering how full it is, so…no sense him running out of something to watch." He hands me a clipboard. "You need to fill this out. I would have, but I don't know most of the information, and you said you'd be here soon. I think it's probably going to be a bit of a wait."

There's an empty seat on the other side of Jamie, so I take it—I don't want to make Aiden move until I have to. "Yeah, well, seeing the guy with the bloody hand and the pregnant ladies, I'd say you're right."

He gestures at a guy who's probably a high school senior, sitting across the room with his foot propped up on his backpack, his head in his girlfriend's lap. "I think he broke his ankle or something, and there's another guy in here with a concussion so bad he legitimately thinks he's Captain America."

"Oh my."

I fill out the necessary paperwork, turn it into the clerk, and sit back down.

Jamie's eyes fix on mine. "I hate that this happened on my watch," he says.

I shrug. "Was there anything you could have done to prevent it?"

He shakes his head. "No, not really. It was just an accident, you know? He went to catch a long toss, went up, caught it, and just landed wrong." He reaches out and ruffles Aiden's hair. "Still made the catch, though."

I roll my eyes. "Wow, I'm *super* glad he still made the catch that injured him."

Jamie rolls his eyes back at me. "It's a guy thing. Right, Aiden?"

"Right, Coach." He holds out his fist, and they bump their knuckles together.

My heart thumps—is it melting or doing flips? I'm not sure. They bump knuckles, now?

Jamie and I lapse into casual chitchat—we talk about students, and college, and how Aiden's team won their first game last week handily, outscoring the other team 44-7; Aiden was the superstar of that game, scoring all but one of the touchdowns. I may or may not have taken several hundred photos.

It's the kind of conversation that never really ends, just morphs easily from one topic to another, and all the while Aiden watches *Ninjago*.

Finally, after an hour and a half wait, Aiden is called back. They bring a wheelchair for him; he pauses the show and hands the phone back to Jamie, but Jamie just shakes his head.

"Hold on to it, bud. You'll need it—hospital time sucks."

"What's hospital time?" Aiden asks, trying to act manly and unaffected.

"Well, time just seems to go slower in the hospital than anywhere else in the world, and nurses always tell you it'll just be a few minutes, which always turns out to be hours."

"Oh. So it always takes this long in the hospital?" Aiden asks.

Jamie chuckles. "Unfortunately, yeah."

"Then I hope I never have to come back."

"All right, you guys," the nurse says. "Time to head back." She smiles at the three of us. "Mom and Dad, are you both coming?"

"Oh, I'm not his dad," Jamie says, his expression carefully blank. "I'll wait out here."

"Jamie, you don't have to stay." Why is my heart

hammering so hard, and why is it so difficult to swallow?

He shrugs. "Gotta make sure my buddy is okay."

"Jamie—" I say, but choke on whatever I was going to say.

"Go. Be with your boy. I'll be out here when you're done."

There's a lot I'd like to say, but I don't say any of it. I accompany Aiden to the room they've assigned him, and the nurse goes through the process of checking him over, taking his vitals, the usual hospital procedures. Which is, as Jamie predicted, followed by another hour or more of waiting. Aiden is a trooper through the whole thing, staying patient and calm, despite the fact that he's obviously in a lot of pain. Finally, the doctor comes in and examines Aiden's ankle.

He orders an X-ray, just to be sure—which means another long wait for someone to take us to the radiology department, get the X-rays, and then another wait for the doctor to look at them and come in and talk to us about the results.

"Good news is, it's not broken," the doctor—a young man fresh out of med school—says. "Bad news is, it is a grade one sprain."

"What's a sprain?" Aiden asks.

"Well, basically, it means you wrenched the ligaments. You twisted them really hard, and now they're all messed up."

"What's a ligament?"

"Ahh…kind of like a tendon." He scratches his jaw-line. "Um, sort of like rubber bands that connect your bones around the joints, where your elbows, ankles, and wrists bend."

"Oh." Aiden frowns. "So, do I get a cast?"

The doctor chuckles. "Do you want one?"

Aiden shrugs, grinning. "I mean, kind of? My friend Bryan broke his leg riding his BMX bike last summer and he had a cast and everyone wrote stuff on it and drew on it and stuff, and it was cool. I don't want a broken ankle 'cause then I'd have to have the cast for like weeks or something."

"I suppose I can see how that might be a fun side benefit in a bad situation," the doctor says. "But no, you don't need a cast. Ice it to reduce swelling, wrap it in an ace bandage, and stay off it. So you will be on crutches for a few days to keep weight off of it, but you'll be limping around on your own soon."

"So when can I go back to playing football?"

The doctor bobbles his head side to side. "Well… it's not something I can sit here and say, oh on this day exactly…" He indicates Aiden's ankle. "It depends on how you heal. If you ice it, compress it, and stay off it, you could be able to start carefully using it in a week or so. Or, it could take longer, up to two weeks or so. No way to know for certain."

"So how will I know when I can use it again?"

"When it stops hurting to walk, basically. Use the crutches and keep compression on it for two or three days at least, and then try carefully limping around on it at home, just to test it. If it still hurts to move the ankle, stay off of it some more. Eventually, you'll be able to use it normally again and you'll be as good as new. You just have to be smart."

"Okay."

"So we can go now?" Aiden asks.

The doctor smiles. "Soon. A nurse will come by and discharge you and get you a pair of crutches."

"Okay."

The doctor claps Aiden on the shoulder. "All right, bud, I guess you're hoping you heal fast and can get back out on the field soon, huh?"

"I hope so. Thank you, Doctor."

The doctor shakes my hand. "You've got a good kid."

"Don't I know it," I say. "Thank you."

Sending a nurse by with crutches and our discharge papers sounds like it should be quick, but...hospital time, so it's not. It's another twenty-five minutes before the nurse even reappears with the crutches and fits them for Aiden, and then fifteen minutes after that before a different nurse comes by with the discharge papers.

By the time we're headed for the waiting room, we've been at the hospital for more than three hours. Aiden is exhausted and cranky and hungry, as well as frustrated with the crutches, which are trickier to use than he thought they'd be.

We find Jamie nodding off in the waiting room.

I gently shake his arm. "Jamie."

He blinks awake, his eyes flicking from me to Aiden and back, and then he sits upright. "Hey. What's the verdict?"

"It's a grade one sprain," Aiden says. "I can't play football for a week or two."

Jamie smiles, nods. "About what I expected. I sprained my ankle like that at least half a dozen times over the years I played football. Just ice it, wrap it, and take it easy. You'll be playing again before you know it."

"That's what the doctor said, too."

"He told me we should unwrap it and ice it again when we get home, and then wrap it before he goes to bed," I say. "But I have no idea how to wrap it."

"Well, luckily for you guys, I have plenty of experience," Jamie says. "I can show you."

"You've done so much already," I say.

"I did nothing. I drove him here and sat with him until you got here." He stands up. "How about this— you head home with Aiden, unwrap his ankle, get some ice on it, and I'll grab some carryout from José's and bring it over. One less thing to worry about after a long evening in the hospital."

"Are you sure? I'm guessing you have other things you could be doing."

Jamie shakes his head. "Not a thing."

"As long as you're sure. I don't want to put you through any more trouble."

"It's no trouble at all, I promise."

"Okay. Well, then, José's carryout sounds fantastic."

"Can we get nachos with extra sour cream?" Aiden says, the prospect of restaurant food exciting him—we rarely eat out during the school year, so getting José's is a treat for him.

"It's like you read my mind, buddy!" Jamie says. "That's EXACTLY what I was going to order."

Jamie and Aiden chatter excitedly about their favorite food all the way out to the parking lot; I trail behind them, watching Aiden hobble on his crutches, glancing up at Jamie now and then, visibly worshipful of everything Jamie says and does.

And...I totally get it.

Without realizing it, I had parked next to Jamie—he drives an older and well-loved gray F-150, rust eating at the edges of the wheel wells, the bed filled with sports equipment, orange cones, lengths of two-by-four, empty water bottles, an unopened case of water bottles, and an old mountain bike. The passenger seat is piled high with papers and folders and binders and a laptop bag sits half-open in the footwell, and an unzipped gym bag with shorts and T-shirts spilling out sits on the backseat bench, along with more empty water bottles and carryout containers—there's a hastily cleared spot in the backseat where Aiden had sat on the way here.

He indicates his truck with a rueful grin. "I sort of half live out of this thing. It's got a hundred and fifty thousand miles on it and it's still going, and I plan on driving it until it gives out completely. So…it's kind of a mess."

I laugh. "Yeah, well, take a look at the inside of my car and see if I'm in any position to judge."

Meaning, there are LEGOs everywhere, Aiden's books, my books, dishes from our house from the days when we end up having to eat on the fly, carryout containers, at least three empty Tervis coffee thermoses, a few ceramic coffee mugs, reusable water containers, and did I mention LEGOs?

Jamie takes a look, and then barks a laugh. "Yeah, so you do get it."

"We live on the run during the school year. I don't have to drive far, but I have to drive to a lot of different places."

An awkward silence settles over us, his eyes on mine, my lungs not quite expanding all the way, my heart jittering with uneasy and unfamiliar emotions.

Aiden tags my arm. "Mom? Can we go? These crutches are hurting my armpits."

I blink, and start. "Wha—? Oh. Yeah, sorry, Aiden. Let's go. You need to rest."

"And watch a movie?" he suggests hopefully.

I laugh. "You're gonna milk this injury for all its worth, aren't you?" I ruffle his hair.

"Yep," he admits. "It's called optimism, Mom."

I snort. "Opportunism is more like it."

I help Aiden into the car, stuff his crutches in beside

him at an angle, and then circle around to my side.

"Elyse?" I hear Jamie say; I glance at him over the roof of my car. "Can I have your address?"

"I suppose you'd need that to bring food over, huh?" I say, and then tell him my address.

"You want anything specific? Or should I just bring a variety of stuff?"

"Bring whatever you think sounds good, as long as it doesn't have any onions."

"No onions. Got it." He slides into his truck. "See you soon."

I drive us home, my thoughts on Jamie.

Jamie, in my house.

Jamie, eating at my table.

Jamie, with my son, taking care of him, looking out for him.

Jamie, with those warm brown eyes that seem to see everything I'm thinking and feeling.

11

I GET AIDEN SETTLED ON THE COUCH, THE ACE BANdage provided by the hospital unwrapped and carefully rewound into a neat coil, a towel and icepack on his ankle. I turn on *Teenage Mutant Ninja Turtles*, and place a boxed set of a cartoon series my parents got him for his birthday last year on the coffee table in front of him.

I call my parents and update them on what happened with Aiden, and have to spend several minutes calming my mother down, reassuring her that Aiden is fine, I'm fine, we're all fine.

And then...

I fly into Hurricane Elyse, cleaning the house at literal warp speed—dishes in the dishwasher, counters wiped off, mail and random papers stacked in a corner, Aiden's LEGOs swept into a pile and scooped into the handcrafted wooden chest Dad and Aiden made together—it's a four-by-two-foot replica of a LEGO brick, complete with hydraulic piston arms to keep it up and lower it down safely, a project Dad and Aiden did together over this past summer. Once I've got our rooms picked up, I run the vacuum over the place and sweep the kitchen and…

Aiden frowns at me as I vacuum the living room. "Mom, it's Coach Trent coming over, not, like, God."

"He's a guest, Aiden, and our house was in bad shape. I want to make a good impression."

"You never pick up for Aunt Cora."

"Because she's basically family," I tell him.

"Well, I think you've already made a pretty good impression on Coach Trent." Aiden goes back to watching his show once I'm done with the vacuum.

"Oh?" I ask, going for nonchalant and merely curious. "Why's that?"

"He talked about you a lot on the way to the hospital."

"What did he say?"

Aiden shrugs. "You know, just…stuff." He's a little too dismissive, and his eyes are locked a little too squarely on the TV.

"Aiden."

He sighs. "He just was like asking questions, and talking about how he likes talking to you."

"Asking questions? What kind of questions?"

"I dunno. Just…what kind of stuff you like to do, and…I don't know. Just questions."

I suppress a groan of irritation. Getting an eight-year-old boy to recount a conversation is like trying to herd cats in a dark room. "If he was asking questions, how do you know I've made a good impression?"

"I mean, if he wants to know stuff about you, doesn't that mean he kind of…likes you? Not *likes* you likes you, but… you know. Likes you."

I laugh. "Oh, Aiden." I ruffle his hair as I put the vacuum away. "You're cute."

"Why? What'd I say?"

"Nothing. You just are." I perch on the arm of the couch beside him. "How's your ankle?"

He shrugs. "Hurts, and the ice is getting drippy, and it's cold."

I see headlights approaching our house, and rush into the bathroom: I've gotten all sweaty in my cleaning frenzy, so I change my top and rinse my face with cold water and dab it dry…but then I've messed up my already messy makeup, so I have to reapply at least my lipstick because I can't face Jamie without lipstick at least, and I hear his truck door close and my hair is still a frizzy mess, so I yank it out of the updo I had it in and drag a brush through it…

I hear the doorbell, then.

"MOM! Coach Trent is here!" Aiden yells.

"I know, buddy, I heard."

I grab the ponytail holder, stick it in my teeth, and work my hair into a ponytail as I head for the front door. I'm still gathering my hair back as I open the door. Jamie is on my front porch, two big paper bags in his hands. His eyes lance into me, and then rake down. And I realize, in my haste to get out of my sweaty top,

I forgot my bra is leopard print, and the top I changed into is a thin white V-neck, so now my bra is visible. Great.

"Hi," I breathe.

He blinks, dragging his eyes back up to mine. "Hey." He lifts one of the paper bags. "I've got burritos and chimichangas, two chicken and two beef each." He lifts the other bag. "In here, we have two orders of nachos and, I quote, 'a vat of sour cream,' and a couple of side salads."

I boggle. "Have you ever had the nachos at José's?" I ask.

He shakes his head. "No, why?"

I laugh. "Because an order of nachos there is *huge*. It's what most people go there to get. When Cora, Aiden, and I go there we get one order to split."

Jamie makes a face. "I guess that's why the girl taking the order asked me three times if I was sure I wanted two orders."

"I think we've got enough food there to feed at least six people," I say, laughing.

"Well, then, I hope you guys are hungry."

"I am!" Aiden calls. "Mom—are you gonna let him in or what?"

I blush, embarrassed. "Yeah, good point, kiddo." I step aside so Jamie can sweep past me—his scent rifles through me—masculine and woodsy.

He sets the food on the dining room table, and shoots a glance at Aiden. "How you doing, Aiden?"

"Fine. The ice is making me all wet and cold, though." He's using his *acting tough for Coach Trent* voice; I can see his ankle is hurting him, but he's too proud to admit it.

I remove the ice pack and then the towel. "Oh, crap," I grouse. "It leaked all over the couch."

"I *told* you it was making me wet."

"I know, you're right, you did."

He shoots a look at Jamie. "You were rushing around cleaning like a crazy woman, so you forgot, huh?"

I frown at him as I mop up the wet spot with the towel. "Aiden! Rude!"

"What? Papa said that to Grandma once, when she was having her friends over."

I snort. "Well, a good rule to follow is don't repeat most of what Papa says, especially if he says it to Grandma."

Aiden tilts his head to one side, nodding. "Grandma does whack him after he says that kinda stuff. So maybe you're right."

"Grandma and Papa have also been married for forty-six years, so Grandma knows Papa is teasing. It's disrespectful for you to speak to me that way."

Jamie uses what I would call his "coach voice" on Aiden. "Hey, don't be disrespectful to your mother, kid. She does more for you than you'll ever know." For such an unfailingly kind man, that was a surprisingly firm order.

"Yes, Coach," Aiden says, abashed. "Sorry, Mama."

Jamie glances at me. "You didn't have to clean up for me."

I grin, blushing again. "You know how the inside of my car looks?" I indicate the house around us. "Sometimes, things around here get like that."

"Hey, no judgment here. I still haven't completely finished unpacking." He indicates the food. "Go crazy, you guys. I'll get out of your hair."

Aiden sits up fast, looking almost panicked. "What? No! You have to stay and eat with us."

Jamie glances at me. "Well, I don't know. You guys have had a long day, and—"

I want him to stay.

I don't dare ask him to stay, because I've already turned him down and rejected him so many times, and I can't risk ruining my objectivity.

Who am I kidding? There's no objectivity.

"Stay, Jamie." I grin, and try a teasing tone of voice. "Why do you think I bothered cleaning in the first place?"

He shrugs. "When I offered to get you guys food, I wasn't trying to invite myself over..." His eyes go to mine, fix there, intent and serious. "I haven't forgotten what you said the last time we talked."

I wince, and play with my ponytail. "Jamie, I— that hasn't changed. But this is a different kind of... situation."

He nods. "Understood."

Aiden is watching us carefully, trying to decipher the hidden meanings in our phrasing. "Is it time to eat yet?" he asks, a little too loudly.

He moves carefully to the edge of the couch and starts trying to get up off the couch; Jamie rushes over to help him. "Whoa, there, kiddo—you have to be careful. Why don't you just stay there and eat?"

Aiden lets Jamie help him hobble without his crutches over to the dining room table. "Because I'm a messy eater and I'm not allowed to eat on the couch. I always spill something."

I sigh as Aiden sits down. "I would have made an exception this once, Aiden."

He rolls his eyes at me as he lifts his foot to rest it on a chair—I prop a pillow under it. "Why didn't you say something before I got up?"

I laugh. "Because you'd have spilled something."

So, I find myself at my table with Aiden on my left and Jamie on my right. There's enough food for a dozen people, it turns out, because Jamie got the mega burritos, which are a pound each, and the three-piece order of chimichangas, on top of the two orders of nachos *and* two side salads. It's comical, actually, how much food he got.

He laughs as we unbox the food. "I haven't eaten there yet, so I guess I didn't realize how big the orders were."

I nod as he passes a chicken burrito to me, and a beef to Aiden. "His food is more expensive than

Vinnie's or Field's, but it's all fresh and homemade, and his orders are massive."

Jamie takes a few exploratory bites. "And delicious," he says, around a mouthful.

"If you're serious about food, you go to José's. It's really the only decent place to eat in Clayton. Vinnie's and Field's both just have basic bar food to fill up drunk bellies."

It's shockingly, achingly easy to sit and eat a meal with Jamie and Aiden. It's natural. The conversation between the three of us is constantly flowing, changing—Jamie always includes Aiden, speaks to him as if Aiden is an adult, asks his opinion and listens, doesn't dismiss him as just a kid, and he makes him laugh. His eyes flick to mine frequently, but he's careful to not let his gaze linger too long, and I do the same. It'd be too easy. Too intimate.

I catch his eyes flicking up to mine now and then, having stolen downward; it makes my belly flip, and my thighs clench. And my heart ache. I like the way he looks at me.

But I don't dare allow myself to want his gaze, his touch, his presence.

This is just two friends sharing a meal. Nothing else.

It takes us over an hour to eat, and when we've all eaten our fill, there are mind-boggling amounts of leftovers. I put some leftovers in Tupperware and stuff them in the fridge, and then make Jamie promise to take the rest to the teacher's lounge at school the next day.

By this time, Aiden is yawning, blinking hard, and rubbing his eyes.

I squeeze his shoulder. "You should get to bed, buddy. Been a heck of a day for you."

He nods, and I know he's tired when he doesn't wheedle and bargain for a few more minutes. "I'm so tired, Mama." He peers at me blearily. "Can I brush my teeth in the morning? I'm too tired."

I laugh gently. "Sure, Aiden. Just get into bed. You need the rest."

Jamie winks at him. "I have a feeling your principal would suggest you sleeping in tomorrow."

"What about my coach?" Aiden asks.

"Your coach would also suggest extra rest—it's the fastest way to let your body heal."

"Can I sleep in tomorrow? Go to school a little late?"

I roll my eyes. "We'll see. Just get to bed, and we'll see what ends up happening. But yes, I imagine I'll let you sleep for a while."

He rises from the table unsteadily, hobbling on his crutches, and then hops over to me, and gives me a big, long hug. "Love you, Mama." He then goes to Jamie and they bump fists. "Good night, Coach."

"Night, bud," Jamie says.

I help Aiden change and get into bed, tuck him in, and kiss him on the top of the head. "Love you, Aiden.

Sleep well."

Aiden just nods sleepily as I shut off the light and rearrange his crutches. Within seconds, he's snoring, and I head back out into the living room.

"Wow, that was fast," Jamie says.

I shake my head. "No kidding. Usually he tries to get me to let him stay up a few more minutes. One more episode, a few more minutes of playing with his LEGOs, or he just dawdles over brushing his teeth and getting ready for bed. And when he is finally in bed, he usually reads for a while."

"So he must be pretty bushed."

I nod. "It was a lot for him, today."

Silence between us.

Jamie is leaning against the dining room table, fiddling with the top of a chair. "I, um…"

"Thank you again, Jamie." I let my eyes rest on his.

He shrugs. "I'm his coach and his principal. Plus, I just like the kid."

I lift an eyebrow. "You're an educator and a principal. Don't you like all kids?"

"You know, I feel like, professionally, I'm obligated to say yes, but…" he laughs, "personally speaking, no, I don't. Some kids are just…little buttheads. Their parents haven't taught them manners, or how to just be decent people. My job is to treat them all the same, to show them the same considerations and make sure everyone receives the best education possible, but…I don't personally *like* every child."

I make a face. "Yeah, I get that. It's not that I have favorites, but..."

"Kids are people, and we click with some people and not others. Kids are no different, they're just not finished developing. I've had kids I taught come back a few years later and they've grown up a bit and changed, and I like them more than when I taught them. But others...just rub me the wrong way every time I see them." He glances at his feet, and then up at me, his gaze on my cleavage for a moment before finding my eyes. "I just...Aiden is one of those kids I just genuinely like. I truly enjoy hanging out with him, talking to him. He's a really, really great kid, and that reflects on you as his mom."

I blush. "He makes it easy. He really is great. Even as a baby, he wasn't difficult. He didn't cry much except for the usual stuff, you know—needing a diaper or a bottle—and as he's grown up he just...he's just cool." I roll my eyes. "I mean, I'm his mom, so I guess I have to think that. But I also just think he's a cool kid."

"He is."

I feel the tension between us like a physical presence, a tangling object.

I feel him wanting to look at me, yet constantly forcing his gaze away. I feel his presence, his gaze. I feel my own pull to him.

A visceral memory of him assaults me—his lips, his hands. Darkness around us, skin sliding on skin. Moonlight on his back as it ripples and undulates above me.

I turn away, chewing on my lower lip.

"What?" Jamie asks. "What it is?"

I swallow hard. I'm not sure what to say. "I just… you being here, being alone with you like this…"

He goes very, very still, his eyes locked on mine, his expression unreadable, carefully neutral. "Elyse, I know what you've said, and I haven't forgotten."

"I'm just so confused, Jamie." I say this not looking at him, but at his feet, his dirty, battered running shoes.

"Confused about what?"

"You, me…this."

Jamie nods. "I know what you mean. It's a weird, confusing situation." He sucks in a breath, holds it, and then lets it out slowly. Hesitating, thinking about what to say. "Elyse, I…I'm trying to just be your friend. I really am. But it's the hardest damn thing."

"You're so great with Aiden. He just absolutely worships you, and…" I swallow hard. "I can't deny I'm attracted to you, that I like you."

"But…" he prompts.

"But Aiden needs you as his principal and his coach. He has my dad, and Dad is a great male role model for him. But Aiden needs something else. Someone younger to teach him things Dad can't. To be there for him in a way Dad can't, just as his grandpa. And now Aiden has you as that, and I…I can't risk that. I can't risk taking that away from him for my own selfish reasons."

"Wouldn't it be adding something? If you and I

were…if we spent more time together, I'd be able to be around more, if you wanted that. If you allowed it. I'm not assuming anything, I just…" He sighs, hunting for the right words. "I feel like it could add to the roles I could play for him. And I won't mince words, Elyse: I'd like that."

"It's tempting, Jamie. You have no idea how tempting." I have to close my eyes, I can't look at him. "But what if…"

"You can't live your life scared of the what-ifs, Elyse," Jamie says.

I shake my head, pacing away from him. "How do you *not*? It's all I think about. What if I let something with you and me happen, and Aiden gets even more attached to you than he is, and then something happens between us? What then, for Aiden? And for myself, I ask the same question, you know? Like, what if I let something happen, and *I* get attached, and then something happens. It was hard enough with what happened with Daniel and me. You and me, we would be…different. Which is why it's so tempting." I find myself facing the window beside the front door, staring out into the darkness beyond, my arms wrapped around my middle. "But the what-ifs run through my head, and I think back to how devastated Aiden was when Daniel left, and how he thought it was his fault, and how hurt he was, how hurt he *still* is, and I just…I get so scared. And it freezes me up. And I just…*can't*."

I hear his steps, feel him standing behind me. Smell

him. Sense his heat. "Elyse…" His voice is so close, his breath is on my ear. He's nearly touching me; he's standing so close. "You're not asking the reverse what-ifs."

I twist in place, and I'm staring up at him. So close. So, so close. His hands lift, hover over my waist, then settle on my hips. "What…" My voice cracks, breaks, drops to a helpless whisper. "What do you mean?"

"What if, you say…what if something happened. And I say, yeah, what if something *did* happen? What if we were great together? What if we lasted? What if you got attached and Aiden got attached, and I got attached to the both of you—more so than I already am, I'll be the first to admit—and it was a wonderful, beautiful, lasting thing?"

I blink hard. He swims in front of me, blurred and hazy. "Jamie, dammit, not fair."

"Just asking the same question you are, from the opposite perspective."

"How do we know which it'll be?"

He shakes his head, shrugs. "You don't. We wouldn't. We'd be taking that risk."

"And that's the risk I'm afraid of."

"Wouldn't it be worth it, if it was the what-if I'm suggesting?" he says, closing the space between us, so our bodies are touching. "Wouldn't it be worth the risk, if things worked out?"

"Yeah," I breathe, "it would be." I inhale sharply. "But the cost if it doesn't…that's what stops me."

"There'd be a cost for me too, Elyse. I've been hurt and abandoned, too—I've felt like I wasn't enough."

"If there was some way of just...*knowing*..." I whisper.

"I wish there was, too." He shrugs. "But there's not, is there? So we just have to risk, and trust."

I stare up into his eyes. Swallow hard. Fight for breath.

"Dammit, Elyse." His whisper is hoarse, frustrated.

"What?"

He shakes his head, his jaw flexing. "I just..." He lets out a sharp huff.

"What, Jamie? Just say it."

"It's not something I need to *say*." His brown eyes aren't just warm, now—they're hot, eager, fiery, blazing and intense.

"Then what?"

His hands lift from my waist, and wrap around my face, thumbs brushing my cheekbones, palms on my jaw, fingers tracing the tender skin behind my ear and under the fall of my hair.

"I need to kiss you," he says, his voice strong and confident.

"Jamie..."

He shakes his head, brow furrowing. "I *have* to kiss you. I need to know."

"Need to know what?"

"If it's like I remember it being."

"How do you remember it?"

He brings his mouth to mine, whispers with his lips brushing mine. "Like...heaven. Like home."

I blink hard, and then my eyelids remain shut and all I feel is him, his body against mine, his palms on my cheeks and his fingers dancing along my skin and his lips against mine.

The kiss is everything that is sensual. I'm lost in it immediately. Instantly. I breathe him, taste him, feel him. Only him. Jamie is everything, everywhere. The cool panes of glass against my back, his hips hard against mine, my breasts crushed between us, I lift my face to his and open my lips and take his tongue, strong and hungry, against my teeth and lips and tongue.

His thumbs brush my cheekbones and my heartbeat is a hammering drum in my chest. I lean into him, gasp through the kiss and drown in it.

My skin heats, and tightens. Tingles. I throb. My hands tangle in his hair and catch at it, pulling him closer.

God, kissing Jamie Trent is incredible.

His words: Like heaven, like home.

My words: Sweet, delirious perfection.

My heart throbs, pounding with frantic intensity— my heart opens like a flower spreading her petals for the sunlight. I clutch at him and I whimper, and I kiss him for all I'm worth.

God, I could kiss him forever.

His palms slide down my cheeks, and our lips move, meld, shift, lock and seek and hunt and slide. His tongue dances along mine. His hands are at my waist, on my hips.

I'm not breathing, only kissing Jamie.

I'm trapped between Jamie and the window, and I want nothing in this moment but to remain here like this, trapped thus, his lips devouring mine.

His heartbeat slams in his chest, each beat going *thumpthump...thumpthump* against my ribcage, against my breasts.

He palms my backside, and I lift up, press against him, lean into his touch and cradle his head in my hands and lift up on my toes and I kiss him, and I kiss him, and I kiss him.

"Mom?" Aiden's voice is so confused.

12

JAMIE BACKS AWAY, DRAGGING HIS WRIST ACROSS HIS LIPS. He doesn't turn around to face Aiden; my eyes flick down to his fly, and I see why.

I'm on fire.

Heart palpitating, head throbbing, lips tingling, core tight and hot, thighs shaking. My emotions are everywhere.

"Aiden, I..." I push away from the window and look over to see Aiden standing in his doorway, sagging against the doorframe, staring bleary-eyed at me and Jamie.

"Mom, my foot really hurts," he says. "I can't sleep."

"The painkillers must have worn off," I say as I rush over to him. "Let's get you back in bed and you can take another one of the pills they gave us at the hospital." My mind is a blur, but I try to sound normal.

I get Aiden settled back into bed, his nightlight glowing softly, and he cuddles his well-worn bunny. "I'll be right back with a pill and some water."

By the time I arrive back in his room, Aiden is almost asleep. I shake him gently, give him his pill, and tuck him in with a kiss.

But before I leave his room Aiden says, "Is Coach Trent still here?"

"He's just leaving. Now close your eyes and have a good sleep. See you in the morning, honey."

I'm a hot mess as I shuffle slowly back into the living room. I look sheepishly at Jamie who is standing near the front door.

"Elyse, I—I'm sorry that happened. Is Aiden okay?"

"Yeah, he is sleeping again. He just needs his rest." Suddenly I feel awkward, and all the excitement and passion I was feeling ten minutes ago has been replaced with anxiety and guilt. "I think we should call it a night, Jamie. Thanks again for all your help…and for dinner."

"I got carried away and I'm sorry things ended this way. I know this is not what you wanted." And with that, he slips quietly out the front door.

I stand alone in the dimly lit living room, having gone from exhilaration to the depths of despair in the blink of an eye. I lock the front door, turn off the lights, check on Aiden one last time and get into bed myself.

It's a long time before I fall asleep.

My alarm goes off at six thirty the next morning and for a minute or two I don't remember anything—the injury, the hospital, Jamie, the take-out dinner, the kiss. I'm blissfully happy for about two seconds. And then it all comes back to me in a hot, hammering rush. Suddenly, anxiety threatens to overwhelm me. I lay in bed for a few minutes, strategizing, and then I check on Aiden, who is still in a deep sleep. I decide to let him sleep in, and head to the shower and get ready for the day.

I whip up some pancakes, and at about eight Aiden limps into the kitchen. He looks at the time and says, "Wow, I never thought you would let me sleep this late." After reporting that his ankle isn't too bad, he heads back to his bedroom to get dressed. Clearly he is relishing the idea of going to school on crutches.

By the time Aiden sits down to breakfast, I've called his school to let them know he'll be a bit late, and I've called my school secretary to tell her the same thing. My mom has called for an update and, satisfied that there is nothing she can do this minute, promises to make Aiden's favorite dinner tonight—chicken fingers and cucumber and strawberry salad.

Things almost feel normal for a school day—almost, but not quite.

As Aiden tucks into a big stack of pancakes he says, rather nonchalantly, "What were you and Coach Trent doing last night, Mom?"

I turn to face him. "We—um…"

"Were you kissing?"

I stare into his eyes—I can't fathom what he's

feeling in this moment, but I've never been the sort to lie to him. "Yes, Aiden, we were."

"I thought so."

I blink at the statement. "Um. We…it's…" I shake my head. "It's hard to explain, Aiden."

He's silent a moment. His brows furrow deeper. "Can I have some more pancakes?"

Oh, brother. What is he going to say next? I won't varnish the truth for him but, at the same time, he's a kid and I need to be careful about telling him too much…and not enough. I decide to let him lead this conversation.

"You know, I think we all had a nice time last night, even though you got injured. Coach Trent and I do like one another. How do you feel about that?"

"I dunno. Okay, I guess. He's pretty cool but…" Aiden stops to think.

I give him a minute before asking, "But what? Is there something bothering you?"

"You like Coach Trent?" he asks, his eyes sharp and inquisitive.

I sigh. "Yeah, I like him. He's a really great guy."

"Do you like him more than Dad?"

"Aiden, that's not…it's not like that. I can't say more than or less than…because it's just…*different*. I loved your dad."

"But not anymore."

"He's gone, Aiden. He left, and it's hard to love someone who…"

"Who goes away and doesn't come back?"

I swallow hard. "Yeah, exactly."

"Is…" Aiden's eyes fill. "Is Coach Trent going away too?"

See? This is *exactly* why I can't let anything happen with Jamie—one kiss, and Aiden is all mixed up.

"No, baby. He's your coach, and he's your principal. He's not going away."

I sigh, hang my head. "It's really complicated and hard to explain, Aiden."

"You say that when you just don't *want* to explain something to me. I could understand."

His eyes are on me, inquisitive, a little confused but thoughtful. "If you…if you and Coach Trent like each other, and you kiss each other, does that mean he'll be my stepdad?"

I try to follow his leaps of logic. "Ummm…no." I breathe deeply, let it out. "I mean I guess that's a possibility—meaning…it happens sometimes, to people. A couple gets divorced for whatever reason, and then they meet new people and get married. But I don't…I don't know if that's going to happen for Mr. Trent and me."

"Why not?"

"Would you want it to?" I counter.

He shrugs. "I don't know. I saw you guys kissing and I was confused and little scared. But Dad left a long time ago and he's never coming back. Right?"

I nod. "Right. But—"

"And sometimes I feel like maybe you're lonely. You have me and Grandma and Papa, and Aunt Cora, but sometimes I feel like you're lonely. I thought maybe it was because you miss Dad, but you don't, do you?"

I have to think hard about how to answer that. "I… god, Aiden, you're full of tricky questions this morning aren't you?"

"Let me say this. I loved your father. And the reasons we got divorced are adult stuff, things that I'm not ready to explain to you right now. But what I *can* say is that your father and I divorced for reasons between the two of us. It was *never* anything you did or didn't do. It wasn't your fault in any way whatsoever."

"Mom, I just meant—"

"Hold on—just listen, okay?" I touch his lips, and he goes quiet. "So…I miss us being a family. And I miss the way I used to love your father. But that changed, like it does sometimes, but yes, I do miss family life. Do I miss your father, the man, right now? No, not at all. He changed, and I guess we kind of stopped loving each other."

He frowns at that, his eyes seeking mine. "You stopped loving him too?"

"Once things were over, yeah. He left, Aiden. I had to let go. I had to move on. So yes, I stopped loving him."

"But you didn't *want* to stop loving him, right?"

I sigh. "God, Aiden. This is stuff I have trouble figuring out myself, so it's really hard to put in a way

you'll understand." I spend a moment considering. "I…
um…I mean, no. I wanted us to be a family."

He stares off into the distance for a moment, then
back at me. "Will you ever stop loving me?"

I grab him in a tight hug. "God, no, Aiden. *No!*
Never! Not in a hundred million years." I kiss his cheek,
his forehead, his cheekbone. "No matter what happens,
never *ever* think I could *ever* stop loving you."

He blinks hard. "You said you stopped loving Dad,
so I thought maybe—"

"No, baby. No. That's different. You're my son—
my baby. Even when you're all grown up, you'll be my
baby boy. And I'll love you as much then as I do now, if
not more! Nothing could ever happen to change that."

"What if Coach Trent got in love with you?"

My heart aches, stings. "Aiden, I…I don't know."

"Could you love him *and* me?"

I laugh. "Of course, Aiden!" I poke his belly. I tickle
him. "And do I love Grandma *and* Papa?"

He nods seriously. "Yes."

"And do I love Auntie Cora?"

"Yes." I see comprehension dawning. "Ohhhh."

"So, I can love lots of people all at the same time."
I tap his chest. "Your heart can hold love for as many
people as you want."

He's quiet, and I find myself hoping the barrage of
questions is over.

"Mom?"

Crap.

"Yes, Aiden?"

"Did you like kissing Coach Trent?"

"I'm not sure that's any of your business, Aiden."

"Did you?"

I sigh. "Yes, Aiden. I did."

"Do you want to kiss him again?"

"I...I don't know." Lies—yes, I do: I know without a doubt that I want to kiss Jamie again.

But I'm scared. So, so scared. The confusion in Aiden's eyes...the probing questions he's asking...I just don't think I can handle this.

He frowns when he senses my hesitation. "Mom, you know how you tell me you always know when I'm lying?"

"Uh-huh...?" I really don't like where this is going.

"Well, I can tell when you're lying too."

I laugh. "You're too smart for your own good, buster. Or mine." I sigh, tapping his nose. "Aiden, the thing with me and Mr. Trent is complicated, and I don't know all the answers. But I do know that I love you, that I'll always love you, and that no matter what happens, we'll always have each other."

Aiden gets up from the table to go brush his teeth, and I think I'm finally off the hook, but it seems he has something else to say. "Mom?"

I sigh. "Yes, Aiden?"

"You know, if you did want to kiss Coach Trent again, you could. Just maybe not where I could see, because it's a little weird and yucky. But...I don't want you to be lonely just because I saw something you don't think I should see."

"God, Aiden." I blink back tears. "It's not that. It's…" I don't have anything to finish that statement, though.

Aiden does, apparently. "It's complicated?"

I laugh. "Yeah. Exactly."

"Everything is complicated," he mutters, sounding irritated at adults in general.

God, that kid.

I love him so fiercely it hurts. I want to protect him, shelter him, let him stay innocent as long as he can. And I'm afraid I've already messed that up, that he understands things he shouldn't have to understand at eight years of age.

Will you ever stop loving me?

Do you want to kiss Coach Trent again?

I don't want you to be lonely…

Yeah…it's complicated, all right—too complicated. There are so many pitfalls and landmines.

But I can't make myself wish I'd never met Jamie, because the memories of our night together are some of the most amazing and sensual of my life, but… if this is how it's going to be, trying to navigate being Aiden's mom and figuring something out with Jamie…

Then I can't see how anything can happen with Jamie.

13

A LITTLE OVER A WEEK LATER, AND IT'S ALMOST BUSI-
ness as usual. Aiden is not attending football
practice regularly because of his ankle. My
mom and dad have been picking him up after school,
and sometimes the three of them go over to the field to
watch part of the practice. Aiden hasn't said anything
else about Jamie, so I've just left the topic alone.

The past week has been super busy and I've barely
had time to think, never mind think about Jamie Trent.
To be honest, being so busy has been a relief. I'm transferring handwritten notes from a counseling session
with a troubled sophomore into my computer. It's a
half-day today, and I'm hoping to be able to get out of
my office on time—Cora and I have tentative plans to
go to lunch.

I finish transferring my notes, wrap up some other
paperwork, and then I have one last appointment—a
follow-up with a junior who was on academic probation last year which prevented him from playing basketball for part of the season...and he was one of the star

point-scorers. He's doing better this year, partly due to tutoring sessions with Jen in the mornings. We go through his grades, check for missing assignments, discuss upcoming tests and projects, strategies for success, and which colleges he plans on applying to this year—he has a good chance of getting some decent scholarships for basketball, so keeping his GPA up and getting good scores on his entrance tests is vital.

Once that appointment is finished, the bell is about to ring and I still have few other items on my to-do list before I can leave. It's another twenty minutes before I'm done, and as I'm shutting down my computer and turning off my light, Cora sweeps into my office, purse on her shoulder, carrying a backpack by the handle, typing a text message one-handed.

"You ready, Elyse?" she says without looking up at me.

"Sure am."

"I've barely seen you this past week. We're still going to lunch, right?" She finishes her text, sends it with a *bloop*, puts her phone to sleep, and stuffs the device in her purse. "I'm hungry, so the answer had better be yes."

I laugh. "Yes, Cora, we're going to lunch."

"Where should we go?" Cora asks, her voice thick with sarcasm. "Wait, I know! José's!"

I laugh. "A wealth of choices, indeed." I lock my door and wave at the principal as I pass his office.

We almost always park next to each other, so we

walk out to our cars together and I follow her to José's. We get a booth near the front—it's busy this afternoon, as most of the staff at the high school had the same idea we did. We order iced tea and burritos, and fill up on chips and salsa while we wait for our food.

"So." Cora gestures at me with a chip. "What's the latest on you and Jamie?"

I sigh. "There is no latest."

"Bullllllllll-shiiiiiiit!" she says in a singsong. "There is too. I can tell just by looking at you."

"Cora."

"Elyse."

"I'm not gossiping with you."

She rolls her eyes. "It's not gossip if it's about *you*, ya dork."

"Fine. Then I just don't want to talk about it."

She leans forward, her eyes gleaming as she seizes my avoidance like a dog with a bone. "Something happened." She pounds the table with her fists in time with her words: "*Tell* me, *tell* me, *tell* me!"

"Cora!" I hiss. "Quit making a scene!"

She cackles as she dips another chip into the salsa. "It's like you don't even know me! I live to make a scene." She crunches on the chip, and then shoves the bowls away. "God, make me stop! I'm already full and we haven't even gotten our food yet!"

"I know, right?" I take one last chip and then resolve to not eat any more.

Cora's voice is quieter, but still intense. "Elyse

Thomas. You *have* to tell me what happened."

Our food arrives just then, and I'm spared having to answer for a few more minutes as we dig into our food. We eat in silence for a while, and then Cora finally gestures at me with her fork, speaking around a mouthful of food.

"All right. Talk."

I sigh, poking at the last few bites. "I told him nothing could happen, that I wasn't ready, that I needed to focus on Aiden, protect Aiden, all that."

"Right, I remember all that."

"So then Aiden sprained his ankle, right? And Jamie was just…amazing. He brought Aiden to the ER and sat with him until I got there, and he bought an entire season of *Ninjago* so Aiden would have something to watch to take his mind off the pain. He sat in the ER waiting room for *hours*. And then he got carryout for us all, and…" I shrug. "Aiden just absolutely *adores* Jamie. He worships him like he's a superhero or sports star or something. And Jamie genuinely likes Aiden. He listens to him, talks to him like an adult, plays with him."

"Well, to be fair, it's hard not to like Aiden." Cora grins. "It's also hard not to like Jamie."

"Exactly." I take a bite, thinking. "So…Jamie gets us food and was going to just drop it off and leave. But Aiden was like no way, of course. So Jamie ends up eating dinner with us at our house."

Cora blinks in surprise. "Wow. Really?"

I nod. "Really."

"He's the first single male you've had your house since Daniel left, right?"

I nod. "He's the only man, period, except Dad, who has ever even been in my house."

"So that's a big deal."

"Huge. What's weird though is that at the time, it didn't really feel that way."

Cora frowns. "It didn't?"

"I know, but it didn't. It felt...totally normal. Sitting, eating, and talking to Aiden and Jamie in my home was just the most easy, natural, normal, and comfortable thing."

Cora's eyes widen, almost comically. "That is pretty significant! Elyse, don't you realize what that means?"

I roll my eyes and shake my head, and hold my palms out to stop her. "Cora, no. Stop. Don't. Just... don't."

She ignores me. "It means you're meant for each other."

"No, we're not."

She gives me a look of utter disgust. "You're delusional! Does lying to yourself like that come easily, or do you have to work at it?"

"I'm not lying to myself," I say, poking at my food again, finding it hard to look at her.

"Okay, well I can't win against stupid, so I'm not going to try," Cora says. "What happened next?"

I sigh again. "Aiden went to bed. Which left Jamie and I alone."

"Uh-oh."

"Yeah." I close my eyes, duck my head. Drop my voice to a whisper. "We talked. About…us. He really wants to see if we could…if there could be something between us—"

"Well nothing could be more obvious, but continue."

I ignore her statement, opening my eyes to meet her gaze again. "And I explained why I'm so afraid."

"Aiden. You're worried you and Jamie would break up and he'd be upset."

"Not upset, Cora—*devastated*. Daniel leaving really messed him up. He thought it was his fault." I suck in a shuddery breath, letting it out slowly.

Cora leans forward, her eyes piercing mine. "You didn't…sleep together again, did you?"

"No." I look away again, down at the table. "But he did kiss me."

"Oh." She blinks, hesitates. "Wow. So…how was it?"

"Even better than I remember it being."

"Which, considering you used the word 'magical' when you told me about it the first time, is really saying something."

It's hard to breathe, hard to swallow past the lump in my throat and the butterflies in my belly. "Magical is the only word that applies." I hesitate, chewing on my lip. "Other than…home. Or heaven. Or…perfect."

"And you still deny that you guys are made for each other?"

I squeeze my eyes closed, refusing to cry in the middle of José's. "Stop, Cora. *Please*…just stop."

She grabs my hand. "This is a really big deal for you, isn't it?"

"You don't understand."

"I'm trying to."

"We *can't* be perfect for each other. Because I can't have him."

"I think you could."

"No! I can't! Aiden can't handle it, and I can't handle the risk—I couldn't handle it if it didn't work out and Aiden had to go through all that again."

"Elyse—"

I cut her off, my eyes on hers. "Aiden saw us kissing, Cora."

She winces at that. "Oh. Oh dear. How'd he react?"

"He was confused, and he had so many questions."

"What kind of questions?"

"Oh, you know, nothing big. Just…did you love Dad? Did you fall out of love with him? Could you fall out of love with me? If Jamie and I got together, would Jamie be his stepdad? Stuff like that."

"Jeez." She swirls her iced tea with her straw. "That must have been tough."

"How do you explain to a confused eight-year-old why Daniel and I are divorced?"

"Saying Daniel was a loser and an asshole probably wouldn't work, huh?"

"No, Cora, it wouldn't," I say. "He wasn't always a

loser and an asshole. The miscarriage really messed us both up, and we didn't handle it well at all, either of us."

"He should have been there for you. He should have understood, and been supportive and loving and strong for you."

"It was hard for him, too, Cora."

"Why the *hell* are you defending *him*? He basically abandoned you to deal with the emotional trauma alone. You should have seen a therapist, and he should have insisted." Her eyes water. "I should have insisted."

"Cora, stop. Don't you try to take that on yourself."

"Then don't you either."

I shake my hands, blowing out a shaky breath. "No more of that. The point is, Aiden saw Jamie and I kissing, and he was confused, and he had a lot of very difficult questions."

"So he wasn't cool with it."

I can't lie to her. "Well...the last thing he said was that if I wanted to kiss Coach Trent again I could, but maybe just do it where he can't see because it's weird and yucky."

"That's kinda funny, but it's not an outright rejection of the idea."

"He said he thought I was lonely, and he didn't want me to be lonely just because he saw us kissing and I didn't want him to."

Cora claps her hands over her heart. "Oh, my god, that boy. He's the actual sweetest human being on the planet."

"He sure is."

"So it sounds like he'd be okay with you and Jamie being together."

I shake my head. "You didn't see the look in his eyes when he first saw us…" I glance at the ceiling, remembering.

Cora winces again. "Ooh, ouch. That's a tough one."

"Yeah, exactly."

"I tried to be honest with him without overwhelming him or giving him more information than he could handle. I don't know. I'm just so worried I messed that up, that I should have had better answers." I roll a shoulder. "I lay awake at night thinking about all the different answers I could have given him."

"You did the best you could, Elyse."

"I know, but what if my best wasn't good enough?" I tap the table with a finger. "And all this is exactly why I can't date Jamie. This all resulted from Aiden seeing us kiss *one time*."

Cora nods. "Yeah, I guess I get that."

"You guess?"

"But kids are adaptable. If parents handle these difficult situations with honesty and openness, then I think the kids can manage change. It was new and confusing. He loves you, and he wants you to be happy."

"That is just it. My happiness isn't his job—*his* happiness is *my* job."

"Elyse—"

"I need to pee." I can't handle this conversation any longer. "Just...give me a minute, okay?"

I leave our booth and head for the bathrooms at the back. I keep my head down and focus on getting to the bathroom and into a stall—I allow myself a few quick, sobbing breaths, and then shut it down. This is why I can't be with Jamie. I can't fall apart in public like this, and I can't let Aiden see me like this...being his mom and taking care of him requires everything I've got, and I can't afford any distractions.

Even kind, handsome, thoughtful, caring, and amazing distractions like Jamie Trent.

I spend a few moments in the bathroom stall, breathing, getting myself under control. And then I do my business and leave the stall, wash my hands, and exit the bathroom. This time, on the way back to our booth, I see something I wish I hadn't.

Because there, in a booth in the back of the restaurant, huddled close and talking in low tones, are Jamie...and Debra Eisenhart.

Debra is a fifth-grade teacher, another Clayton transplant. She came to Clayton from California, with California good looks: tall, perfect wavy blond hair and pretty blue eyes, and a trim, tight body with curves in all the right places.

Sweet, funny, a great teacher.

Single. Young.

Looking for a husband.

She laughs at something Jamie says, leaning close

and touching his arm.

My heels clack loudly against the tile floor. Jamie's eyes go up, find mine, and he blanches.

My heartbeat trips, and then my stomach squeezes and my throat closes.

I shake my head, stand up straight, and let out a short, sharp breath. Lift my chin, and head for my booth.

I slide in opposite Cora, and I focus on breathing slowly and evenly.

Cora sees how upset I am and leans forward. "What? What happened? You look pissed, Elyse."

"Jamie is here." I close my eyes, but all I see is Debra laughing, leaning close to Jamie and touching his arm. "With Debra Eisenhart."

"Ohh boy." Cora rubs the bridge of her nose. "Like, *with* her, with her?"

"Seemed that way to me, judging based on body language."

"Elyse, there could be—"

"I know—there could be all sorts of explanations," I say, "but in the end, it doesn't matter, does it? I've rejected him three or four times now. I snuck out on him after we slept together, and I told him we couldn't be together next time we saw each other, and I've told him so again several times since. And then we kissed last week and I kicked him out of my house, telling him it just wouldn't work."

I close my eyes, breathe in slowly, hold it for a few

seconds, and let it out just as slowly.

"He's…" I shake my head, open my eyes. "He's allowed to go to lunch with another woman. I rejected him, and he's moving on. I have no right to be jealous or upset."

"It *is* a bit soon."

I shake my head again. "No, it's not. We slept together *one* time, weeks ago. We kissed once, a week ago. More than a week, actually. So…it's fine. I'm fine." I fake a smile. "See? Totally cool."

Cora rolls her eyes, snorting. "Yeah, okay. You're a crappy liar, Elyse, and you're an even worse actress."

"I am not."

Cora laughs. "You are. You're terrible. You couldn't lie your way out of a paper bag. It's a good thing, but it means you just shouldn't ever try."

I laugh, sniffling. "Aiden said something similar. He asked if I wanted to kiss Jamie again, and I said I didn't know. Which was a lie, because I did know I wanted to kiss him again. And he asked if I knew how I told him I always knew when he was lying, and I was like yeah, and he said, well, Mom, I know when you're lying too."

Cora barks a laugh. "Oh—my—*god*, he did *not* say that."

"He did."

"What a little punk!" She shakes her head in disbelief. "So, what'd you say?"

"That it was complicated."

"Cop-out."

I shoot her a look. "Cora—do you really expect me to tell my eight-year-old son that I wish I could kiss Jamie and never stop? Oh… hi Jamie." He's standing at our table, arriving just as I was making that admission to Cora.

"Hi."

I wish I could truthfully say I feel nothing, that I'm cold, that I'm unaffected, but it wouldn't be true. I'm none of that.

"Having a nice date?" I hear the snarky vitriol in my own voice.

He rubs the back of his neck, wincing. "It's not like that, Elyse. I swear. It's a working lunch. She asked for help adding some things to her curriculum, and we—"

I stand up, push past him. "Save it, Jamie. You're allowed to do whatever you want."

"Elyse, wait."

"Can you get the check today, Cora? I'll get you back next time."

She eyes me warily. "Yeah, I've got it." She grabs my hand to stop me. "But Elyse, I think you should hear him out."

"No point. Nothing has changed for me. I can't get into anything with anyone, and I've made that clear. So…Jamie is allowed to have lunch with whomever he wants, and he owes me zero explanations." I try to put some casualness into my voice as I look at him, meeting his eyes. "Honestly, I hope it is a date, for your sake. You deserve good things, Jamie. I want you to be happy, and I'm sorry I can't be a part of it."

He reaches for me. "Elyse, now hold on a second—"

I shake my head and back out of his reach. "I have to go."

I hustle out to my car, ignoring both Cora's and Jamie's voices as they call after me.

I drive away, pretending even to myself that I'm not crying, that I'm not hurt, that I'm not being unreasonable, that I'm not jumping to conclusions.

But, like Cora said—I'm a crappy liar, even to myself.

14

I HAVE TO PUT THE SCENE AT JOSÉ'S OUT OF MY HEAD. I can't let it shake me, can't let it consume me.

But…it does.

I pick up Aiden from school, and I force myself to be as normal and cheerful as possible. I ask Aiden about his day, how his ankle is feeling—fine, and fine, respectively.

"Mom?" he says, as we're heading to our doctor's office to get the all clear from his doctor to go back to football.

"Yeah?"

"What's wrong?"

I smile at him in the rearview mirror. "Nothing, baby."

He narrows his eyes. "We talked about this, Mom. I know when you're lying."

I sigh. "Nothing you need to concern yourself with, Aiden, and that's the truth."

He nods, accepting my answer. "So, do you think Dr. Pritchard will let me play now? We have a game coming up and I want to be in it."

"I think probably, yes," I tell him, truthfully. "You've been off the crutches for a few days, and you're moving without much pain, right?"

"It doesn't hurt at all."

"Well, we will just have to see what the doctor says, but I'm hopeful, for your sake." I meet his eyes in the mirror again. "Even though I'm worried you're going to get hurt again."

"Coach Trent says I'll get hurt a lot in football, but that getting hurt is different than getting injured."

I frown. "I see. And what's the difference?"

"Coach said hurt is something you can play through, injured is something that takes you out of the game."

"And how do you know the difference?"

He shrugs. "I dunno. I guess if you can still play, you're just hurt. Like, I *injured* my ankle because I couldn't walk it off."

I nod. "I see. Well, I don't want you getting hurt *or* injured. So be careful, okay?"

He rolls his eyes at me. "Mom, you can't be *careful* in football. You have to give it everything, every play. If you hold back, or try not to get hurt, that's when you get hurt."

"Let me guess, Coach Trent said that?"

He grins. "Nope, actually that was Coach Barnhart. He told us that the first day we started tackling." His grin fades. "Is it weird for you when I talk about Coach

Trent because you guys kissed?"

Gahhhh. "Nope!" I say, lying through my teeth.

"Mom," he drawls.

"You know what, buster? You need to let your mom get away with a lie now and then. Sometimes it's for your own good."

He frowns at me. "But, Mama, you told me a million times that lying is never okay, and that it never solves anything. Even if it saves someone's feelings right then, in the end it's always better to just tell the truth."

I groan. "I get the one kid who remembers everything I tell him, and he uses it against me." I meet his eyes in the mirror. "Okay—the truth is, Aiden, yes, it's a little weird for me sometimes."

"Oh. So should I stop talking about Coach Trent, then?"

I sigh. "No, Aiden. He's your coach, and your principal, and your friend. This is my issue, not yours. So you talk about him all you want, okay?" I opt for more honesty. "And, really, this is why we won't kiss again."

He frowns. "Because of me?"

"No…because it complicates things that don't need to be complicated."

He frowns more deeply, as if he doesn't quite buy my explanation. "But what about you being lonely?"

I smile at him, touched by his love and concern. "Baby, I'm *fine*, I promise. I have you, and I have Grandma and Papa, and I have Auntie Cora. I'm fine—I'm *not* lonely."

He doesn't answer, but he still seems skeptical. He stares out the window as we finish the drive to Dr. Pritchard's office. He unbuckles after I park, and we head in. We're in the waiting room, and he's watching the fish in the fish tank in the waiting room—it's designed to look like the tank from *Finding Nemo*, including the same sea creatures.

"Mom?" he says, still watching the fish.

His tone of voice tells me he's got another question.

"Yes, Aiden?" I say, flipping through an old *Good Housekeeping* magazine.

"Are you sure you're not lying about why you won't let Coach Trent kiss you again? Because I think it's about me, and you just don't want me to feel bad."

"Aiden..." I trail off, though, because I need to think about my answer.

How do I get out of this one? He's right, in a way.

I put my magazine down and look at him. "Aiden, honey. I'm your mom. It's my job to do what's best for you. I have to protect you, and try to make sure you're happy and healthy. And I'm going to do that, no matter what."

"Even if it means you don't get to do something you really want to?"

"Even then, Aiden. Being your mom is the most important thing I could ever do, and I won't let *anything* get in the way of being the best mom I can be."

"Not even Coach Trent?"

I laugh, softly. "Not even Coach Trent."

He frowns. "So…it *is* me."

"Sort of, yes," I say, knowing he will appreciate the honesty. "But it's something I'm *choosing*, Aiden. You being happy is most important, and I can be happy without Coach Trent."

"But you like him?"

I sigh. "I think it's time for me to say we're not talking about this anymore, okay?"

"Okay." He looks at me thoughtfully. "But, Mama—"

I quirk an eyebrow. "Aiden." I make my voice firm, indicating that there will be no more discussion on this.

He sighs in irritation. "Fine." He glances at me. "One last question."

"You can ask, but I reserve the right to not answer."

"What does Aunt Cora say?"

I groan, but it's also a laugh. "Aunt Cora wants what's best for you, too."

"But she *also* wants what's best for *you*, right? So whose side is she on?"

"There are no sides, Aiden. There's me saying Mr. Trent and I are just friends and that's all we will ever be, and that's it. That's the only side there is."

"But what if—" he starts.

"Aiden, *enough*." I keep my voice low but firm. "No more, please."

His eyes meet mine, and he sees something more convincing in them than my words. "Okay, Mama. No more questions. I'm sorry. I just...what if you could be happy in a different way, *with* Coach Trent, and not just as friends?"

"Aiden, you're only eight years old. You shouldn't be worrying about this kind of thing at your age."

"Papa says I've got an old soul."

"Papa is right," I say, relieved to be on safer ground. "But you're still an eight-year-old boy. So you just worry about football and LEGOs, and remember that girls are gross, and put the seat up before you pee and down when you're done."

"Papa says if he can put it up, Grandma can put it down, because that's only fair."

I laugh. "Well, again, Grandma and Papa have been married longer than you and I have been alive combined, so they can make those kinds of compromises. But I think if you asked Grandma, she'd tell you a different story."

Aiden laughs. "Grandma says half of what Papa says is bunk, the other half is nonsense, and the *other* half is the rambling of a crazy old man." He frowns. "But that's too many halves, and Grandma just said that's because Papa is so full of himself he has a whole 'nother half, and I said maybe that's because he has a big belly, and Grandma just shushed me and said Papa is sensitive about his belly."

"What else does Papa say?" I ask, eager to distract Aiden.

"Well...? He says a lot of stuff. He talks pretty

much all the time. I guess I just only remember the funny stuff, or the really smart stuff."

"Papa *is* pretty funny," I say. "And he likes to tease, so remember that he's not always being serious."

"I know when he's teasing," Aiden says. "He gets this look in his eye, which I think is a twinkle. I didn't think eyes could actually twinkle, because stars twinkling is just something about the light taking a long time to reach us or something, but Papa's eyes *actually* twinkle when he's teasing."

I laugh. "His eyes *totally* twinkle! Especially when he thinks he's being crafty and thinks we don't know he's teasing."

"That's when it's easiest to tell he's teasing!"

"I know!" I say. "I figured that out when I was…oh, about your age."

"Aiden Thomas?" The nurse appears then, calling Aiden.

After a thorough examination of his ankle, Aiden gets the all clear to go back to sports, but with a caution to take it easy with the first few practices, but that he should be good to go for the game later this week.

As we leave the doctor's office, Aiden wants to go to practice right then, since there's still a good twenty minutes left.

So, being the sucker I am, we head to the field. His team is practicing a play, and while there's not time for him to dress out in his gear and practice with them, at least he can watch from the side and chat with Coaches

Barnhart and Trent.

Unfortunately, it also means I can't escape Jamie, who walks Aiden over to me after the rest of the team ends the practice and heads for the equipment shed.

"So, our guy got the all clear to play?" Jamie asks.

I nod, offering him a tight smile. "Yeah. He needs to be a little cautious at first, but he should be fine."

"Great—we'll need him at the game this week. Our opponent is gonna be tough—they've got a really good running game and a solid defense."

"Well, here he is, ready to go."

Aiden is talking to his teammates, tossing a ball around. Jamie glances at him, and then back to me—making sure Aiden is out of earshot.

"Elyse, listen, what you saw this afternoon at José's—"

"Jamie, stop, please." I hold up both hands. "I meant what I said."

"It wasn't a date. I'm not interested in Debra like that. For one thing, I'm the principal where she's a teacher. Intra-district dating is fine with me, but intra-school is not. I wouldn't ever date anyone I directly work with, and especially not an employee of my own." His gaze is open and truthful. "So, please, just—"

I close my eyes and back away. "Jamie, *stop*. Honestly, I just…it's not worth wasting any more time talking about this."

He winces. "So that's it?"

"That was it before this afternoon, Jamie. I can't…I

can't—God, I've already explained this half a dozen times. We can be friends, but that's it."

He sighs, and his eyes reflect conflict. "I know what you've said, Elyse. And I do respect that. I promise I will try, because I truly do respect and honor where you're coming from." He doesn't look away, and his eyes are intense, direct. "But just in the name of honesty, I'm not sure I can totally forget what we're like together. I'm not sure I can forget how it felt to kiss you...how great it feels to be around you—I can't just turn off how I feel about you."

"That's going to seriously complicate things, Jamie."

He nods, shrugging. "I know. I wish I *could* shut it down, because that'd honestly be a lot easier—it'd sure as hell hurt less. But I can't. What I can do is promise to try my best."

"Your best, huh?"

"Yeah. And, for the record, I don't believe you really want it to be like this, but you're scared. I think we could be great together. I think it would be something amazing, something truly lasting. I have to say that—you have to know that."

I swallow hard. "God...Jamie. I hate you, sometimes."

"I'm sorry, I'm just—"

"AIDEN!" I call, cutting him off. "We have to go!"

"Elyse—"

I shake my head. "No more, Jamie. Please, I can't."

He sighs, holding his hands up palms out. "Okay, okay. I won't say I'm sorry, because I'm not—you have to know my truth. But I will respect your stated desires, even if I disagree with them and think you're making a mistake for both of us." He clamps his jaws together a moment, and then speaks again. "I *want* you, Elyse Thomas. I want to be *with* you. I'm not going to just... stop, or forget. I'll keep my peace, and keep my distance after this out of respect, but I'm going to hold out hope that you'll change your mind someday. And if you do, I'll be there."

"You should move on, Jamie," I whisper.

He shakes his head. "Not a chance. I know a good and perfect thing when I see it and feel it, and I'm not the type to just let it go without a fight."

Aiden jogs over, then, and I take his hand and walk away.

"Mom?" he asks, as he gets in. "What's wrong?"

I shake my head. "Nothing," I whisper.

"Mom—"

I hold up my hand to stop him. "Don't, *please*, okay?"

He sighs. "Okay, Mama."

And this time, he listens.

15

THE AUTUMN DAYS BOTH CRAWL BY AND FLY PAST. Days can last for hours, and the weeks can vanish at lightning speed. I create a new habit in my day: I drop Aiden off at school fifteen minutes early. It means getting up earlier and getting us moving faster, but Aiden likes to help his teacher get ready for the day, and he helps Jamie get the kindergarteners off the bus and into their rooms—the opportunity to volunteer and help out makes Aiden feel important, and the extra time lets me get into my officer sooner which, in turn, means I can leave closer to the final bell.

And, by dropping Aiden off fifteen minutes early, I avoid having to see Jamie, as he doesn't come outside for drop-off until eight fifteen.

I tell myself it's for the extra office time, and so Aiden can volunteer, but really, it's about avoiding Jamie; I'm not a morning person and never have been, so getting out the door fifteen minutes early when mornings are already hard enough is a pretty major thing for me.

It's worth it, though.

I barely see him, now. Maybe the odd wave from a distance in the morning, and another wave after football in the afternoon; I watch practice from my car, now, and I don't even pretend this isn't about avoiding Jamie.

Aiden doesn't ask about Jamie anymore, and I notice there's a discernible reduction in the number of times Aiden quotes Coach Trent; I feel guilty about that because, on a platonic level, Jamie is a wonderful influence on Aiden.

But I try not to think about that too closely either, because letting myself think about what a wonderful influence Jamie is on Aiden only leads me down a what-if spiral:

What if it *could* work…

What if Cora is right?

What if Jamie is right?

"I know a good and perfect thing when I see it and feel it, and I'm not the type to just let it go without a fight."

What if I really am just using Aiden as an excuse, and I really am denying myself a good thing out of fear of getting hurt? And not just hurt *again*, but hurt even *worse* because, deep down, I know Jamie has the capacity to hurt me worse than Daniel ever could.

What if I'm denying myself the possibility of finding real, true, lasting, beautiful love?

What if I'm denying Aiden the chance to have an amazing father figure?

These thoughts flicker through me, and I shy away from them—recoil from them, more like. I shy away, I recoil, I deny, and I hide from them. They say the truth hurts; maybe I'm just pathologically unable to allow myself to think too deeply about it, to let myself really pick apart my truth from my fears.

I have to protect Aiden.

I'm fragile. I can admit that much—the miscarriage and my subsequent brutal depression, Daniel's withdrawal, our eventual divorce…it all damaged me much more deeply than I think I ever understood, until Jamie waltzed into my life and made it all painfully apparent.

It's all too much.

And this, friends, is why I don't allow myself to even approach the edge of the what-if spiral; once I start spiraling, it's nearly impossible to pull myself out of it.

I close my eyes and breathe, focusing on my breath, hold it, then breathe out. Focus on Aiden. Focus on Mom and Dad. Focus on Cora.

My students.

Push away thoughts of Jamie, his warm brown eyes, his ready, charming, boyish grin, his lean, muscular body. Push away thoughts of his gentle, strong hands sliding across my skin…

"Dammit," I whisper to myself.

That's *not* pushing the thoughts away, that's daydreaming.

Ugh. Why is it so hard to stop thinking about him?

I've had Jamie on the brain all day, and it's made work especially difficult.

Flu season is approaching and feeling queasy all day hasn't helped. I know of at least six students who are currently out sick with stomach bugs, and the school secretary went home early. Schools are great big petri dishes; I'm denying that I have anything, or that I'm coming down with anything. I've just avoided eating, and have been sipping on peppermint tea all day. Once I feel better, I'll make sure I get the flu shot.

Feelings will fade, desires will eventually go away. Need will subside. I'll eventually stop missing him.

Right?

A gentle, timid knock on my door jolts me back to the present. "Mrs. Thomas?" It's Tina.

Her belly is rounding a little, and I've heard rumors about her pregnancy rumbling through the school.

"Hi, Tina. Come on in. What's up?"

She comes in, closes the door, and settles in a chair. "I know it's close to the bell and you probably have to go, but…I got a pass to the bathroom and I just…I need to talk to someone."

"No need to explain, honey—it's why I'm here." I shuffle papers, set them aside, bring up my notes on Tina on my computer, and then tug a notebook and pen over in front of me. "Having trouble with the rumors?"

Tina snorts, waves a hand. "No—god, no. I accepted the fact that there would be rumors a long time ago. I could have hidden my pregnancy with baggy clothes and stuff, but that's not me. I don't hide. So I just…wear what I wear, and let people talk."

"Very brave of you, Tina." I doodle on the notebook. "So, what's bothering you, then?"

She sucks in a deep breath, lets it out in a shuddering sigh. "I'm worried I'm getting attached."

"To the baby?"

She nods, sniffling. "Yeah. I try to think of it as *it*, you know. Not assign a gender, or think about a baby, or any of that. But it's hard. And I can't—I know I can't afford to get attached, because I'm determined to give it up for adoption. I've already started the process—the agency has several prospective couples lined up, and they're narrowing it down." She picks at a thumbnail, not looking at me. "I can't get attached, but how do I not?" She blinks back tears. "It's hard, Mrs. Thomas. It's really, really hard, and I have no one to talk to. No one supporting me. Except you and Ms. Pearson, I mean."

I set my pen down and consider my response for a few moments. "Tina…" I sigh, chewing on my lower lip. "The honest answer here is that I'm not sure I'm qualified to give you advice on this. I'm a guidance counselor, but I'm not a licensed therapist."

"I'm not asking for advice, just…" She shrugs. "If I wanted a therapist, I'd go see one. I want to know what *you* think, because I know you and I trust you."

I nod. "Okay." Another long pause as I think. "Well, the truth is…I don't think there's any way around the fact that you're going to become attached. Your biology and your hormones are working against you, because your body *wants* you to be attached. It's the maternal instinct. I wish I had a better answer than this, but...I think you just have to mentally and emotionally prepare yourself for this to—to get worse before it gets better." I grab her hands in mine and squeeze. "You have a hard, painful road ahead of you, and I don't think I'd be doing you any favors by pretending otherwise."

Tina nods. "I know." She sighs, wipes away tears with one hand. "I got myself into this, and there's no easy way out."

"It wasn't just you. You had help getting into this."

"Yeah, but Jake is useless. He's ignoring me in the hallways. I've been shunned by my circle of friends, because they were *his* friends before they were mine. He wants nothing to do with me. I'll get no money from him, not a damn thing. I could take him to court, put him on the birth certificate, fight for child support, but that's going to get me nowhere and nothing but trouble and headaches—I've looked into it. I'm better off just writing him off and knowing I really am in this alone. So, yeah, I know he is partly responsible, but I knew the risks of having sex with him, and I still did it. I thought we were covered, but apparently there was an accident with the condom and he didn't tell me."

"Asshole," I mutter, and then wince. "Sorry. Not a great example, am I?"

Tina laughs. "No, you're right about that, and I think everyone knows it." She waves a hand. "But, whatever. I'm not even thinking about him anymore. I have more important things to spend my time and energy on than Jake Emerson."

I smile at the firm, dismissive tone of voice. "Good for you, honey. Although part of me wants to tell you to do whatever you can to stick him with his responsibility, I know how futile that can be."

"It's just not worth it. I've spoken to several caseworkers about this already, and I'd spend all this time on court cases and hearings, and trying to track him down, and trying to force payments out of him...so I see no point in any of it." She sighs. "I mean, if I was planning on keeping the baby instead of giving it up for adoption, it'd be a different story. But as it is? No. Jake can go...well, you know."

"Yeah, I do." I pat her hand. "I'm here whenever you need to talk, okay? You know that—no appointment needed. You're going to be fine. Believe that."

She sniffles, nods. "I'm trying."

The bell rings then, and Tina takes a long, slow, deep breath, holds it, and then lets it out, shaking her hands. "Okay. I'm good." Another quick deep breath, and then she pastes a smile on her face. "I'm good!" Her smile brightens and I'm impressed by her ability to push it all away and present a calm, controlled appearance. "Thanks, Mrs. Thomas!"

"Absolutely my pleasure, Tina. Whatever I can do,

just let me know, okay?"

I watch her go, and she absently rubs her belly with both hands.

Something I've thought but haven't said to her is that there's no way I could do what she's doing. I can't imagine not having Aiden. I couldn't possibly have carried him for nine months, birthed him, and then given him away. Granted, I had a husband at the time, but still. It's unfathomable to me, but I'm proud of her for making the decision.

I lock up my office, and I'm actually somewhat surprised when I'm able to get out the door without any last-minute surprises.

Today is Aiden's game, which means I need to head home and put on my jersey with the matching number to Aiden's jersey, and write his number on my cheeks in lipstick—his team colors are red and white, so I'm doing red lipstick on my cheeks. Just so there is no doubt as to which team I am supporting, I will also bring my red-and-white pompoms, my stadium seat cushion, and my red-and-white team mascot to-go coffee mug.

Aiden is always embarrassed when I show up to games decked out in all my gear, but he's my baby boy and it's my duty as his mom to embarrass him with overly exuberant support. He once asked me if I could choose, like, one or two things instead of the whole embarrassing get up; I responded by threatening to paint my entire face half white and half red, and he promptly shut up.

Mom and Dad meet me at the high school stadium where the game is held: we take football very seriously around here, so even the youth teams play on the nice field. Mom and Dad already have a little section of bleachers spaced off, front and center right at the fifty-yard line, and Mom is as decked out as crazy as I am while Dad, like Aiden, is probably wishing he was allowed to sit with less embarrassing people.

"It's just kiddy football," he'll grouse. "No point in getting all worked up about it. Not even a championship on the line, so just calm down."

Mom will laugh and pat his cheek, because she knows as well as I do that there's no human on the planet who loves and supports Aiden more than Dad... he just has his own way of showing it.

I take a seat by mom, with Dad on her other side. He's got a Styrofoam cup of concession stand coffee in his hands, despite the fact that it's unseasonably warm for this time in the fall. As far as Dad is concerned football games equal crappy concession stand coffee and nachos and hot dogs and paper bags full of popcorn. The boys are warming up in the end zone, kicking their legs high, clapping and shouting in unison, and doing all sorts of funny-looking calisthenics. The scoreboard shows there is less than a minute before the game begins, and I have the jitters for Aiden.

Aiden is one of the team captains, so he and two others meet at the fifty-yard line with the referees, umpires, line judges, and the other team captains to determine who kicks off first and in which direction. After a brief discussion, the teams take their places on opposite ends of the field.

Apparently the other team has chosen to kick off first, which means Aiden takes his place on the field well behind his team, since he'll be the one to receive the ball. This, of course, assumes the other team's kicker can get the ball in the air, which isn't always the case.

The whistle blows, and then there's the soft, distant thump as the kicker sends the ball flipping end over end in a high but short arc. Aiden's teammates surge forward, and both coaches shout for Aiden to get under it, to move forward. Aiden launches himself into motion as the ball hurtles toward the ground...he catches it neatly and cradles it in his arm, his other hand placed over the top of it protectively.

"GO, AIDEN!" I hear Jamie shout.

"UP FIELD!" Coach Barnhart shouts. "NORTH AND SOUTH, NORTH AND SOUTH!"

Which, I've learned, means Aiden is supposed to run toward the end zone instead of heading for the sidelines. Aiden angles away from the largest group of opposing players as if heading for the near sideline, and the onrushing players try to head him off—but Aiden, instead, cuts back toward the middle of the field, dances around one tackle, dodges another, trips out of a third...and then he's gone. Sprinting full speed, Aiden is running so fast that he's steadily putting yardage between him and the nearest player from the other team.

His whole team is chanting, shouting, Barnhart is clapping—and Jamie is jumping up and down excitedly, pumping his fist as Aiden jogs into the end zone to score a touchdown, turning to accept the pile-on hugs of his teammates. His team line up for the two-point conversion. There's the count, the hike, and the quarterback, one of Aiden's best friends, plugs the ball into Aiden's belly and Aiden darts right up the middle. I lose him in the crowded jumble of players, and then I see the refs raise their arms over their heads—the two-point conversion is good!

Mom is shrieking like a banshee, Dad is on his feet and clapping, and I, predictably, have lost every bit of my dignity as I shout Aiden's name, whistling, clapping, and just generally embarrassing myself.

As our offense jogs off the field and the kick-off unit takes its place, Aiden is engulfed in a back-slapping round of hugs from the players on the sidelines.

And then I watch as Jamie approaches him. Instead of hugging him or doing the weird football player butt slapping thing—which I've never understood—he kneels in front of Aiden, catches his helmet by the face mask in one hand and slaps him on the helmet with the other. I can't quite tell what he's saying, but it's a deeply personal moment, somehow. Intimate. A man encouraging a boy whom he cares about very much.

Mom glances at me, watching Jamie and Aiden.

She leans close. "Elyse...is there something I should know about the new principal?" Her eyes cut into mine, knowing and suspicious.

I shrug, attempting nonchalance. "Ahhh...no."

"Elyse." She glares at me, using the Mom voice—which still works on me, even though I'm thirty-two.

"No, Mom. There's nothing you need to know about Jamie."

"Jamie, is it?"

Crap. "Um. Yeah. Jamie Trent. We've...spoken a few times."

Mom's eyes are narrowed to slits. "Aiden talks about him all the time. Practically worships the man, it seems to me."

"He's a great principal and a great coach."

"And he's giving you quite a look, if you know what I mean."

I glance at Jamie—he is, indeed, staring at me in a telling way; I look away and meet her eyes. "Mom...no. Just let it go, please?"

She shrugs. "It's just that he's awfully handsome, and he really seems to have taken a shine to Aiden."

"Handsome, is he?" Dad mutters. "He ain't so pretty."

I roll my eyes. "Oh stop, Dad."

"He's a darn sight better than that pathetic worm of a loser you were married to. That boy was as useless as a screen door on a submarine."

"Dad."

"What? He couldn't find his ass with both hands and a flashlight. Didn't know what he had with you, never appreciated you, and I never liked him." He gestures at Jamie. "I ain't even met that boy, and I like him a hell of a lot better."

"*Dad*," I snap.

He lifts an eyebrow at me. "Elyse?"

"Can we not?"

"You been divorced from Daniel for three years. About time you moved on, sweetheart. Aiden needs a father."

I suck in a sharp breath. "He's got you."

"I ain't gonna be around forever." Dad's firm, unforgiving hazel eyes fix on mine. "And I'm his grandpa. I love that boy somethin' fierce, but I can't ever be his dad. Daniel made it clear he don't give a hoot, which means there's got to be someone else." He gestures at Jamie. "That fella down there seems interested in the job."

"He sure does," Mom agrees.

"Neither of you know him," I argue.

"So? Don't need to meet him to be able to tell he cares about Aiden," Dad says. "That's about all anybody can ask for, from where I'm standing."

I shoot to my feet. "I—I need some coffee."

I leave the bleachers and head for the concession stand. Mom and Dad both know I never drink coffee past noon, so this is an obvious gambit to escape the conversation. Fine. I'm avoiding the topic. I just...I can't do it.

I want to, but I can't.

I just can't.

I have a visceral memory of signing the divorce papers.

Of watching Daniel's car drive away for the last time.

Of Aiden sitting in our living room, his overnight backpack packed and resting on his back, ready to spend the night with Dad…who never showed up.

Of Aiden sitting with my cell phone in his little hands, on his birthday, waiting for his dad to call and at least wish him a happy birthday—he didn't even care that Daniel didn't send so much as a card, he just wanted a call. And he got nothing.

I know, rationally, that Jamie is a drastically different sort of person. But I just cannot and will not risk putting Aiden through all that. Bottom line is that Daniel didn't fight for me, and he didn't fight for Aiden.

So how I can begin to trust that Jamie would? Or that Jamie would choose to fight for a woman he barely knows, a single mother, a closed-off woman who has rejected him so many times, and who continues to push him away.

Why would he fight for that? What is there for him to even fight for?

I'm tapped out, emotionally drained, and I spend several minutes alone, watching the game from the concession stand.

"Moping, are you?" I hear Cora say.

I don't turn to look at her; I just bump her with my hip. "Jamie gave me a look from the sidelines when Aiden scored, and Mom caught it, and now Mom and Dad are putting pressure on me to…" I break off with a hissing sigh. "To *move on*, like it's this easy thing to do."

Cora takes my coffee from me and sips at it, knowing I won't actually drink it. "They love you and they want to see you happy, and they know how things were with Daniel and, they can see, even from a distance, what the rest of us see when Jamie looks at you."

I groan. "CAN WE *NOT*?!"

Jess, a classmate of Cora's and mine, and the mother of Carter, the quarterback, is inside the concession booth, scooping popcorn into bags—she has, up till now, been pretending she can't hear our conversation. "Oh man, he really does look at you in…*ahem*…a certain way," she says to me.

I sigh. "Oh, no. Not you, too."

Jess is a volunteer at the school, working the lunchroom and the pickup line—she's one of *those* moms, the "involved in *everything* at the school" type. She just rolls her eyes. "If you haven't seen the looks he gives you, you're blind, Elyse Thomas." She leans over the counter. "There are rumors about the two of you, you know." Jess is a fledgling member of the Busybody Society—she's not as gossipy as Cora or Yvonne, but she'll talk your ear off if you let her.

I push away from the concession stand. "And on

that note, I'm going back to the bleachers."

"I'm coming too!" Cora says.

"You missed his touchdown kickoff return," I scold as we clomp across the noisy bleachers to where Mom and Dad are sitting.

"I know, but Tina was having this hormonal sobbing episode about something," she waves at someone in the stands, "so I had to talk her down before I could leave her alone."

"Will she be living with you permanently?" I ask.

Cora shrugs. "Not permanently, but just until this whole thing is over. She needs a support system, and having been kicked out by my own parents, I understand more than most what it's like to try to make it in this town, alone, as a teenager—and I wasn't even pregnant."

"My parents all but adopted you," I remind her.

She nods. "Oh, I know. And that's why I'm all but adopting Tina. Paying it forward."

Cora is suspiciously silent as we take our seats next to my parents. We settle in to watch the next play on the field but then I realize that Cora and my mom are whispering conspiratorially.

I lean against my dad and clutch his arm dramatically. "Dad, help. They're cahooting."

Dad cackles gruffly. "Good luck to you, darlin'. Once those two start jawing, ain't much can stop 'em." He pats me on the side of my face with a big, rough hand. "They just love ya, girly. You know that. We all do. Just want to see you happy, and you been letting what that—"

"Dad, please," I whisper.

"Aiden ain't here to hear me, so I'm gonna say it," he grumps. "A piece of moldy moose shit. That's what Daniel was, and what he is. He hurt you, and you been lettin' that hurt fester in you ever since. Now, you're right—I don't know that Jamie Trent fella from Adam, but your son fairly adores him, and that says somethin'. And I'm just sayin', maybe you oughta give some thought to letting bygones be bygones and…well, as much as I hate using clichés…maybe you oughta start a new chapter in your life."

I shake my head. "It's not that simple."

"Ain't nothin' ever *simple*, Elyse." He indicates Mom. "You think it was simple when she and I had that big fight? We had to choose to get past the hurt. You and Cora were just girls when it happened, and we kept how bad it really was from both of you. We nearly didn't make it, Elyse. I said things I regret, she said things she regrets, she left and I let her…it took a whole hell of a lot of work to get past it. To trust each other again, to not keep seein' and hearin' all that old mess."

"It's not the same thing, Dad. It's not like I'm trying to get Daniel back."

"No, and thank god for that, 'cause he never deserved you. Point is, takes time and effort and willpower to get over some things, baby girl. It don't just magically happen all on its own one day. You gotta *work* at it."

I shake my head and focus on the game, and Dad knows better than to push it. And, bless him, he shushes Mom and Cora when they try to bring their guns to bear on me.

I know they mean well, but...the harder they all push, the more determined I am to keep Jamie at a distance.

16

THERE'S NO PRACTICE THE DAY AFTER THE GAME—
Aiden's team won in an absolute slaughter:
64–8, and Aiden scored the majority of the
touchdowns. After such a great game, the coaches gave
the players the next afternoon off, so once my appointments are done and the bell rings, I skedaddle out of the
office in a hurry: I plan to pick Aiden up from school
and take him to get ice cream at the pharmacy—which
still doubles as the town ice-cream shop, as it has since
the inception of the town. After ice creams, we are going to a movie at the theater in Hanover.

I'm excited for my impromptu day out with Aiden,
since the two of us haven't really had a chance to go
out just for fun since school started.

I've even cleaned out the car, *including* a forty-min-
ute session with Dad's Shop-Vac. Basically, the car is as
clean as a secondhand car that gets heavy usage as a
mobile restaurant and equipment storage unit can get.

And, just for fun, I've gotten a little dolled up for
Aiden. Which just means nicer jeans and a dressy top

and my favorite fall boots with a sweater duster, and maybe a little more makeup than usual.

It's all for Aiden, and it has nothing to do with the fact that I'm about to see Jamie in the pickup line.

That would be stupid and immature, especially considering I most assuredly do *not* want, need, or crave his attention, or the way those big warm sexy brown eyes look at me.

GAH. I am such a liar.

I turn into the elementary school parking lot and merge in with the line of cars waiting to pick up their children. I idle forward inch by inch as the line crawls through, occasionally glancing at my phone or fiddling with the radio. I'm third in line, and I see Aiden standing with Jamie just outside the front door.

Jamie is his usual preppy principal self, with pressed khakis and a white button-down and a Transformers tie. He has a walkie-talkie hanging from his hip pocket, and his eyes dart here and there, overseeing the progress of the line. If he sees a child waiting too long, he gets on his walkie-talkie and alerts Mrs. Emory, who knows literally everyone in town, and she will contact the parent in question and find out their ETA. While the child is waiting, a teacher or other staff member takes the child aside and stays with them until their parent arrives.

I pull forward few more inches and Aiden surges forward, intending to jump into the car with me as fast as possible. But the next few seconds happen in slow motion.

I see Jamie's eyes widen, and then I see him lunge forward, grab Aiden by the backpack and yank him forcefully backward. Jamie's eyes are locked behind me, and then they go to me.

I glance in the rearview mirror just in time to see a pair of headlights and the chrome grille of a pickup fill the mirror. And the vehicle is not stopping.

My foot, instinctively, slams down on the brake pedal.

But it's not enough.

I feel the impact, hear it—a deafening *BANG-CRUNCH* accompanied by the squeal of metal on metal and I'm sent jolting forward, the impact too forceful for my brakes. Even with my foot on the brake pedal, I'm sent flying up onto the curb and into the landscaping. The red brick of the school wall fills my vision and I'm surging forward with momentum. I'm still trying to slam on the brakes even though my foot is already fully depressed—

CRASH.

My car slams into the brick wall, my windshield splinters and spiderwebs, my hood accordions, and I'm thrown forward as I abruptly, violently come to a halt.

My seat belt has already caught, I feel it constricting painfully against my chest, slamming me back in my seat.

Time returns to normal.

My ears ring in the silence.

My head throbs.

My neck and back are aching from the whiplash.

It's hard to breathe.

Aiden?

Aiden.

I blink, but it hurts to do so.

Something is hissing.

"...Lyse? Elyse?" I hear a warped, distorted voice, blink again. "Elyse? Are you okay?"

It's Jamie. He has my door open and he's kneeling in the opening, brushing my hair out of my eyes, his brown gaze worried, scared.

I groan. "Unh—" I swallow hard. "Yeah. I...Yeah, I think I'm okay."

"Who am I, Elyse?"

"You're Jamie. Aiden's principal."

"Do you know who you are?" he asks. "What's your full name?"

I wonder why he's asking me this...

Oh—he's worried I have a concussion.

"I'm Elyse Gabrielle Thomas."

"Do you know your address?"

I tell it to him and then wave him off. "I'm okay. Just...help me out of the car, please."

"The police are on the way. I want to make sure they're sending an ambulance." He grabs his walkie-talkie, adjusts the channel, depressing the talk button.

I stop him with a hand on his. "Don't. You know the insurance we get won't cover an ambulance. I'm fine."

"You need to be looked at, Elyse," he says, his voice brooking no argument. "That was a really bad crash. You were rear-ended and then you slammed into a brick wall." His eyes are worried. "Give me your insurance card, I'll handle the police and insurance." I gratefully give him my insurance card and let him deal with Mrs. Quincy and the police and everything.

He comes back once that's all dealt with and takes my hands, but I put a few inches of distance between us, unnerved by his proximity, by the obvious concern in his voice and eyes. His hands are on mine, and his thumbs are probing my forehead, his eyes tracking mine carefully. I realize, as a football player and coach, he's probably very familiar with signs of a concussion.

"I didn't hit my head," I tell him. I wince. "But it does ache."

"The impact and the whiplash can cause headaches." He brushes my temple with a gentle thumb. "I don't think you have a concussion."

"No, just bad whiplash."

"You need to see a doctor to be sure, though."

"Aiden." I glance past him, and then through the passenger window. "Where's Aiden?"

"Inside with Mrs. Emory. I wasn't sure how hurt you were, and I didn't want him to see you if you were bleeding or something."

I swallow hard. "Th-thank you for that."

His smile is tender, and it makes my heart hurt. "Come on. Let's get you up out of this car."

"Was anyone else hurt?"

He shakes his head. "No. The person who rear-ended you is fine. Mrs. Quincy, I think it is? Thank god one of the first things I did as principal was make sure no one is ever on the sidewalk over there during pickup and drop-off—for exactly this reason."

"Smart guy."

He reaches in and unbuckles me, and I smell him, feel him—he makes me dizzy. Or maybe that's just the adrenaline and the headache. "Come on."

His hands are gentle but strong, guiding my legs out of the car and helping my feet hit the ground, and then he has one hand in mine and the other around my waist—far too intimately—and he's helping me to my feet.

I'm shaky, unsteady; my legs are wobbly, and my hands are trembling. I'm grateful Jamie is beside me, thankful for his arm around my waist as he helps me away from the car with its hissing radiator. I want to lean into him, press my head against his chest, and let him wrap me up.

Instead, once I'm on the sidewalk, I grip his hand hard and push away from him so I'm walking on my own, standing on my own. My head throbs and my neck aches, and I just want to lie down, curl up into a ball and cry.

Aiden.

"I need to see Aiden. I need him to know I'm okay."

"Mrs. Emory has called your parents. They're

on the way to come get him so I can take you to the hospital."

"I need to see him."

"Okay, this way." He doesn't let go of my hand; his palm is warm and dry against mine, keeping me upright as I wobble on shaky legs.

I'm still three or four feet from the front door of the school when Aiden barrels through it at a dead sprint, arms wide, tears running down his cheeks. "Mama!"

I get down to my knees, and let Aiden slam into me for a hug. "Whoa, careful, bud."

"The car hit you and Coach pulled me back and I thought you were—I thought—" He's sniffling, sobbing, close to hyperventilating.

"I'm okay, honey. I'm fine." I wipe his cheeks and cup them. "Look at me, honey. Not a scratch on me. I'm shaken up and my neck hurts, so I'm gonna have a doctor look at me to be sure. You're going to go with Grandma and Papa, okay?"

He shakes his head. "No. I'm going with you."

I smile, and hug him. "Aiden, baby. Do you remember how long it took at the hospital when you hurt your ankle?"

He nods, sighing—I can see the resignation in his eyes. "Yeah."

"I promise you I'm *okay*. I'm not injured. I'm barely even hurt. It was scary, but I'm okay. I just need to see the doctor to be absolutely sure." I hug him again. "I want you to be with me too, buddy, but there will be a lot of hospital time, and you'll get bored. Go with Grandma and Papa. Have some dinner, watch a show, build something with Papa in the barn, and I'll be back before you know it, okay?"

"All right." He frowns at me. "You're not just being tough because you don't want me to be scared or worried?"

I laugh. "I won't lie to you, Aiden—I'm pretty shaken up. It was scary as heck, and I have a headache and my neck hurts. But that's all minor stuff. Remember what you told me about the difference between hurt and injured?"

He nods. "Yeah." He glances at Jamie. "Coach told me that."

"Right. So, buddy, again, look at me: I'm a little hurt, but I'm not injured. Have I ever lied to you?"

He shrugs. "Not that I know of."

I laugh. "Not that you know of, because I've never lied to you, and I never will. And I'm not just being tough. But I don't want you to be scared or worried because I'm *okay*. I just have to get checked out to be a hundred percent sure."

"Okay, Mama." I hug him again, and then I hear the telltale rattle of Dad's ancient Chevy pickup as it enters the pickup/drop-off circle.

Dad hops out, and while his expression is neutral, I know him well enough to know he's worried. "You all right, kiddo?" His voice is low, gruff, and angry.

"I'm fine, Dad." I stand up and hug him. "Whiplash

and a headache."

He glances at Jamie. "You're taking her in?"

Jamie nods. "Yes, sir. Right now. Or as soon as I can get her into my truck."

"Good luck with that," Dad huffs. "She's as stubborn as they come."

"Dad!" I snap.

He shrugs. "You are. Just like your mama."

"Mama's not stubborn," Aiden says. "She just knows what she wants."

Dad laughs at that. "Well, I can't say you're wrong there, pal." He claps Aiden on the shoulder. "Well, buddy, I've got a carburetor needs fixing so my ol' tractor will work, and I need your help."

"What's a carburetor? Is it like carbohydrolates?"

I laugh. "Carbo*hydr*ates, bud."

"Yeah, that," Aiden says.

Dad snorts. "Not even close. A carburetor is a part in older cars and trucks. I'll explain what it does while we fix it and put it back in."

"Okay." Aiden hugs me once more. "Be good for the doctors, Mom."

I wobble a little, and Jamie catches me, his arm surreptitiously bracing my elbow. "I will. You be good for Grandma and Papa."

"I will!"

"And don't learn any more of Papa's crabapple wisdom."

Dad laughs. "I've been a crabapple my whole life.

Ain't about to stop now."

I pat him on the arm. "I know it, Dad. And we love you that way. Just don't turn my son into one."

"Eh. Worse things'n bein' a crabapple. Could be a no-good wussy."

"Like my sperm donor?" Aiden asks.

I whirl on him. "Aiden Daniel Thomas! Where in the world did you hear *that*?"

He pales. "I didn't know it was bad! Carter said that's what his dad said my dad is—nothing but a good-for-nothing sperm donor."

"Ugh, my god" I sigh. "Do not repeat that, okay? Your father made his choices, but it doesn't mean we get to say nasty or unkind things. We take the high road, Aiden."

"Okay, Mama. I understand. I won't say it again."

Dad squeezes his shoulder. "Let's go." He shoots Jamie another glance. "Get her to the hospital and make sure my little girl is okay."

Jamie's nod is serious. "Yes, sir."

Dad winks at me. "He's respectful. I like that."

"Dad," I growl, my voice full of warning. "*Don't.*"

He raises his hands. "Just sayin'."

He helps Aiden into his truck; Aiden scoots behind the wheel and reaches for the gas pedal. "Can I drive?"

Dad snorts. "Not a chance. Now scoot."

"But you—"

"Would *never* let an eight-year-old boy drive my truck," Dad cuts in, a little too loudly.

I laugh. "You really think I don't know you let him drive? You strapped blocks to my shoes and taught me to drive when I was six."

"Never can start a kid too early, as long as you're careful. We go way out in the north field where there ain't so much as a stump for acres, and I let him toddle around in the grass. He's a champ. He'll be the best driver on the road by the time he's got his license."

"Just be careful, and don't let him go too fast."

Dad slides behind the wheel, makes sure Aiden is seated properly on his booster and is buckled in, and then he rattles away, waving at me through the open window.

Mrs. Emory and a few other teachers have taken over directing traffic and getting kids to their parents while Sheriff Johnson writes a ticket for the driver of the truck who rear-ended me. A flatbed tow truck rumbles up, waiting as the last few parents pick up their kids, rubbernecking, and then the flatbed backs up, beeping loudly, right up to the back of my car. He lowers his bed and sets about attaching the chain and hooks while Sheriff Johnson takes my statement.

And then, finally, Jamie escorts me to his truck, not letting go of me for a second. I slide up and in, slowly and carefully, my neck aching and protesting with each movement.

Once I'm alone in the truck, I allow myself a quick, quiet sob. And then Jamie is climbing behind the wheel and starting it up and heading out of the parking lot.

An old Randy Travis song is playing on the radio, the volume down low.

"You don't need to be strong right now, Elyse," Jamie says.

"I'm fine."

"That scared *me*."

"Thank you for pulling Aiden out of the way."

He shrugs. "It was instinct. I didn't even think about it." He growls. "I've heard more than one person say Mrs. Quincy needs to stop driving, and that's why."

Mrs. Quincy is at least eighty years old, but she's the only living relative Victoria Quincy has, seeing as her parents died in a car accident and left Victoria with no other relatives except her great-aunt, Mrs. Quincy. And Mrs. Quincy has been driving…erratically, shall we say…for at least ten years.

I sigh. "People have tried stopping her from driving on and off for the last decade, and she just refuses to give up her license. Plus, she's Victoria's only way to and from school."

"Well, she could have killed you, or others." He frowns. "What's she doing driving that huge truck anyway? She can barely see over the wheel!"

"Her husband bought it with cash about six months before he passed, and she won't sell it. She's had offers, but it's Herb's truck, and she's clinging to it."

Jamie taps his fingers on the steering wheel. "There's got to be something we can do. That can't happen again."

It's quiet the rest of the way to the hospital. Jamie is deep in thought, and keeps glancing at me as if to make sure I haven't developed a sudden injury or passed out.

"What?" I ask.

He shakes his head. "Nothing. Nothing."

"I'm *fine*, Jamie."

"I know. It was just…" He sighs roughly. "Scary. Watching that happen and being helpless."

"You weren't helpless—you were right there, taking care of Aiden."

We pull into the ER parking lot, and he finds a spot near the back. He puts the truck in park, but glances at me before shutting it off.

"There's so much I want to say, but…" He shakes his head, scrubbing his hand through his hair. "I won't open that can of worms right now."

"Probably best," I say. "I don't think I can handle that conversation at the moment."

Jamie exits the truck and circles around to the passenger side, opening my door and holding my hand to help me down.

I want to hold his hand; I want that comfort. I'm shaky, trembling, more from residual adrenaline and the post-trauma surge of fear and anxiety.

Instead, I walk on my own two feet, fists clenched, refusing to lean on Jamie any more than necessary.

He notices, and his jaw tightens, the corners of his eyes wrinkling, tightening with…irritation? Hurt? Frustration? I don't know.

We find a pair of seats together near the entrance to the ER, and Jamie brings me a clipboard with paperwork to fill out. Instead of letting me do it, however, he asks the questions and circles the correct answers and writes in the correct information—much of it he remembers from our visit here with Aiden.

After a fairly short wait, a male nurse opens the door to the examining area and calls my name, "Elyse Thomas?"

I rise, slowly, shakily, and Jamie helps me to my feet. "That's me."

The nurse glances at Jamie. "You're the husband?"

Jamie blinks a moment. "Um. No, but—"

"He's with me," I cut in, quickly; the thought of sitting back there alone waiting for a doctor...my stomach flips with anxiety just thinking about it. "He's coming with me."

"Okay," the nurse says, not really caring either way. "This way. Room four."

I follow him, with Jamie at my side.

Holding my hand.

I don't want to let go, but...I can't let myself think this is normal. I just need the support in the moment.

The problem is that whenever I need someone to support me, Jamie has been there, since the first day we met.

We reach room four, and I sit on the hospital bed, and the nurse takes my vitals and tells me the doctor will be right with me.

The doctor finally arrives about forty minutes later and after asking several questions he begins to poke and prod my neck, has me roll it this way and that, checks my pupils and has me follow his finger up and down and side to side, and asks me more questions.

When he's finished, he sets his computer tablet aside and frowns at me. "I'd like to have an X-ray on your neck, just to err on the side of caution. It sounds like it was a rough crash, and your neck is pretty well tweaked."

"Okay."

He asks a few questions about allergy to medication and such, typing my replies into his tablet.

"Okay. I'll get someone from radiology in here as soon as possible, get your neck scanned, and see what we see."

"Sounds good," I tell him.

"Great. I'll be back in to talk to you once we get the scans back."

Another wait, and then a young woman from the radiology department comes in, and she has more questions, most of them straightforward, and most of which I've already answered at least once.

"Any allergy to medication?"

"No."

"Any family history of cancer or high blood pressure?"

"No."

"Are you pregnant or is there any possibility you

could be?"

I blink. "Um. No?" I wasn't expecting that question. "Why?"

The young woman eyes me. "Standard procedure. We wouldn't X-ray you if you were pregnant unless absolutely necessary."

"I'm not pregnant."

She smiles. "It can't hurt to be sure. A quick urine test and we'll have you under the X-ray in no time. Okay?"

I shrug, nod. "Sure, I guess."

I glance at Jamie, but his expression is carefully blank.

So...I follow her out of the room and to a bathroom, where she gives me a quick rundown of clean-catch procedure and I procure the sample.

I return to the waiting room...and wait.

And wait.

Finally, after about forty minutes, the doctor comes back in—not the nurse, not the girl from radiology, but the actual attending ER doctor.

He stuffs his hands in his lab coat. Adjusts his stethoscope around his neck.

Smiles at me.

At Jamie.

"Congratulations, Mom and Dad."

17

"I...w-w-what?" I stammer. "What do you mean, congratulations?"

Jamie, who had been pacing restlessly, sinks to the chair, his hand over his mouth.

The doctor tugs on the ends of his stethoscope. "You're pregnant."

"I—no, I'm not."

He smiles patiently. "Yes, you are. The results were unequivocal. Your hCG level says you're about...oh... seven, maybe eight weeks along."

"I...I haven't—um." I blink, swallow, try to think, to remember. "I haven't had any symptoms. Not one."

He shrugs. "You don't always get early pregnancy symptoms. Some women have terrible symptoms for one pregnancy, and essentially none for the next."

"You're positive?"

He nods. "I mean, I'll administer a blood test if you want, but I'm one hundred percent certain, Mrs. Thomas." He smiles again. "You're pregnant—I'd say just over seven weeks."

I stare at Jamie and he stares back.

I'm pregnant.

I'm pregnant.

I'm...*pregnant*.

━━

Jamie hasn't said a word since we received the news. Of course, there's barely been time.

I don't get the X-ray, but an ultrasound is ordered. Since they can take me right away, we are shown into an examining room right away.

Sitting in the darkened room, a brusque but kind older nurse slides the wand over my stomach, Jamie is in a chair in the shadows, watching with a carefully neutral expression as the technician smears the jelly around and adjusts the wand, taps a button, and then there's a distorted whooshing sound, which warbles and distorts further as she wiggles, tilts, and twists the wand, and then the staticky whooshing sound turns into a sound which is familiar to me...and absolutely terrifying:

Ba-BUMP-ba-BUMP-ba-BUMP-ba-BUMP-ba-BUMP...

Steady, rhythmic, quick.

The technician smiles at me. "There it is. Nice strong heartbeat."

I feel like I could pass out. "Yeah..." I mumble. "A heartbeat. Guess I didn't have the flu after all."

Her eyes go from me to Jamie and back. "Not

expecting this little nugget, huh?"

I shake my head, speaking for both Jamie and I, "No…no, we weren't."

Jamie is visibly pale, even in the dark ultrasound room.

"Well there it is, ready or not." She taps a button again and the heartbeat goes silent, and then as she taps some more and adjusts the wand she says, "Let's see if I can get some measurements."

She does whatever it is ultrasound technicians do, making certain things light up, measuring, labeling, taking still shots and printing them out. She freezes the wand in a certain position and points at the screen. "There's the heart, left side and right side, contracting and expanding beautifully."

She takes the stack of printed glossy ultrasound photos, puts them in a folder, and then uses a new clean towel to clean the worst of the jelly off me before handing me paper towel to take care of the rest myself.

"You have a nice healthy fetus, Mom. We'll see you in a few months for the gender ultrasound."

"Thank you," I say automatically.

She helps me off the table and I finish adjusting my clothing as she turns the lights back on, and then Jamie and I are alone in the hallway. Fluorescent bulbs bathe everything garish white, and Jamie's shoes squeak on the linoleum while mine clack noisily. There's a strong smell of antiseptic.

A male nurse appears. "This way, please."

We follow him through the maze of hallways to another room, this one not in the emergency department. We wait in silence for whatever is happening next.

There's no sound in the small, cold hospital room. Even my own heartbeat seems muted.

Jamie looks at me as if trying to find something to say.

I give a small shake of my head. "Not here, not now. Let's talk, but later."

"Elyse, I—"

"Jamie, please, let's just get through with this whole hospital business and go home. We'll talk at home."

After what feels like two hours, but was probably less than half an hour, the original ER doctor bustles in, leans against the door and toys with his stethoscope. "So. We found a heartbeat, got some measurements. Things look great. I would've liked an X-ray on your neck, but I'm confident it's just a case of moderate whiplash, so it's not really serious enough that I'm willing to order an X-ray anyway. Just take it easy, maybe put a hot pad on it, or some Ben-Gay. If it hurts bad enough that you have a hard time sleeping, you could probably get away with a low dose of aspirin, but I'd recommend against it unless absolutely necessary."

"I'm fine. I can tough it out." I try for a smile, but don't quite manage it.

"Do you have a primary, or an OB we can send the ultrasound results to?"

I sigh. "I...I have a primary. Dr. Pritchard in Clayton.

But no, no OB. I, um—I wasn't expecting this, so I haven't seen my OB since my last routine checkup."

"Well, I'd get with her and get started on prenatal care vitamins and all that."

I nod, another automatic response—I'm shell-shocked right now and operating on autopilot. "Yeah, yes. Of course."

"Do you have any questions for me?" He smirks. "Aside from 'how did this happen,' I mean. I trust you're aware of that, regardless of your obvious shock."

I just nod again, and then blink. "Um. No, no questions. I just want to go home and try to process this."

"Well, you're free to go. You were never admitted, so there's no discharge papers." He eyes Jamie. "You're driving?"

Jamie nods, as shell-shocked as I am. "Yes."

"Good. Because she's in no shape to be driving anywhere."

"I've got her."

The doctor's smile is sympathetic. "Are you okay yourself?"

Jamie nods, stands up, visibly shaking off and putting aside his shock. "Yes. I'm okay. Thank you, Doctor." He holds out his hand to me. "Ready, Elyse?"

Without thinking, I nod and take his hand, let him help me to my feet. His hand stays in mine as we exit the room and wind through the hallways to the check-out desk, where I pay my co-pay and then let Jamie lead me out to the waiting room.

"Stay here," he says, pausing by the exit. "I'll grab the truck and bring it around."

I settle gratefully down onto the bench. "Okay."

In less than a minute, his truck squeals to a stop under the ER awning and he's in front of me, taking both of my hands and helping me outside, and up into his truck. He even leans across me to buckle me in. Shock has worn away to numbness, and a little voice in the back of my head warns it is only temporary.

More tense, resounding silence as we exit the hospital parking lot; but within a couple of minutes we're leaving Hanover, going from a wide, relatively suburban four-lane thoroughfare onto the narrow, quiet, dark, tree-lined rural two-lane highway that is the more direct route between Hanover and Clayton.

The only sound is the crunch of Jamie's truck tires on the road, and the occasional frog croak or cricket chirp through the open windows.

A Jason Aldean song murmurs low on the radio, and Jamie hums along.

He drives with his left hand, his right wrist hanging over the column-mounted gear shifter, fingers twitching to the beat now and then. His brow is wrinkled, the corners of his eyes tightened—his telltale sign of stress, I'm learning.

He glances at me. "What?"

I frown. "Huh? What, what?"

"You're staring at me."

I sigh. "Oh. Sorry." I look away, out the window;

we're passing the quarry on the left, thumping over the train tracks and then the highway is dark and quiet once more.

"Just wondering what you're thinking, is all." Jamie lowers his window a bit more and hangs his hand out; the early fall air is cool and pleasant.

I can't help a laugh. "I'm trying to figure that out myself."

"Same."

Silence for miles, nothing but trees and guard rails and blacktop.

A small, quiet, tightly controlled sob escapes me. "I'm scared, Jamie." I breathe through it, and tamp the sobs down. "Scared and confused."

He doesn't answer for a while. "Elyse, I..." He shakes his head. "I have so much in my head right now, and I just...I don't know how to—"

"Can you just...just turn up the radio? I'm not sure I can handle conversation, yet."

"Shit, me neither," he says, relieved, and turns up the volume on "Would You Go With Me" by Josh Turner.

Country music serves to cover our nerves and the raw, anxious, thick silence between us. The trees give way to farmland, and farmland to large rural home plots, and then those get smaller and closer together, and there's the occasional neighborhood, and then the prefab and single-wides. The front yards get smaller and smaller, and then we're slowing to enter the traffic circle at the center of town—home.

Jamie glances at me as he trundles slowly around the circle. "I...um. Am I taking you home? Or are we getting Aiden from your folks? What do you want to do?"

I can't think. I can only shrug and try to hold back the tears. "I don't know," I whisper. "I don't know."

He angles away from the traffic circle and pulls to a stop in a parking spot outside the general store. "Can I see your phone?"

I dig it out of my purse and hand it to him without thinking.

"Passcode?"

"One-zero-two-one-one-zero," I say. "Aiden's birthday."

"October twenty-first, twenty-ten, huh?" he muses. "Mine's the thirtieth."

I glance at him, a faint hint of amusement whizzing through me. "Devil's Night?"

He laughs. "Yup."

"That must've kept your childhood interesting."

He chuckles. "Nope. Totally boring. Never got into any trouble on my birthday. I was a boring, innocent child completely devoid of any mischievousness whatsoever."

I laugh. "I bet."

"I definitely did not *ever* get arrested for vagrancy and trespassing. Nor for climbing the water tower, or stealing Old Man McClary's tractor."

"I thought you grew up in Nashua?"

"On a farm outside it, actually. We only moved into the city itself after my dad passed when I was fourteen. Mom couldn't handle the farm by herself, so we sold it and moved into the city. Just me, her, and our Schnauzer Border Collie mix, Hurley."

I smirk. "And you got into all that trouble before you were fourteen?"

He laughs. "And then some. Most kids who lose a parent get into trouble afterward as a way of lashing out at life. I actually stopped getting into trouble. Mom needed me, so I put my focus into being there for her. Which kept me out of trouble. Otherwise, I'd probably be fixing cars in a highway-side auto body garage in the middle of nowhere in the New Hampshire countryside. I'd have long greasy hair, a scraggly goatee, and prison tattoos."

I laugh and frown at the same time. "I can't picture that."

He chuckles. "I just described my uncle Stu. I idolized that guy growing up. Dad was always busy running the farm, so I spent all my time with Uncle Stu. Who, looking back, wasn't the best influence." He wiggles his phone. "I'm going to call your parents. I think you need some time alone to rest. I'm sure Aiden will be fine there overnight."

I can only nod.

But a word keeps tolling in my head: *alone...alone... alone.*

It takes all I have to keep the horror at bay. I absolutely cannot be alone right now, but I don't know how to say that. I can't bear to face Mom or Dad, or even Cora. Not now. Not yet.

I hear Jamie talking: *"...Shaken up, needs to rest... check on her..."*

I'm spacing out—my head is buzzing, heart palpitating; it's hard to breathe, my ears hum, my hands shake and my fingertips tingle. I feel the truck moving again but I'm not sure where we're going. Things are blurry, and I'm not sure if I'm dizzy or if there's fog in the air.

We stop.

A door thunks.

"Elyse?"

I twist and see Jamie; he's concerned, worried—I can see that much even through the haze. "Hmmm?"

"Let's go in."

I blink, look past him. We're at my house. Lights off—everything's dark and lonely.

He unbuckles me and helps me out. I follow him across the driveway to the side door by the garage; still operating on blind instinct, I unlock it, and let Jamie go in first. He flicks on lights as he heads into the kitchen. I stop in the middle of the kitchen, staring without seeing.

"Elyse?" His warm voice is close.

"Hmmm?" I don't see him. I feel faint.

"Do you want some tea?"

"Sure."

I hear him rummaging around the kitchen. He finds my electric kettle, fills it, turns it on. I'm still standing in the middle of the kitchen, purse on my shoulder. I feel…blank. Not numb, not panicked, just… strangely, eerily blank.

He puts his hand on my shoulder, and I flinch at the unexpected contact. His eyes are deep and brown and worried. "Do you want to change?"

"Change?"

He waits for me to respond further, but that's all I've got. "Yeah, change. pj's? Something more comfortable?"

I glance down at my nice jeans, form-fitting top, and my best sweater duster. "I was supposed to take Aiden on a date. We were going to dinner and to see the new superhero movie."

"You can reschedule. He'll understand."

"He didn't know. It was going to be a surprise."

"Then he won't miss what he wasn't expecting. For right now, you just need to relax."

"Relax." The word comes out dripping with sarcasm.

I still can't move. My legs and arms won't cooperate. I don't even know what to do, how to be me. Right now, I'm just a hole in the world shaped like Elyse.

Jamie sighs. "Come on."

He tugs me by the hand toward my room. I'm too blank to even care that it's a disaster—dirty clothes hanging out of the hamper, bras hanging four deep off the closet doorknob, clean clothes in another basket, rifled through. Makeup and beauty products cluttering the bathroom sink, curler plugged in but off, a towel rumpled on the towel rack.

He lets go of me once I'm in my room, but I still can't find the brainpower to function beyond following him. Once he lets go, I just stop.

"Elyse?"

I blink at him. "Huh?"

"You need to change."

I shake my head. "I don't know how." I sniffle; sobs lurk behind the numb, blank wall of shock. "I'm in shock. I can't function."

He frowns. "Do you need help?"

I nod.

"Okay." He tries to meet my eyes. "I'm going to help you get changed, okay?"

I nod. "Okay."

There is absolutely nothing erotic whatsoever about the way he helps me undress. He removes my sweater and tosses it into the hamper. Kneels and helps me out of my shoes, then my socks. He lifts the hem of my shirt, and I hold my arms over my head. He keeps space between us—a fact I notice absently—as he helps me out of my tight jeans. I step free of them and stand shivering in my underwear, a mismatched bra and briefs, not at all sexy or cute.

"Where are your pajamas?" he asks, turning away

from me slightly.

I point at the top left drawer of my bureau. He pulls out a thick pair of fleece sweatpants and a baggy T-shirt. I step into the pants, and he ties the drawstring loosely, just enough that the ends don't dangle. He starts to help me into the shirt, but I mumble a negative.

"What?" he asks. "Not this shirt?"

I'm frustrated by own inability to formulate words, but the numbness is wearing off and I'm scared of the impending breakdown. "Bra."

His expression tightens, and his jaw sets. "Ah. Um... yeah, okay."

He goes around behind me and unhooks my bra. I let it flop to the floor and stand topless, waiting for him to put the shirt on me. He does so while standing behind me, tugging the neck hole over my head and gently helping me find the sleeves with my arms, all without touching me any more than necessary.

Once I'm clad in pajamas, he moves back around in front of me. "Do you want to sleep, now? Or...I don't know. Watch a movie or something? I can get you some tea and leave you be."

That slices through my blank haze of numbness. "No! Don't—please. Don't leave."

"You don't want me to go?" He seems surprised.

"I...I can't be alone right now," I whisper. "I'm going to freak out soon. And I—I...I'm going to need you."

"Elyse, I…" He sighs. "Yeah. I'm here."

I hear the hesitation in his voice, but handling it is beyond my capabilities right now. I shuffle to my bed, using the last of my energy to climb under the covers and sit upright against the headboard.

I stare unseeing across the room—holding off the breakdown requires every ounce of focus I have.

Jamie leaves, and I hear him moving around the kitchen. Water pouring into a tea mug. The toaster rattling. He returns with an English muffin slathered with a liberal amount of peanut butter, and two mugs of tea.

"You have, like, three packages of these muffins, which I took to mean they're a favorite around here," Jamie says, handing the muffin halves to me on a strip of paper towel.

"Comfort food," I mumble. "Thank you."

I hand him one of the halves, and he takes it; we munch in silence. The tea steeps, steaming, on the table next to my bed.

Once the snack is gone, I glance at Jamie. "My iPad is in the drawer there," I say. "Maybe we could watch something funny."

He leans over and opens a drawer. I don't have time to freak out when he opens the wrong one; I meant the top one where I keep my iPad, a second charger cord for my phone, and general random items. The bottom drawer has my…errr, *helpers*. A large, knobbed, purple dildo, a small but powerful clitoral stimulator, and a

Hitachi wand with various attachments.

He opens the second drawer, stares into it for a split second, and then slams it closed. "I, um. Sorry. Wrong drawer."

"I should've specified," I say, choking on my embarrassment. "Top drawer. The iPad is in the top drawer."

Silence, acute and awkward. Jamie withdraws my iPad, opens the red leather case, and props the device on his knees. I tap in my code, bring up Netflix, select a comedy special, and the introduction begins.

Jamie is restless. "Elyse," he says, turning to look at me.

Emotion bubbles up inside me—thick, hot, potent. I shake my head, biting my lip hard enough that I taste blood. "Not—not yet, Jamie. Please. Not yet."

He looks at me, staring at my face. He sees the emotion I'm desperately fighting back. "Elyse, you don't have to…" He struggles for words. "You can let it out. I'm here."

"That's part of it," I whisper. "That you're here."

He fiddles with the corner of the iPad case. "But you don't want me to leave."

I shake my head. "I'm more afraid of being alone than I am of being around you."

"Why are you afraid to be around me in the first place?" he asks.

I just shake my head. Putting it into words is impossible in my current emotional state. Jamie sighs, clearly frustrated and wanting to talk about…*everything*, but

I'm just not ready. I can't.

The comic is onstage, setting up a joke about a priest. I focus on him, and even though he's very funny, I can't seem to laugh.

Jamie lets the silence linger and hang, but he's not laughing either.

"Mr. Nubbins, Mr. Tippy Tickles, and Thundera," I blurt.

He glances at me, confused. "Huh? What are you talking about?"

I blush, gesture at the drawer he'd mistakenly opened. "That's, um. The...the names of the—things—in the drawer."

Jamie holds a straight face for a moment, and then snickers. Snorts. "Uh...wow. Okay."

I cover my face with both hands, giggling hysterically. "I don't know why I said that."

He's trying gamely to suppress his laughter. "Mister...Tippy Tickles?"

I hide my face in my hands. "Cora and I got drunk here one night and gave them all stupid names, and I've just always thought of them by those dumb names." I tip my head back and steady my breathing. "I seriously have no idea why I told you that. I must be delirious."

"But...Mr. Tippy Tickles?"

"That's the..." I hesitate over the name. "The clit stimulator."

"Ah, because it tickles your—um..."

"Yeah."

"And Mr. Nubbins is pretty obvious," he says. "But…Thundera?"

My blush deepens, until I'm certain my face is literally scarlet. "The wand. The big thing. It plugs in, because it's so powerful it requires an actual outlet. It's… um…it feels kind of like being hit by a thunderbolt."

He seems vaguely uncomfortable with this, somehow. "I see."

As weird and bizarrely personal as it is, I welcome the conversation, because it's a distraction. I frown at him inquisitively. "What?"

He shakes his head. "Nothing."

"Does the thought of me using sex toys weird you out, Jamie?"

He frowns back. "No."

"Then what?"

"I just…" but he trails off.

"What? And don't say nothing."

He sighs. "It's a personal thing."

I laugh. "Um…I just told you the names of my sex toys, Jamie. Not sure how much more personal you can get."

"It's about my ex."

I arch an eyebrow at him. "Okay?"

He sighs again. "I think I told you the primary reason for our divorce was me wanting this job."

I nod. "Yeah. But…I guess that doesn't seem like enough of a reason to get divorced."

He shakes his head. "No. We'd been having issues

before that. Um…she was raised very, very conservative. Like, women weren't allowed to wear anything but skirts and dresses, nothing exposed above the elbow or knee, hair worn long, church twice a week. That kind of background."

"Yikes."

"Yeah. Part of a background like that is extreme sexual conservatism. She, um—she was a virgin when we got married. I wasn't, but she was." He pauses, scratches his jaw, sips tea. "So, she'd grown up being taught that sexuality is a sin."

I frowned. *"All* sexuality?"

He rolls a shoulder. "Um? Sort of. Within the context of marriage, sex is acceptable, but not really…celebrated, or talked about. Sex is basically procreation to make children, and that's all."

I grimace. "Wow. Sounds…really restrictive."

He nods. "I mean, it's what they believe, and people are welcome to their beliefs, and I'm not going to try to judge people for their beliefs. I personally think it's kind of closed-minded at best, if not actively harmful psychologically. But that's not the point. The point is, masturbation is a sin, and therefore she grew up a virgin in every way. We kissed for the first time when the pastor told me to kiss the bride."

I blink. "Whoa, wait—really?"

He nods. "We held hands, and that's it."

"But you weren't a virgin?"

He huffs a somewhat bitter laugh. "Nope. I'd had

a few girlfriends before her, and had lost my virginity at…seventeen? Eighteen? Somewhere in there. Which was very late, in the context of my social circle, actually."

"But with your ex, you didn't even kiss?"

He nods. "Yeah. It was her beliefs, and I wasn't going to try to push her out of them. I loved her. I was willing to wait."

I shake my head. "That's…amazing."

"It sucked, to be honest," he says, laughing. "I was so damned horny all the time I was going nuts."

"I bet."

"Not to put too fine a point on it, but…I was, um… raw, by the time we got married."

I laugh, hand over my mouth. "I can only imagine."

He sighs again. "So, we dated, and we had a chaperone for every date—usually her older sister or her aunt. We were allowed to hold hands, and hug, but not too close."

"Jeez."

"Then we got married, and we kissed for the first time at the wedding. Her first kiss, ever." He rubs his face with both hands. "We went on our honeymoon, and our first night together was…" He swallows hard, looking away, struggling with the memory. "It was awful. No other way to put it. She was scared out of her mind. Tense, awkward, frightened, and not at all ready. I told her we could wait, but she insisted. I think she felt it was part of her…duty, or something. I don't know.

Her mom probably had some kind of talk about *marital duties*, or something like that. Like she was obligated to have sex with me, but that she shouldn't expect to enjoy it."

I wince, shake my head. "I can't imagine growing up with such a limited view on it."

"Anyway, I wanted to wait a few days, but it almost became an argument. I wanted to ease into it. Kiss, touch, just sort of...learn each other. Take our time getting her ready for sex rather than just jumping right into it."

I watch him, seeing the remembered pain on his face. "God, Jamie."

"She wasn't having it. She tried to convince me she wanted it, but that she was just scared. But, I could tell she wasn't ready, you know? So, we had this super awkward, super short foreplay. And then...she was like, okay, let's do this. Like, with an air of let's get this over with."

I touch his shoulder in sympathy. "That's just...sad and terrible for both of you."

"I was...I don't want to say pissed, or disappointed, just... I don't know. Upset."

"Um, yeah, I can see how you would be."

"I mean, I'd been waiting and looking forward to being with her for almost three years. We met when we were twenty, and got married when we were both just short of turning twenty-three. That's a long, *long* time to wait. And then when the moment finally comes, she was tense, scared, and not into it at *all*. It was just… hard. Upsetting."

"Did it ever get better?"

He shrugs. "Not really. Which is the point of me telling you this. I hoped that with time and experience, she'd loosen up and learn to enjoy it—learn to enjoy our relationship. But she just…never did. She wasn't… cold, not at all. She was a kind, warm, amazing, sweet, affectionate, wonderful woman. She just wasn't interested in sex at all. She never got past seeing sex as a duty. Once a month, on Sunday evening. She would brush her hair out, put on some makeup, take her clothes off, and just sort of sit on the bed waiting for me. After a while, I sort of stopped trying to involve her, to make it feel good for her, any of that. She just wanted me to finish as quickly as possible and get it over with."

I shake my head. "Wow. Just…wow."

"That's how it was, for a long time." He sighs. "For our whole marriage."

"Once a month? Get it over with, good night?" I ask.

He nods. "Yeah. Pretty much. Once, a friend of mine got married and I was in the wedding party. Open bar, and she got a little tipsy. That night was the one and only time she ever loosened up and seemed like she had an inkling of what it could be. But she felt so awful the next day about drinking that she vowed to never drink again, and she didn't."

I groan on his behalf. "Ugh."

He laughs. "Yeah, ugh. So, my point in all this is that I really have no experience with a woman who desires and enjoys sex. Up until my wife—my ex—my only experiences were the frantic, hurried, fumbling experiences of a teenage boy."

I blink, suck in a breath, and try to sort through and filter the wild tumult of thoughts and feelings inside me. It takes me so long to figure what to say, where to start, that Jamie eyes me with confusion and amusement in his eyes.

"What, Elyse?" he asks. "Say *something*."

"I'm trying. I have so many thoughts and feelings right now that I don't know where to start."

"Anywhere. Say anything."

"Anything?"

He nods. "At this point, Elyse, I just need you to…I don't know—open up to me, whatever that looks like, even a little bit."

I wince at the pained, strained, hurt desperation in his voice. "Jamie, I—"

He cuts in. "I know, Elyse. I get why you've been pushing me away. I really do. I don't like it, it hurts, but I get it. But at this point, considering…? I think you need to trust me at least a *little* bit. Even if it's just a response to everything I just shared."

I owe him that much, don't I? A response, at least.

I blow out a long slow tense breath. "Okay. Okay." I shake my head, as if the movement could dislodge my thoughts and turn them into words. "I think—when you and I had sex, I would never have guessed that your sex life was so…shitty, for lack of a better word. You were attentive, responsive, and…and you made me feel beautiful. Desired. You were focused on me in a way I wasn't used to." Now that I've started talking, words begin tumbling out in a flood. "My experience was with a husband who was…well, your ex would've been happy with him, I think. He was interested in very little other than getting to the finish as quickly as possible, and he never gave a single thought about how that may have felt for me, or for what I wanted."

"Yeah, she'd have been cool with that," Jamie says, bitterness ripe in his voice.

"After he and I split up, I was…lonely. And…needy. But with Aiden being so young and so messed up from Daniel leaving that I couldn't spare the time or attention to even think about dating. Before Daniel, I'd been… not exactly adventurous, but I did have enough fun to discover that I really liked sex." I feel things emerging that I've never talked about, even with Cora. "I, um… things with Daniel were so crappy that I bought those toys to make myself feel good, because I needed it and I wasn't getting it with him." I blush. "I was also sort of ashamed. Or, not really ashamed, just…I don't know."

"Of needing to take for yourself what you should've been getting from your spouse?" He laughs ruefully. "I understand that more than you know. I did the same thing. I didn't dare look at porn, because she'd have sussed that out faster than you can say sin, but I had to find relief more than once a month somehow, you know?"

I nod. "Yeah. For me, it was books. I read romance books on my Kindle, and that provided the mental stimulation I needed to get myself there." I blushed harder, hiding my embarrassed grin behind a hand. "I hid the toys. I had a little purse I never used in my closet, and I knew Daniel would never look in any of my purses, so I'd hide them in there. I would tell Daniel I needed a few minutes for a shower, and I'd turn on the water and sit on the toilet and..." I shrug, blushing harder than ever, giggling. "You know. Then, when we split, I didn't have to hide them."

"Why did you hide them in the first place?"

"It would've caused issues," I say. "It'd have made him feel...emasculated. He wouldn't have understood. And we were having enough issues as it was. I just wanted some kind of status quo, some kind of peace. But things just got progressively worse between us, and the crappy sex we did have started tapering off. And then I got pregnant and it became even less frequent, like not even once a week. And then I had a late-term miscarriage, and it just messed us both up. I went into this horrible depression and stopped trying. Like, totally. The only thing that kept me going at all was Aiden needing me. I gained weight, quit taking care of myself, and I ate crap, didn't exercise, even hygiene was a struggle, I was so depressed."

Jamie frowns. "Damn, Elyse. That sounds awful."

"It was utter hell. Daniel was clueless. He was upset himself over the miscarriage—I was supposed to have a little girl, which was something he'd said he wanted. He retreated emotionally and physically from me, and from Aiden. Eventually he just left, and ironically, once he was gone I started to get over it. Aiden needed me more than ever, and I knew I had to get better for him. So, I did. Slowly, but I got there. Mostly." I laugh. "Cora would say I'm not totally over it still, though."

Jamie's eyes search me. "I'd say I would agree with her."

I frown. "Really?"

He nods. "You don't trust me. You don't trust yourself. You're not willing to let yourself have something you know would be good, because you're still hurt and scared of being hurt."

"I just don't want—"

He interrupts me. "Aiden to get attached. I know—you've told me a million times. But he's already attached to me. And I'm attached to him." He slides off the bed and paces away, a hand raking through his hair. "I'm attached to him, Elyse. I care about him more than I should as a principal and coach. I…" He sighs heavily. "I love that kid."

I choke. "Jamie…"

He whirls, eyes blazing. "I can't pretend anymore, Elyse. I *won't*." His jaw clenches, tightens, and his chest expands as he sucks in a breath. Paces back to stand in front of me, where I sit cross-legged on the bed. He takes my knees and spins me so I'm facing the side of the bed, touches my chin so I'm looking up at him. "I won't pretend anymore that I'm not in love with you."

I shake my head. "Jamie, you're just saying that because—"

"*No*," he snaps, more short-tempered than I've ever seen him, than I thought he was even capable of being. "No, I'm not just saying that because you're pregnant with my child. I'm saying it because it's true, and it was true before we found out. I've been hiding it and pretending it's not true, but it is. I think I fell in love with you the first day we met."

I swallow hard. "Jamie—"

"I'm not done. I've held this in for *months*, and I'm not doing it anymore. I'm sorry if you're not ready, but I can't and won't keep shoving it down. I don't know what's going to happen, now. I don't know how you feel. I know you may not be able, ready, or willing to get into anything with me. If not—I won't say it's fine, because I think it'd be bullshit, but I'd understand as well as I can, and I'd survive it."

"Jamie, I—"

"No, not yet. You can say what you want—or not say anything, if that's where you are —once I'm done." He cups my face in his strong, warm hands. His eyes blaze and gleam, hot and deeply brown and intense. "I am in love with you, Elyse Thomas. I *want* you. The one night we had wasn't anywhere near enough. It felt like a dream, and I want more. I want to be with you with both of us totally sober. In the daylight. Eyes open. I want to know what it can really be like with a woman who's in touch with her body and with her sexuality, the way you are. I don't want to wait. I don't want to be smart or responsible or sensible. I want to give in to being…wild. I want—I want to know you want me, that you need me the way I need you." He indicates the bottom drawer of my nightstand. "I want to play with those, *with* you. I want to explore things, try things, *with you.* I want to love you. I want to love Aiden. I want to be a dad to him." He pauses, swallowing hard. "I…my ex and I—the one thing she wanted, and I think the only reason she kept having sex with me at all was because she wanted a baby. But she couldn't conceive. We were talking about getting tested to see which of us was sterile or whatever, but then this whole thing with my job started happening and that conversation got shelved because we were having so many other issues. But I—I wanted a baby. I wanted—I…I desperately wanted to be a father. I think us not being able to conceive created as many problems as her lack of sexuality, if not more. I don't know. I just know that…"

He turns away, tilting his head back, blinking hard, breathing hoarsely. "I won't be stepping aside, Elyse. Even if you don't want a relationship with me, I'm going to be here for that child." He turns back, and his eyes shine, shimmer. Meet mine. "For you. Like it or not."

I can't breathe. I'm crying. Shaking all over. "Jamie."

He holds his arms out to the side, palms up in a broad, helpless shrug. "That's it. I'm done." He lets out a sad sigh. "Your turn."

I'd speak, but I can't. I'm crying too hard.

Sobbing. Broken, shattered, utterly.

Breathless, snot-streaming, can't-see, ugly crying.

Jamie watches for a moment, and then comes to sit on the bed beside me. His arms go around me, wrap me up.

He holds me as I weep—for my past, for the miscarriage, for my divorce, for my awful marriage, for my son, for the long lonely years of being a single mother, for my pent-up sexuality, for my broken heart, for my fears that I can't shake, for Jamie and all he went through…I'm crying for so many things, and it's a cry that won't stop.

And he just holds me through it. Doesn't shush me. Doesn't tell me it's going be okay. Doesn't try to fix it. Just holds me, stroking my hair away from my eyes. I snatch a Kleenex from the nightstand and he takes it when I'm done without a hint of disgust, and offers me another.

How long I cry, I don't even know.

Slowly, I feel the flood of emotions begin to…not subside, but kind of sort themselves out, at least a little bit.

What settles into place, then, is need.

Raw, furious, unquenchable need.

It's mixed with fear, but leavened with a nascent, burgeoning, swelling sensation of a nebulous, boiling thing I know will become love, once I allow myself to examine it—once I can feel anything but a need for Jamie.

For comfort.

For his arms. His lips.

Jamie feels my tears end, and pulls away to look at me, gauging where I am, trying to parse what I may be feeling.

"Elyse, I hope you don't think I—"

My lips slash across his, and I feel our teeth clack together and our noses bump, and then he tilts his head and cups my face and tilts mine so that our lips align and his breath is my breath and, just like that, I'm lost in him, kissing him in a futile attempt to express the sudden, white-hot explosion of need I feel.

There is no expressing it. No encapsulating it. No containing it.

All I can do is kiss him and let the fire consume me.

18

MY HEART IS AFLAME, AND MY BODY IS BOILING with need; my mind is whirling, and my soul is a maelstrom.

All I know, in this moment, is Jamie. His hands scrape across my cheeks, and his lips seek mine with ravenous fervor. His body is hard and close, but not close enough. Yet, still within me is an awareness of all that's coiled and tangled between us.

I can't process it—the pregnancy, his declaration of love.

I've put off this hunger for him for too long, pushing it away and tamping it down again and again, ignoring it, pretending it's not there—and now the bill is due.

I NEED HIM. I can't deny it any longer. I need his kiss, his mouth, his hands, his skin. His heat, his body. Him. Just him. Whatever else may happen or not happen, I need this. I'm sober and aware, and no longer numb.

The pendulum has swung to the other

extreme—I'm awash with emotions, and they're consuming me. They require expression. I can't put this aside, I can't pretend it's not happening.

I have no choice but to give over to it.

Everything.

Myself, my needs and desires.

Jamie pulls away, staring into my eyes. "Elyse…"

Tears still slip and stream down my cheeks, but I can't stop them. And I don't even try. "Jamie, I'm just—I'm…" I shake my head and whisper, "Kiss me. And don't stop."

"I'm not going to use sex as a way of avoiding talking about feelings, Elyse," Jamie murmurs.

I laugh through tears. "I have too many feelings right now, Jamie. I need physical feelings. I need you, I need—this. Please. I have a million things to say to you, and I swear I'll say them. I just need…I need to connect with you like this first."

His eyes search me. "I just told you I love you."

"And now I'm asking you to *make* love to me," I whisper, although it's nearly more of a hiss than a whisper. "I'm begging you, too. I'm too—overwhelmed by everything to know what to *say*. All I can do right now is—is try to *show* you."

"You're not saying no, though?" His voice is low, as if he's holding back powerful emotions from flooding over him.

I shake my head, pass my hand through his hair and scrape the other hand up his back, under his button-down shirt. "No, I'm not saying no."

"You can't say it back, though."

I laugh again. "I'm saying I—" I burst into laughter, and then fumble and rip at his button-down, get it off, and throw it aside and rake my hands over his chest. "I'm saying I need this before I can figure out what I want to say or how to say it."

He captures my wrists in his hands and holds them between us, his lips grazing mine, his eyes hot and wild. "One last thing, Elyse."

"What?" I breathe.

"You have my heart in your hands. I've never been as vulnerable with anyone in my life as I am with you right now. So just...don't play with me, okay? Don't—" He exhales on a shudder. "Please, don't hurt me—don't break my heart, Elyse."

I don't know how else to make him understand that I have no words just now. They're jumbled and whirling and clotted in my head and my heart, blotted out and blinded by the white-hot nuclear flash of wild need that currently eclipses all else. I'm literally vibrating with need. I feel too much need to feel something real and physical and true.

I push him backward onto the bed and plant kisses on his chest, over his ribs, across his belly. He sucks his stomach in and reaches for me, grazing fingers over my spine but not quite daring to touch me fully just yet. It is as if he is afraid still of taking this, of letting himself have this. Maybe afraid of waking up from a dream he's had a million times before, only to wake up alone.

I understand more than he can know.

I palm his chest and scour his shoulders with my hands as I kiss my way down his body, and then, when my lips reach the waist of his once-pressed and now-wrinkled khakis, I trail my fingertip down his chest and over his navel, pausing at the closure of his pants. His stomach is concave, sucked in with anticipation. I gaze up at him over the plane of his body, meeting his eyes. Unbutton, unzip. I hook my fingers in the elastic of his underwear and pull them away from his body. He lifts his hips off the bed, and I yank his khakis off, along with his underwear.

He's waiting for me, hot and thick and long and hard, and I gasp with need, groan with anticipation. He is utterly still, waiting, as if he can't believe this is happening. I remember what he told me about his ex, and remember that the last time we were together like this we were both half-drunk, filters and inhibitions flooded and overcome by booze. But I remember every single moment, even the half-asleep moments in the early dawn light that resulted in the child inside me.

I remember it all with stark clarity.

I want it all, and I want more.

He's naked, lying on the bed with a mammoth erection, staring at me watchful and waiting, chest heaving, stomach curving in with each inhale, flattening with each exhale. Waiting. Wanting to know what I'm going to do, willing to let me take my time doing it.

His hands are fisted near his hips, as if the effort to hold still requires everything he has.

I kiss his hipbone. His navel. His palms stutter over my shoulders and his breath catches. "Elyse?"

A tornado of words and sentiment and expression blast through me, but they lodge in my chest and bang and tangle in my throat, and I use my lips to kiss instead of speak. Kiss his thigh. Just below his navel.

His hands graze down my back, seeking to go lower—he peels my shirt off, and I'm naked for him from the waist up. The peaks of my breasts graze his chest, the tips stiffening and aching.

I turn my eyes up to his. Smile—a hungry, eager, teasing grin meant to telegraph my intentions.

"Elyse?" His voice is harsh, hoarse.

I curl my fingers around him, groaning in delight at the feel of him in my hands. A slow twisting downward stroke, and then I kiss him, devour him, lips and tongue singing over his salty, firm flesh, and he's gasping in disbelief and arching his back and I'm whimpering at the taste of him and the feel of him—

And then Jamie hauls me desperately up his body and yanks my fleece sweatpants off and my underwear and his fingers tease me and slide into me and circle me into a writhing state of eye-rolling arousal, riding the edge of explosion.

I wrestle his hands away from me and straddle him, and our palms meet, fingers tangle. Our eyes lock.

"Jamie." I lean over him, breasts draping silky soft

with hardened nipples against his broad chest, and I lower myself against him. "Please."

He lifts his head, captures my mouth with his, and our lips slide and mesh, and our tongues wrap like needy serpents around each other, twining and twisting and tasting and licking. I let go of his hand with one of mine, and his palm immediately skates down to cup my breast and then my bottom, and then caresses my back and my shoulders and my hair—everywhere. With my free hand, I reach between us and grasp him, and guide him to me. Nestle him where he belongs, where I need him.

"Ohhhhh god, oh god," he breathes. "Elyse, you—god, you feel so good."

I kiss him, taste his words, absorb them and let them fill me—and then I sink down around him so *he* fills me.

"Elyse, Jesus—Elyse!" he gasps. "God, I love you."

I move, eyes fluttering back in my head, and I tangle our hands and rest my weight on him and writhe. A whimpered wail escapes me as he surges through me, and I'm flooded by feelings, by sensations, by *him*.

There's nothing between us, this time—just skin on sweat-slippery skin, just us bare together; slow lazy familiar perfection.

And yet this is more—so much more than the last time we made love. I feel his lips on my sternum, on my shoulder blade, on my cheekbone, on the swaying slope of my breast, and then his warm wet lips suckle the peak of a breast and I'm whimpering at the feel of his lips on me, and the sensation of his thick hot shaft inside me, and the groan in his chest as I move above him.

"Elyse…" he moans, and cups my cheeks in both hands and brings my face to his, demands my mouth—I give it to him, and in return take his tongue, demanding his breath.

I feel an upwelling within me, a drowning, subsuming, rapturous detonation. I shudder above him, lift upright and his hands scour my hips and my thighs and over my belly and clasp my breasts, and even his hands make me feel absolutely beautiful.

He's chanting: "Perfect, perfect, perfect—"

"What's perfect, Jamie?" I ask.

"You are. We are. This is." His eyes meet mine as I lift up, roll my hips down, and balance on him with my hands on his chest. "You are the most gorgeous and sexiest woman I've ever known in my life. So damned beautiful, Elyse. You are *so* beautiful."

I choke at his words, because the shimmer in his eyes and the movement of his body and the eager relentless sweep of his hands tells me he means it down to his marrow. "You're beautiful, Jamie." It's a trigger, unleashing a torrent. "You're a beautiful person. A handsome, amazing man." I gasp and lift and moan and fall to impale him deeply. "You're everything, Jamie. You're—oh, *ohhh*, oh god, Jamie—you're everything."

His eyes shine and shift and shimmer and burn.

He grips my hips and helps me lift up, yanks me down around him. His hips pivot and drive, and we move together in perfect synch, in perfect rhythm.

"*This* is everything," he grates through gritted teeth. His movements falter, his rhythm stutters.

I whimper. "Not yet, Jamie. Not yet—I'm almost there."

He presses a thumb to my aching, sensitive center and that's all it takes—I'm gone, I'm screaming and wailing and crying as the explosion erupts in my core and expands like wildfire through me, cell by cell, making my skin tighten and my extremities tingle, and my breath rush out in a sob, and my entire body spasm, my core clamping around him.

I don't need to say anything—he knows. He feels it. He sees it.

"Elyse, god...yes! There's never been anything more beautiful than you coming apart for me." He moans and his thrusts quicken, become fast and rough, and I delight in it, speed my own movements, riding him faster. "There's never been anything as beautiful as this. As us."

As the climax rips through me, rips me into a million shivering pieces, I collapse onto him and cling to him. He coils his strong arms around me and rolls us over, and now I'm under him and I'm shaking and shuddering and he's still moving, driving. I wrap my legs around his waist and palm his taut backside and grind with him as he takes his time reaching his own climax.

His fists bury in the mattress to either side of my face and I see his breath coming faster and feel him moving harder and I'm brought to tears once again by the rapture of his beauty as he cries out, his forehead nudging mine. I slant my lips over his and taste his moans—my name, chanted, wept:

"Elyse, Elyse, Elyse—" and then he's coming and I feel it and I'm filled with him and taken by him, and now his chant shifts. "I love you—I love you—god, I *love* you, Elyse!"

His climax triggers another of my own, this one erupting from deep within me, centered somewhere behind and below my belly button, and this one is hotter and deeper and wilder and more intense by exponential amounts, and I can't even scream, can't make a single sound. I'm shredded by this, by him, and I throw myself into the black hole of this climax, this mutual explosion, his body spasming as he shatters above me, crying out and groaning wordlessly, clinging to me, driving into me, lips fumbling at mine as our bodies coil and twist and tangle and braid together.

And then I have my breath and I'm sobbing, broken open by the shared climax. How could I have ever denied myself this? How could I have ever pretended this wasn't perfection?

"Jamie…" I gasp. "Jamie!"

"I'm here," he murmurs in my ear. "I'm here."

I palm his cheek and blink tears away from my eyes and kiss him with trembling aching exquisite tenderness. "I love you, Jamie," I say. "I can't help it. I'm scared, I'm terrified, but I love you."

He laughs, and his voice is emotion-clogged. "You don't have to be scared, Elyse. I'm yours and you're mine and I'll love you like you've never known love could be possible. You'll never be alone again. You'll never—" he cuts off, overcome. "I'll love you like I've always known I was meant to love someone—I just couldn't, because I didn't know how until you. Now I know, and now I can love you the way you deserve."

"I'm going to throw your own words back at you, Jamie," I say. "I've never been this vulnerable with anyone. I've never wanted anyone—*needed* anyone—the way I want and need you. I've never loved anyone like this. Like you." I let him see me, my tears, the depth of my terror. "Daniel hurt me, almost broke me. You—Jamie—you have the power to absolutely destroy me."

"It would be mutually assured destruction, Elyse," Jamie says, still above me, inside me. "Because you have the same power. Instead of talking about destroying each other, though, let's promise to give each other everything we have, everything we are."

"You already have all that, Jamie," I say. "Why do you think I resisted so hard?"

He kisses me. "Fear is a powerful thing."

"It is," I say. "But love is stronger."

"It can be, if you let it."

I push at his chest. "Let's get cleaned up."

Once we're back in bed, I curl up against him, my

head in the nook of his arm. Our breathing is synchronized. I feel the silence like a living thing between us.

There's still one thing we haven't addressed. "Jamie?"

He rumbles. "Hmmm?"

"I'm pregnant." I have to say it out loud. For myself, for him, for us. "I'm going to have our baby."

He sighs long and deep. "I know."

"Just so there are no doubts—I'm keeping it."

"There was no question in my mind." He twists so he's levered over me, angled toward me. "When I told you I loved you, that was a promise."

I sniffle, my emotions at high tide and ready to overflow at a moment's notice. "A promise?" I ask, my voice thick and my eyes wet yet again. "What do you mean?"

"A promise, Elyse. It means I promise to love you, no matter what." He gestures with a nod of his head toward the wall. "It means I promise to love and be there for Aiden."

I choke back more tears. "Oh."

He wipes them away, and then his big warm strong hand covers my belly. "And this little one, too."

That breaks the tears free all over again, and once more Jamie doesn't try to shush me or stop me from crying, he just kisses me as I weep. He holds me, giving me the time I need.

"Jamie, I—" I fight for words, hunt for the right ones amid the maelstrom inside my head and heart. I can't find them. There's too much inside me.

Instead, I again resort to showing him.

I find him ready—more than ready.

Again and again into the small hours of the morning, until I'm sore and exhausted, I show him. And in the process, I discover how much there is for him to show me, in return.

There's everything for us to show each other. Finally, aching and sore and sated—with an extra ache from the whiplash for me, which is painful but not debilitating—we take a shower together and clean each other and brush our teeth and collapse naked and clean together into bed, and sleep.

Wrapped up in each other.

We sleep into the late hours of the morning, and finally greet the day around noon. Jamie woke up early and called in to take a personal day at work, and to call in for me, and also to let my parents know I was okay and resting. Then he crawled back into bed with me and we slept on, drowsy and contented.

19

I KEEP THE NEWS OF MY PREGNANCY TO MYSELF FOR A FEW days. Jamie and I don't get any more time to ourselves in those couple of days—and the night we spent together wasn't anywhere near enough to sate us. But it would have to make do.

The weekend comes, finally—after a week spent on the phone with insurance and car shopping. I know I have to have a family meeting with Mom, Dad, and Cora. I'm not entirely certain how I'm going to handle Aiden—I'll have to talk to Jamie more about it, I just know I'm not quite ready yet. I arranged for him to spend the afternoon on Saturday with a couple of friends from football so I could have some time alone with my parents and Cora.

Jamie called me as I was on the way from dropping Aiden off at my parents' house. We'd snatched a few kisses last night after Aiden went to bed, but I wasn't comfortable having Jamie stay over just yet, so a couple of stolen kisses was all we were going to get for the moment.

"Hey, Elyse," he says, when I answer. "What's up

with your Saturday? I thought you and Aiden and I could go for a ride into Hanover and have some fun."

"I, um—he's with some friends. Jake and Jimmy. I'm headed to my parents' house."

Something in my voice must have given me away—I wasn't excited about the upcoming talk. In fact, I was nervous as hell. But I was also pretty certain it was too soon to involve Jamie in this kind of thing.

Or rather, I was scared he wouldn't go with me, and so didn't invite him.

"To your parents', huh?"

"Yeah. Cora will be there too."

He lets silence build for a moment. "Wait. You're telling them?"

I hesitate. "Um. Yeah. I hate secrets, and they're my support system. They need and deserve to know."

"Without me? That's a conversation I need to be a part of, Elyse. We're a couple now, remember?" His voice is firm. "I'll be there in ten minutes."

"I know, Jamie, but you don't have to—"

"Elyse?" he interrupts, his voice—well, not quite hard, but authoritative. "We're in this together."

"I know, but...I guess I figured it was a little too soon for this, with us."

"It's not." He sighs. "You're looking at this wrong, Elyse. I don't *have* to be there with you holding your hand while *we* tell your parents and Cora—I *get* to."

I breathe out a shuddery breath. "They're my parents."

"Yeah, but this is *us*, Elyse. You can't cut me out of things anymore. I'm in this with you, start to finish, no matter what. I'm your support system too, now." His voice goes tender. "I get that you're used to be independent, doing things on your own. But you don't have to, okay? I don't want to uproot or change your life or Aiden's—I want to make it better. That means letting me. Letting me be part of things like this. All right?"

I nod, but he can't see me. I have to actually respond verbally. "Okay," I whisper. "Thank you."

"Thank *you* for letting me be part of your life."

I arrive at my parents' house, and Cora is already there, sitting on the porch with Mom and Dad, drinking iced tea and chatting.

I exit my car and head up to the porch, wiping my sweaty palms on my jeans. I know they can't, but it feels like they'd be able to tell I'm pregnant just by looking at me.

I take one of the rocking chairs on the other side of Cora and accept a glass of tea from Mom.

"So," Mom says, her voice bright and chipper. "Is this a social call, girls? It's nice, the four of us sitting here together. Reminds me of when you girls were in high school. You'd sit out here on the porch doing homework and cackling about boys."

"*Cora* cackled about boys," I clarify. "I do *not* cackle."

"No, you sound more like a hyena," Cora teases.

"If I sound like a hyena, then I'm not sure I can

come up with a metaphor for what *you* sound like." I grin at her, falling back into old rhythms. "Krusty the Clown on helium?"

"Yeah, well—" Cora starts.

"Girls, girls," Mom soothes, laughing. "Sometimes I swear you two haven't grown up a bit."

Dad eyes me, silent and brooding, wise and insightful. "You got something on your mind, girly?"

Cora catches the note in Dad's voice—she's as adept at reading his moods as I am. "I think she does, Dad. Don't you, Mom?"

I sigh. "Can we just drink our tea and make fun of each other for a minute or two?"

Cora frowns at me. "Did something happen? That accident shook you up worse than you thought, didn't it?" She puts her hand over her mouth. "They found something, didn't they? Cancer? You're not dying are you?"

I sputter. "Oh my *god*, Cora, relax. No, they didn't find cancer, and I'm not dying. Yeah, the accident shook me up, but I'm fine. A little whiplash, but it's mostly gone already."

Dad's eyes bore into me. "Aiden's not here, and the four of us are. Not that I'm complainin', 'cause God knows I appreciate the time with my girls, but you've got something' on your mind. Dad knows. Don't try to lie to your pops."

I need to buy time for Jamie to get here. But stalling for time isn't really my thing. I'm racking my brain for ways to put off the conversation, but I'm saved by the arrival of Jamie in his pickup. Dad sits forward in his chair, and then when Jamie gets out, placing a Pirates ball cap on his head, Dad's eyes cut to mine. I meet them for a moment, and then look away; Dad's eyes see all, if you let him look too long and too close.

Even looking away tells him more than I was ready to reveal, because he sits back, crosses his arms over his chest, and puts on his intimidating Dad glare. Jamie notices, and meets Dad's gaze steadily. He's unsure how to proceed once he's on the porch, though. Does he lean down and kiss me like I can tell he wants to? I smile at him, trying to be reassuring in my own nervousness. He leans back against the railing, facing me and the rest of my family. I stand up and move beside him, and take his hand in mine.

That alone says about as much as I'd need to on that score. Dad's eyes narrow, Mom's fly open, and Cora claps a hand over her mouth, stifling a laugh and a smile.

"So. You sorted your shit out, huh?" Dad says.

"Watch your language, dear," Mom chides.

Jamie laughs, reaching out to shake Dad's hand. "Jamie Trent. Nice to meet you, sir."

"Ken Thomas. My wife, Emma."

"Cora you already know, I think," I say.

"Seen her around town," Jamie says, "but I don't think we've officially met."

Cora's grin is shit-eating. "Looks like he *does* own

something besides pressed and pleated khakis and button-downs."

I glare at her. "Cora Marie."

Jamie just laughs, though. "I was one of the rare species in high school who could fit in with the preps *and* the jocks," he said. "My style does trend a bit towards the dork side, however."

"Well?" Dad harrumphs. "Out with it."

I sigh and roll my eyes at him. "Dad, you think we could ease into this, just a little? It's a big deal for me."

He harrumphs again. "You're holdin' hands like little kids. I ain't dumb—I know what that means."

I shake my head. "I've never brought anyone over to meet you, ever. Be nice, Dad."

"You brought over that snot-headed turkey turd."

I shoot him a look. "Dad. That snot-headed turkey turd is Aiden's father."

"For all the good it's done him."

"Dad!"

Dad sighs, scratching the silvery stubble on his jaw and staring hard at Jamie. "But, I watched the way you were with Aiden at the game. You have a soft spot for the kid, that much is obvious. It's also obvious he adores you."

Jamie's smile is bright and bold. "I love the kid." He glances at me, and then meets Dad's eyes. "As a matter of fact, I have the privilege of loving Aiden...and Elyse."

"I KNEW IT!" Cora crows. She points double

finger guns at me. "You did it! You got over yourself!"

"Cora, chill. Quit shouting," I say. To Dad, and Mom as well. "It's true, though. It took some time and some work to get over some of my hang-ups, but... Jamie and I are together."

Jamie eyes me, waiting. "We both have hang-ups. I'm divorced, and it...it wasn't pretty, so it left some scars."

"Nobody gets out of life without scars, son," Dad says.

"That's the truth," Jamie agrees.

Mom is eying me very, very carefully, and she alone hasn't said a word since Jamie got here. "There's something else," she says, her voice subdued. "Isn't there?"

I sigh. Nod. Gulp. Lick my lips; knot my fingers in front of me... "I, um. We—I'm pregnant."

Dad's eyes couldn't get any narrower, nor his jaw harder. "You just now told us you're in love."

"Dad, I..."

"That ain't how I raised you, Elyse."

"I'm not a child, Dad." I knew he'd be upset, but still; his recriminations hurt.

"Ken," Mom chides. "She's an adult. She doesn't owe us explanations or answers."

"I just want to know whether the cart came first, or the horse."

Jamie lets out a breath. "It wasn't planned, if that's what you're asking. But still welcome." He meets Dad's eyes. "I'm not just claiming to be in love with her because she's pregnant, which I know is what you're really afraid of. I was in love with Elyse long before we got this news."

It's Cora's turn to give Jamie a hard time. Her eyes are hard as diamonds, her voice harder. "Dude, listen to me, and listen well. Elyse is my sister in ways you'll never understand. I stood by and let her get her heart broken by one asshole, and I'm not letting it happen again. So if you're not all in, one hundred percent, forever, then you can just fuck off right now. Because if you hurt my girl, I will have your balls. Are we clear?"

Jamie's eyebrows lift. "Yes ma'am. Perfectly clear." He smiles, taking some of the sting out of his next words. "And you can listen to me: I don't make promises or commitments easily, not after what I've been through. When I say I'm in love with Elyse, I mean that with every fiber of my being. I've only known her a few months, but I know that my heart belongs to her, and I know that no matter what happens, I'll be there with her, at her side, loving her with everything I am, and everything I have."

He speaks over Dad's voice. "And as for Aiden, I'm not going to jump in and try to take over as his father, but that is my goal. I want to be the dad for him that he deserves. So that commitment goes for him, too. I don't answer to any of you on this, at the end of the day—only to myself, to Elyse, and to Aiden. Don't take that to mean I don't care about your thoughts and opinions, because I do—you're all important to Elyse.

You're her family, and I want to join this family and be a contributing part of it. But at the end of the day, my job is to make Elyse happy, and to make Aiden happy, and that will be my number one priority."

Dad lets out a harsh breath. "Son, you just said all the right things." He nails Jamie with a hard stare. "I sure hope you aren't just blowin' smoke up my backside."

"I realize none of you really know me from Adam," Jamie says, his voice even and unfazed, "but I'm not in the habit of saying things I don't mean. I will earn your trust, respect, and hopefully love…in time. It doesn't come easily or immediately, and I know that. Especially not after how Daniel betrayed you all."

Mom stands up, faces Jamie at arm's length. "Here's a test for you, Jamie." She smiles gently, but there's no mistaking the seriousness in her eyes. "I've always thought you can tell a lot about a person by the way they hug."

Jamie's smile is warm. "Mrs. Thomas, I'm an elementary school educator. Hugs happen to be one of my specialties."

He initiates the hug, wrapping Mom up in his arms—it's a warm, platonic embrace, his arms around her shoulders, holding her close. I know the comfort in those arms, and I know my mom—the look on her face as she accepts his hug transforms from skeptical to welcoming within a heartbeat.

She backs away after a minute or so, and smiles

up at him—this time, her smile is the kind that reveals how much of a saint the woman is, full of love and acceptance without any kind of guile or hesitation. "You'll do," she says, patting his cheek. "Welcome to the family."

She moves to me next, leans into me, putting a hand on my still flat belly. "You're giving me a granddaughter this time, right?" she asks in a whisper.

"I hope so," I whisper back. "I'm scared and excited at the same time, Mom."

She laughs. "Good. I think that means you're doing something right." She pulls back and looks at me. "Will there be a wedding soon?"

I shrug. "You know, Mom, I honestly don't know. We haven't really talked about it. We're not in a hurry. I know it'll be a scandal in town, me being pregnant out of wedlock, but I just don't care. I'm not going to marry Jamie just because I'm pregnant. We'll marry when it's right for us to marry."

Jamie tangles my hand in his and winks at Mom. "Don't worry, Mrs. Thomas—I love her too much to wait *too* long before putting a ring on her finger."

"I hope you know we do things the old-fashioned way around here," Dad says, still trying to play the gruff, tough guy, even though I know he's as taken in by Jamie's effortless charm as I am. "So, I expect you to talk to me before you go putting any rings on anyone."

Jamie just laughs. "I wouldn't dream of doing it any other way, sir."

Dad huffs. "Sir." He grins at me. "I like this one, baby girl. Good job."

"This one," I snort. "Like there's been *sooo* many to dislike."

"Just the one, but I dislike that one so much you could spread the hate around to at least a dozen other assholes and still have plenty of hate leftover for him. And that's how I felt *before* the shitmonkey abandoned his wife and son." He glances at Jamie. "You don't have any kids back where you came from, do you?"

Jamie winces. "No, sir. That's part of why we divorced. The strain on our marriage from not being able to conceive just…was too much, on top of other issues. Short answer—no, no children, no secrets. I'm an open book, sir. Ask me anything."

Dad shakes his head. "That answer tells me what I need to know."

"Does Aiden know?" Mom asks.

I sigh. "No, not yet. We're going to tell him soon. I just wanted to tell you guys first." I glance at Jamie, smiling. "We'll tell him together."

Jamie's answering smile tells me he appreciates the reassurance that I won't try to cut him out again. We're in this together: he proved to me today, as if he hadn't already, that I can trust him, that I can lean on him and rely on him to be there with me for everything.

Dad claps his hands on his knees and then stands up. "Who wants ice cream? I'm buying."

We all pile into Mom's aging minivan, and Dad

drives us downtown for ice-cream floats at the general store—pulled the old-fashioned way on machines that have been in service since the '40s. We sit at the counter and Mom and Cora and I chitchat about local gossip, while Dad and Jamie talk college football stats, rankings, and strategies.

I've never felt so happy, so at home, as I do in this moment…

And the swelling feeling in my heart tells me this is just the first of many such moments to come.

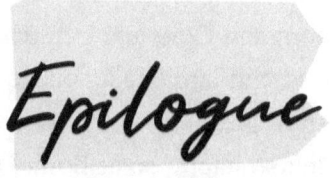

Epilogue

Six years later

"I CAN WALK IN BY MYSELF, MOMMY," EMMA INSISTS. Jamie laughs. "Too cool for Mom and Dad, huh?"

Emma just rolls her eyes. "No. But I'm six and a quarter, and I can walk into the first day of first grade by myself." She holds up her arms. "But you can give me a kissy, though."

"Oh, we can, can we?" Jamie scoops her up and gives her kisses until she's squealing and thrashing. "There—is that enough kisses?"

Emma pats his cheeks with both hands. "I think that's about fifty thousandy hundred too many, *Daddy*." She nuzzles his cheek. "But I love you, so it's okay."

Jamie extends his hand to her after he's put her on her feet again. "Can I walk you in? I mean, I *am* the principal."

She shakes her head resolutely. "No. You can go in after me. Besides, Mommy is going to cry, so she'll need you to give her kisses, too."

I laugh, trying to pretend like I'm not already choked up. "I am not!"

Emma just gives me her patented eye-roll. "You're already almost crying and I haven't even gone in yet."

I sigh. "Fine. I'm going to cry. But you're my baby girl, and I'm allowed."

"Do you cry this much on Aiden's first day of school?"

I nod seriously. "Every year."

"Even this year?"

I nod again. "First day of high school? You bet I did. Like a baby. Didn't I, dear?" I say, addressing Jamie.

"She sobbed. It was pathetic." Jamie winks at me, teasing. "Mom's a crier, babe, so you better get used to it."

Emma shakes her head. "You're silly, Mommy." She wraps her arms around my hips, and I squat down to give her a long, squeezing hug. "Okay, okay, you're gonna squish me, Mom."

I let her wriggle free, take two steps away, and then I yank her back for kisses. Finally, I actually let her go. "Have a good day, Emma. I love you."

"I love you too, Mommy." She points a finger at Jamie. "Give her extra kisses, Daddy."

Jamie pulls me into his arms and dips me backward, kissing me passionately, dramatically. Teachers cheer through open windows, children make grossed-out sounds, and I...well...I kiss him back and work on restraining myself from ripping his tie off and dragging him back home for round two.

Because round one happened around five this morning, before anyone was awake. Even little Cora, our two-year-old daughter stayed asleep, miraculously. Right now, she's babbling up a storm and smacking the tray of her stroller, trying to get Emma's attention.

I call Emma back. "Em, wait! Cora wants you to say goodbye to her, too!"

Emma runs back, backpack bouncing noisily, and gives Cora half a dozen kisses. "Bye, Cora! Be good for Mommy! Don't break any of my toys!"

A futile reminder—Cora has been in full Destructor mode lately, crushing, shredding, ripping, stomping on, and otherwise destroying anything and everything she gets her hands on. Definitely living up to her namesake's reputation, I'd say.

Although, come to think of it, Cora's mellowed out since she married Lewis Calhoun. She's a few feet away from me, walking their son Alexander inside for the first day of preschool. Lewis quit dealing pot and did eventually start selling his junk art. But then, that's a story for another time.

Jamie kisses me once more, softly, tenderly, and then kisses Cora and snuggles her close, and then follows Emma in to the school at a distance.

At that moment, my phone beeps with a text from Aiden: *Give Emma and Cora hugs for me. Have a good day, Mom! ILY!*

God, what a sweet boy. What fourteen-year-old is so open and loving? One with all the love in the world around him, that's who.

I watch Jamie head into school, broad shoulders swinging. He greets children with crouching hugs, listens to stories of weekend highlights, high fives the janitor, and vanishes into the school, where he'll shine as the best principal…pretty much ever.

When I saw him across the bar that day, I'd never have guessed that six years later, we'd have two children together, and have been married for five years.

Or that we'd have another baby on the way.

But *ssshhhh*, he doesn't know yet.

The End

Visit me at my website: **www.jasindawilder.com**
Email me: **jasindawilder@gmail.com**

If you enjoyed this book, you can help others enjoy it as well by recommending it to friends and family, or by mentioning it in reading and discussion groups and online forums. You can also review it on the site from which you purchased it. But, whether you recommend it to anyone else or not, thank you *so much* for taking the time to read my book! Your support means the world to me!

My other titles:

The Preacher's Son:
Unbound
Unleashed
Unbroken

Biker Billionaire:
Wild Ride

Big Girls Do It:
Better (#1), Wetter (#2), Wilder (#3), On Top (#4)
Married (#5)
On Christmas (#5.5)
Pregnant (#6)
Boxed Set

Rock Stars Do It:
Harder
Dirty
Forever
Boxed Set

From the world of *Big Girls* and *Rock Stars*:
Big Love Abroad

Delilah's Diary:
A Sexy Journey
La Vita Sexy
A Sexy Surrender

The Falling Series:
Falling Into You
Falling Into Us
Falling Under
Falling Away
Falling for Colton

The Ever Trilogy:
Forever & Always
After Forever
Saving Forever

The world of *Alpha*:
Alpha
Beta
Omega
Harris: Alpha One Security Book 1
Thresh: Alpha One Security Book 2
Duke: Alpha One Security Book 3
Puck: Alpha One Security Book 4

The world of Stripped:
Stripped
Trashed

The world of *Wounded*:
Wounded
Captured

The Houri Legends:
Jack and Djinn
Djinn and Tonic

The Madame X Series:
Madame X
Exposed
Exiled

The Black Room
(With Jade London):
Door One
Door Two
Door Three
Door Four
Door Five
Door Six
Door Seven
Door Eight
Deleted Door

The One Series
The Long Way Home
Where the Heart Is
There's No Place Like Home

Badd Brothers:
Badd Motherf*cker
Badd Ass
Badd to the Bone
Good Girl Gone Badd
Badd Luck
Badd Mojo
Big Badd Wolf
Badd Boy
Badd Kitty
Badd Business
Badd Medicine

Dad Bod Contracting:
Hammered
Drilled
Nailed
Screwed

Standalone titles:
Yours

Non-Fiction titles:
You Can Do It
You Can Do It: Strength
You Can Do It: Fasting

Jack Wilder Titles:
The Missionary

JJ Wilder Titles:
Ark

To be informed of new releases, special offers, and other
Jasinda news, sign up for
Jasinda's email newsletter.